So Gone Over You

HERE I LAY PART 2

SO GONE OVER YOU

KIMANI LAUREN

Here I Lay Part 2: So Gone Over You

By Kimani Lauren

Copyright © 2021 Kimani Lauren

Published by Perfectly Polished Words

To request permission, contact the publisher at kimanilauren@kimanilaurenbooks.com.

Ebook ISBN: 978-1-7369539-5-2

Print: 978-1-7369539-6-9

First e-book edition September 6, 2021

Edited by The Brain Bakery

Cover art, layout, and interior art by Nicole Watts of kreationsk.com

For the beautiful and talented Kaye Dupree, who lended her patience and expertise so that Monaysia Denise Giles could have a fruitful career.

CHAPTER 1

"hat's your name?" A sheriff with his hand on his holster approached the SUV I was riding shotgun in. Sweat poured down his tawny face. He deserved to melt right at the bridge's entrance where he stood.

Even though my boyfriend answered, "Rahshaan Bailey," just about everybody called him Banger. He handed the sheriff his driver's license along with his other adult passengers'.

The sheriff took them and peered inside at each of us. His eyes rested on me while he took a pen and notepad from his pocket and prepared to write down answers. "Who's in the car with you?"

"My baby's mom, Monaysia Denise Giles, our son, NyQuest Wise Bailey, and a family friend, Rize Darnell Revolution." Banger stared at the Aliners River to keep himself from barking at the sheriff for ogling me.

"Why are you leaving South Sanford?"

Banger turned his head toward me and cracked a half smile that I didn't return. "My girl's a model. If I wanna keep her, I gotta show her something different from what's on this side of the bridge."

"Don't get cute," the sheriff warned him.

Eyes back on the water, Banger's voice turned robotic. "We're going to the grocery store in Sapphire Cadre."

The sheriff came to the passenger's side of the vehicle before continuing his interrogation. "You must be Monaysia Giles. How are you today, Miss?"

"Fine." I tried to focus on the river water, but it always looked like it was bubbling when I stared at it for too long."

"Yes you are," the sheriff commented before examining the next row of passengers. "Why can't you go to the one in South Sanford?"

Banger turned around and watched the sheriff carefully while he answered. "Because it ain't but one on this side of the bridge, and it's out of the food we need. Before that, we're going to Jackson's Department Store so that my girlfriend can model for a catalog that we can't even get delivered on this side of the bridge."

After pulling his hat off his fat head and wiping the sweat from the top of it, the sheriff replaced it and tapped the logo painted on the side of the SUV we were riding in. "That Geno's Auto Sales logo on the side of your car, you get permission from Mr. Dumakis to take one of his vehicles?"

My boyfriend's good mood was snatched away with each question the sheriff asked. He handed the sheriff a note from his boss, authorizing him to drive the vehicle along with his work ID. I rolled my eyes and huffed while I sulked into the headrest. Banger squeezed my knee and then my hand. I sighed again. The sheriff came back to me.

"Ain't you the girl from the Lovely Tresses perm box?" he questioned me.

I nodded my head.

"Well, how'd you end up on the wrong side of the bridge?" He handed back our licenses and then stepped back and motioned for Banger to proceed. "Go ahead. Your life can't get no worse if you're still collecting checks from the perm box, yet still wearing green contacts and settling for life over here with somebody who can't take you further than North ."

As he drove across the bridge, I wondered why Banger insisted on taking those humiliating trips across that bridge every week. Being interviewed to prove he wouldn't commit crime in other parts of the county wasn't worth the aggravation, to me. He said it was to lift my mood, but the only thing that would do that for me would be a plane ticket to Paris to find out what happened to my designs and the collection I created before getting expelled from college. Of course I'd worked on more ideas since then, probably better ones, but Monaysia Denise Giles was too pretty to work for free. Deep in my heart I knew somebody was making big money off of two college semesters' worth of work, and I planned to get back what was stolen from me.

I wasn't much of a dreamer, but from the last month of my pregnancy on, I had intense dreams about somebody counting big dollars from the clothing concepts my mind created. They were so real that I woke up with itchy palms. The tingling yanked me from my bed every night and into my sewing room to sketch and create. Banger followed me in there on nights when he was off from work and watched me from a corner, smiling with pride, telling me that he could feel my big break coming any day. I had this man's baby, and he was going to get me back to the fashion guru I was becoming right before we met. He whispered it to me every night when he thought I was asleep.

Until then, I rode across a bridge to get out of a city I hated to end up in a suburb I hated even more.

The catalog photoshoot brought a smile to my face. Being in front of a camera put me in my natural element. Having my boyfriend nearby with his chest poked out, telling whoever would listen that he had a baby by a model tipped my mood between total bliss and complete irritation. The fact that none of the clothes I modeled were designed by me tanked my frame of mind. It made the rest of the photoshoot a blur until the end when a three tier nameplate with a braided chain was secured around my neck. I traced the gold letters of my name, my boyfriend's name, and our son's name. That put a smile on my face until we got to the white picket fences and uniform split level houses of the suburb I grew up in called Sapphire Cadre.

After confirming my mother and her fickle moods weren't home, I checked the mail to see if there was any word about NYU reconsidering my expulsion or where to pick up the work I'd been conned into shipping to Paris. Nothing. We left pictures of our baby on my mom's dining room table and slipped out of my childhood home. That gave her something to brag about to her friends at Red Lobster that night. Saturday morning, there would be messages on our answering machine saying how badly my mom's friends wanted her daughters to find men to give them the lives my man gave me. That never stopped being funny to me. Only one of them deserved anything that came close to the life I lived: my best friend Siraya. She was so busy working and going to school that I never got to see her during my weekly trips. I missed her.

Next on Banger's agenda was taking a walk around Diamond Park as a family. After that, Banger and Rize took NyQuest to the grocery store to shop for our households and Banger's grandmother's apartment. People waited for them to leave before approaching me to ask me why I came home to get knocked up instead of going to Paris. They tried to get me to tell them Geno's Auto Sales was a money laundering scheme. I rolled my eyes in response and jogged around the park's trails twice, once for the exercise, and two times to show them they needed to mind their business and hope to find a man like the one they were asking so many questions about. Those people would faint if I told them what Geno's Auto Sales really provided transportation for.

Jogging drummed up happy thoughts. The first was how fatherhood turned Banger into a light of love. It made me wish I could go back in time and redo things to see if I could be the reason for the light beaming from his normally scowling face. Even though I wasn't a jealous person, I wanted to be a part of the unbreakable bond my son shared with his father. Banger gave NyQuest a smile warm and nourishing enough to live in. Most days, they left early in the morning for Banger's G-Ma's house to help her get kids ready for school and to the bus stop. Banger talked to NyQuest like a grown man as he dressed him, and NyQuest cooed back at him. I wouldn't see them for hours. He said he was just trying to give me some time to sleep or some time to myself. I wanted to learn how to find a place in their world, but it felt like my purpose had been served. That realization pulled my mood back down and brought my jogging to a halt.

Since it was Friday, Rize's parents picked up NyQuest as soon as we got home. Chillz and Selena were the greatest honorary grandparents ever. They took NyQuest every Friday night, and didn't return him until the end of the Saturday night fish fries at Big Grams's house. Taking me to his great aunt's house satisfied Banger's checklist of getting me to the other side of the bridge. Although the ugly black shutters on the house still looked like they were reaching out to choke me, his family's cooking, the endless Crown Royal cocktails, the weed, the card games, and the party after we ate felt like the Saturday nights I used to know. I thoroughly enjoyed myself while my baby was spoiled rotten by his family.

Somewhere between the food and the partying, I spent my time building my business with Peaches. Her dream of owning a department store that could compete with the Barney's and Saks of the world directly aligned with mine. I found out she was more than just a top employee at the family's escort service. They treated her like she was part of their family. Being part of that family meant they did whatever they could to help her accomplish her goals. Somehow they hooked her up with people who had access to fabrics from all over the world. I taught her what I could about designing, and she let me into her network that included some pretty heavy hitters in the fashion industry. That was the longest and happiest I'd ever been in Sanford County.

And then Best paged me.

I don't know what made him remember that number after all of those months. The conversation we had the day I went into labor sounded like it was our last.

My pager sat on the coffee table while Banger and I sat on the couch in the middle of a heated drawing competition. We both had smiles on our faces, though his picture of NyQuest put mine to shame. More love was put into his details. I expected it to be my sister, Kidra, when my pager vibrated across the table and didn't pay attention. It vibrated four more times.

"You ain't gonna hit that number back? Sounds important," Banger commented.

I shook my head. "I don't want no problems, and that sounds like a problem. A drunk one."

Banger nodded his head and went back to drawing.

The number continued going off, so when Banger got a call for work that night, I waited about 20 minutes and then returned the call.

"Long time no talk," Best slurred into the phone.

"What do you want, Best? Go live your life. You're about to get me in trouble, and I'm happy as hell with my boyfriend," I said and hung up the phone.

My mistake was forgetting to hit *67 to block my phone number before I dialed his. He called back several times until I barked for him not to call me anymore.

"Nay-Nay, just let me taste it one more time! I miss you!"

I hung up the phone again. He called back. The phone ringing so much woke NyQuest. I cussed when I heard him on the baby monitor and went down the hall to get him.

"I only called you back to tell you to stop calling me. I'm a mother and a wifey now," I declared.

Best laughed obnoxiously. "A *wifey*? That nigga know I was poking his baby in the head a couple of months ago?"

While I lifted NyQuest from his crib, Banger's voice came over the phone, "I know now. I'm settin it on your ass when I see you."

I dropped the phone. Banger hung up the cordless extension that he'd taken from the house with him. We stared at each other. He kept his eyes on me while he took NyQuest from me and took him to the rocking chair to rock him back to sleep.

"We need a bottle," Banger demanded.

I couldn't find anything to say, so I just went to the kitchen to make the bottle, shaking the whole time. The phone rang as soon as I finished making it. I snatched the main phone from the cradle and yelled, "I told you to stop calling me!"

There was a pause on the other end. "I knew I should've waited until the morning to call you. My fault."

There was a woman's voice on the phone that time. I looked at the Caller ID. The number was listed as private. I didn't usually answer those.

"Who is this?"

"Peaches," she replied.

"Oh. What's up?"

"Two things. Number one, my boo just took a trip from Italy to Shanghai and came up on some denim and a few other fabrics. I really want to bring your denim sketches to life. Chillz said he would buy us each a Juki and a Brother Serger."

I screamed so loud that Banger picked up the phone again.

Peaches giggled, but she didn't understand. I hadn't sat behind a Juki since before I got expelled from college.

She went on, "I know Banger ain't tryna pay the water bill for washing all of that, so I'll take care of that at my house."

There was a click and a beep, letting us know the conversation was uninteresting to him.

Peaches sucked her teeth. "You got that man going out of his mind over you. Congratulations." She giggled and continued, "Anyway, on to the second thing. Girl, Selena took our lookbook down to The Green Balloon with her, and Iris Campavhore wants to talk to us about working on the costumes for their next show!" Peaches exclaimed.

"The Green Balloon?" I repeated. "The Broadway wannabe?"

Peaches sucked her teeth. "Girl, you better act like you know. The Green Balloon ain't just 'Wannabe Broadway.' People from the actual Broadway come to watch the dancers Selena choreographs and take them with them."

"So you think they'll be looking at the costumes we make too?" I asked.

"Girl, yes. And even if they don't, *everybody* in Sanford County who needs to be dressed will be there. If we get our names on the programs and our shit on the stage, it's a wrap!" Peaches declared.

"Are you sure?" I asked. "I heard those chicks who own it don't do nothing but fight over their husbands and try too hard to be like Broadway."

Peaches sucked her teeth. "You sound like one of those stupid snobs in DPD. I really feel like we shouldn't sleep on this. The last crew they took stayed in Paris and got permanent jobs in theaters over there. When I first met you, you said you were trying to get back there. Let's go!"

I perkily asked her, "When you wanna meet?"

"I gotta go out of town for work for the rest of the week. Will you be ready Monday?" she asked.

"If Banger doesn't strangle me by then," I said, and hung up the phone. I squealed and skipped to my sewing room to get to work on some things.

The next day, Banger didn't say a single word to me. I didn't know what to say to him after telling him I didn't want anybody but him, so I blasted Monica's "Ain't Nobody" on repeat for the rest of the day. I didn't care if my neighbors got tired of me and that song. Monica knew how to say things that I didn't want or know how. When Banger couldn't stand hearing the song anymore, he told me to get in the car so that we could have dinner at his grandmother's house.

Once we got to G-Ma's apartment building in the Nat Turner Projects, we stopped and showed off the baby to the boys on the stoop. Rize's brothers three older brothers — Trigga, Nyir, and Rico — along with his cousins Ken-Ken, PeeWee, and Moosie were out there, as usual. Banger took a place between Rize and Nyir, beaming while every thug out there melted at the sight of his baby. Their friend Squeak sat out there with his girlfriend Shanae, who was pregnant yet again. I couldn't believe how many times she went through that. She was so happy to have another woman to talk to.

A girl pulled up in a white Audi and smirked at us. "If Your Girl Only Knew" by Aaliyah clamored from the speakers. Another girl was in the car, so she left it running and the song playing while she ran up to the door and hit the buzzer for one of those apartments.

That let me know she wasn't from around there, because everybody knew those buzzers — just like the elevators and doorbells — never worked. Chillz went in there quite often and used his own tools to fix them. Then, somebody went behind him and snipped whatever cords he put down there.

The girl continued to stand there and press the buzzer. The guys out there were so busy looking at her booty hanging out of her shorts in the second summer in October that they didn't bother to tell her she was wasting her time. I cut my eyes at Banger to see if he was staring at her like the other boys were. He buried his face against NyQuest's and kept talking about "Daddy's baby," not paying that girl any attention. The girl went and got back in her car and honked her horn. A girl stuck her head out one of the windows and yelled that she'd be out. This one, who was skinny and brown with a pixie cut, spoke to everyone as she came down the stairs in an even shorter pair of shorts. She lingered while waiting for Rize to say more than hello to her. She and her sable skinned companion stomped off when they didn't get the attention they wanted.

When the car of girls in coochie cutter shorts pulled off, Banger and the older guys took NyQuest up to G-Ma's house. I went back to talking to Shanae, shouting to compete with the girl driving back around, playing that same song.

"Bitches be suck jobbin," Shanae remarked after the fourth time.

"What you mean?" I asked.

"That girl fucked Banger when y'all broke up, and she's been coming back around ever since she heard about that nameplate he bought you. I heard she was supposed to be confronting you, but that's a stiff ass North Sanford bitch. She really ain't tough enough to confront anybody."

Even with the tension from Best's phone call hanging between us, the news about Banger cheating on me had me hot. He could get dealt with later. That bitch came down there to confront me, so she was going to have to do it.

"Go tell Mavis to watch your kids, and walk to the store with me," I commanded her.

Scurrying to obey, Shanae asked, "What you about to do, bitch?"

"I'm about to let that bitch confront me," I told her.

I waited in the middle of the street for the girl to drive by again. The white car stopped a block away with that stupid ass song blasting. Shanae walked with me toward the place where every hoe in the hood went when they wanted attention: the basketball court. The girl was sitting on the roof of her car. I snatched her backward by her drawstring genie ponytail. Hearing her scream made my toes curl. Clutching her hair, I locked pupils with hers.

"You supposed to be confronting me?"

She swung at the air, but I pulled her backward and sliced her face open with my butterfly knife. I carried that thing for years to protect me from jealous bitches but never had to actually use it. That blood leaking from her face while her friends screamed instead of doing anything excited me. I pulled the knife from the corner of her mouth to her ear. My fingers tingled from feeling it break her skin.

"You should've went to your man about the issue, not her!" her friend screamed.

I flexed at her, and said, "Bitch, shut up before I slice you too." While I waved my knife, all the people on the basketball court rushed to me and yelled for me to chill. They kept saying Banger's baby mama should've called this person and that one to get the girl for me. I wasn't supposed to be lifting a finger to fight, but it felt so good after the tension filled day and night I had.

"What's wrong with you all? Call the police!" the girl with the pixie cut screeched while her other friend begged for someone to get her something to stop the bleeding with.

While Shanae followed me, cracking up, I stomped back up the street to G-Ma's building. I felt tougher with each step. Everyone knew I was Banger's baby mama, and I'd sent the message to everybody in those projects that my Sapphire Cadre ass was not to be messed with.

The closer I got to G-Ma's apartment, the more pissed I got. My life did not involve fighting over men. I wasted a whole night feeling guilty when I was just returning his action.

"What's wrong with your hair?" Banger asked when I appeared in G-Ma's doorway, probably looking as crazy as I felt. The kids G-Ma babysat that day snickered at me.

I ignored his question and asked, "When did we break up?" He didn't answer.

"That bitch on the stoop came down here to confront me over you, so I had to cut her ass," I let him know.

G-Ma came shuffling her slippered feet out of the kitchen with Rize following her and admonished me, "Don't you come in my house cussin!"

"What? Why would you do that?" Banger asked with a flat voice, eyes on the knife. I thought I saw him lick his lips and got confused.

"Because you fucked her, and she thought coming around here playing that song was the thing to do!" I yelled. His lack of a display of guilt was making my blood boil.

"It was just a song. It was probably on the radio," he tried to reason.

Why the hell was me making excuses for this bitch when he cheated on me with her? My blood boiled and then froze.

"That song is two years old! Why would it be on the radio? And since when can you put songs on the radio on repeat?" I snapped and started toward him with the knife still in my hand.

"Yo! We ain't even know if Quest was mine! You was doing your thing, too! What about the nigga who called the crib last night?" Banger panicked.

"She better put that knife down before I fuck her up," G-Ma warned.

Instead of backing down, I kept charging toward him. Rize's brother, Rico, was sitting on the couch, holding the baby, so I could have really done some damage to Banger if not for that boot hitting me in my face with a blinding force.

G-Ma was a tiny woman of five feet and four inches, but her accuracy should have had her running practice drills with the

Buffalo Bills. I saw stars when that thing connected with my face and stumbled backward. I heard everyone laughing at me. When I regained my balance and vision, I put the knife away before anything else embarrassing happened. G-Ma told me to get out of her house since I couldn't keep my hands to myself. I told Banger to stay there. Instead, he followed me to get me home.

Desperate to get away from him, I tried calling my friend Siraya to see if I could pay her a visit. She wasn't home, as usual. I took NyQuest into the bedroom with me and closed the door. He fussed until Banger opened the door with his arms extended. I gave Banger his baby and his bedroom, and went to sleep on the pull-out couch.

In the middle of the night, I woke up to Banger whispering in my ear about how turned on he was by hearing about me cutting a bitch over him. The phone rang off the hook with his family asking about it. He just hung up on them, coming closer to me every time. By the time he put NyQuest down after his 2AM feeding, it seemed as though everyone in his family called twice.

"Come get in the shower. You still got blood on your fingers."

He yanked me off the couch, carried me into the bathroom, and threw me against the shower wall, both of us fully clothed. After licking each of my finger tips, he ripped our clothes off of us. Then he hoisted me against that wall and told me not to move or let go of him. He banged up against my g-spot and didn't tap out until sunrise. Part of me was scared, but the other part wanted more.

CHAPTER 2

*D*ad had been begging to see NyQuest, but had it in his mind that he was going to run into Mommy if he came to my house, so I visited his house in East Terrace for breakfast. He had all kinds of sports-themed toys that NyQuest wouldn't be able to use for a few years. Meanwhile, NyQuest was just barely able to hold his head up. I guessed that was just a minor detail in Dad's world. He even bought him toddler-sized boxing gloves.

For gifts that he could actually get a use out of in the first year of his life, he bought Buffalo Bills everything. There were bottles, diaper bags, onesies, snowsuits, and an obnoxious wardrobe filled with the team's logo. He told NyQuest about all the games he planned to take him to. I was a little jealous. He hadn't taken me to a game since before I left for college.

Melinda came into the room with a strange look on her face. Dad scurried out of the room when she entered. She curled her lip while she watched him run with the baby.

"He shows me off to everybody and then acts like a punk bitch in front of you. Let's get out of here and get some lunch, girl. I heard some shit about you, and I can't wait to hear the story. Leave the baby." She rushed to get her purse and called out, "Eddie, we'll be back a little later!"

"Okay, beautiful!" he called back.

Her car was junkier than ever. I told her we were stopping to clean it out, because that shit was annoying. We took it to a place near her house called Reemus' BBQ & Oil Change. That business seemed too ghetto to survive in East Sanford. I had strong reservations about eating in a place connected to car maintenance. Melinda assured me that Chillz taught the owner how to cook. That was the only outing she ever let me pay for.

"Now what the hell are you doing, slicing bitches' faces open in the PJs?" Melinda asked when we sat down to eat ribs.

"We'll get to that in a minute," I said. "Why did your brother blow up my pager the other night? He caused so many problems for me and Banger."

Her face dropped. "You're not a dumb girl. I'm sure you've figured out by now that I kept him abreast of what was going on with you and Banger. It wasn't to throw salt in your game with Banger; I just hated how easily he got off. He ain't have no business turning his back on you then getting mad when I told him you weren't thinking about him. He made it sound like y'all had more history than what he originally said. He kept telling me he loved you. That nigga don't love nobody but himself."

"Well, him loving himself had me apologizing to Banger all night. I hate apologizing," I complained.

The way Melinda snapped, I thought her head was going to do 360-degree turns and then roll off her body.

"I will bust my brother upside his head if he messed y'all up. Y'all have been doing so good since that baby got here!"

I waved her off, and said, "Best ain't mess up nothing that Banger didn't already mess up himself."

"Why you say that?" Melinda asked.

"Because of the bitch whose face I had to slice open," I replied.

Melinda slammed her hands on the table. "Yeah. Get to the good part. Because I heard some shit, but I knew it was gonna be even better coming from you."

Whenever I began a story with the word, "Girl..." and held onto it for a long time, Melinda crossed her legs and leaned in for a good story. She let me get as far as telling her about Shanae before she interrupted.

"Please stop listening to Shanae's dumb ass. That bitch ain't shit but a hater, and she's fake as fuck. She stays in your face when you come around, but she's more jealous over you than any bitch down there because of Banger. Banger put in that work immediately to get you out of Nat Turner as quickly as possible while Squeak's lazy ass still got her living in somebody else's house and pregnant a-fucking-gain. You ever notice that every time you're around her, you and Banger end up arguing?"

I thought about how right she was, but felt the need to defend Shanae for some stupid reason.

"That's because she's the only one keeping it real with me. Nobody else was gonna tell me that Banger crushed that girl."

"That's because nobody else has told themselves they have anything to gain from starting shit between y'all. All Banger wants is to tell people his baby's mother is a model. You make him look good as hell. He got right up out of Nat Turner when he knocked you up, and even if the police were watching, they definitely understood. Ain't nobody gonna keep nobody fine as you in the PJs. All that running back to him to tell him what you did puts him in a bad mood. Whenever Banger's in a bad mood, the whole hood gotta feel it."

"So why does Shanae do what she does then?" I asked.

"Because her and Squeak are some type dumb, weak ass links. They don't even like each other. Squeak is using her for something to nut in, and Shanae thinks if Squeak keeps her around, she can be up in his friends' faces until one of them takes her off his hands."

That jolted me back to Thanksgiving night with all the ballers in VIP. No way did I share a thought process with Shanae.

Melinda kept going. "The only reason why either of them is around is because Unc felt sorry for Squeak when his parents put him out the house. They tried to call him a problem child, but they were just too trifling to take care of him and just left him on the streets."

"But that's what they say happens to all the boys that get reported missing on the news," I said.

"And that's the number one reason why Chillz and Unc made sure it didn't happen to him. Chillz doesn't get money to be flashy; Chillz got all that money to make sure people in Nat Turner never go without. No kids go hungry, homeless, or without clean clothes that fit. Everything you ever heard about South Ridge is a lie, because Chillz and Unc spend every second they're breathing making sure that everything the news says isn't true."

I wrinkled my face. "Chillz has mad kids of his own, plus Banger, plus Marcus when he comes over. He doesn't think he did enough?"

Melinda wrinkled her face at me. "Do you pay attention to anything that goes on around you? You talk about how many kids are at G-Ma's house all the time. Why do you think she takes care of all them damn kids? Could you live knowing your grandchildren were latchkey kids?"

I shrugged. "I was always out on modeling jobs, so my parents never had to worry about that. I don't think I would stop living my life just because my grandchildren had to watch themselves after school."

Melinda shook her head at me with her teeth gritted. "That's that damn Sapphire Cadre attitude. Whatever happens to your kids is what happens. That's one thing I hate about that place."

The urge to make a comment about her relationship with my dad came, but that would have just proven her point.

"Anyway, Squeak moved into that building with Mavis and clung to Banger from that point on. He was tiny for the first summer he stayed in that building, and then he started eating Chillz's, Mavis's, and G-Ma's food and wouldn't stop growing. But for as much as he ate, he ain't do too much in return. He'll stand behind Banger and look scary, but that's about it. You see how many jobs Banger worked when he found out you were pregnant with a baby that might not have been his? Squeak didn't do that, none of them times that he knocked up Shanae, but he's mad about not living where you and Banger live at.

"And Shanae? I never met a more useless, more miserable bitch in my life. I ain't just talking shit behind her back. I've said this shit to her since she first got pregnant. She had that same type of plan as you did— get pregnant by one of them niggas, and get him to take care of her — but she couldn't land nobody but Squeak. The most she does is strip in between pregnancies. I think she might have been boosting too, but that don't work with what Peaches got going on. So long story short, they hate you and Banger cuz they ain't you and Banger. They want what y'all got without putting in the work that y'all did. You go to work and school full time, Banger does his thing, and the whole hood could eat a little more."

"You always talk about Banger like he's the illest nigga alive. Why is that?" I wondered.

"It ain't hard to tell, Nay. When Unc and Chillz retire, they're gonna hand all their shit down to Chillz's sons and Banger."

I snickered. "That's a hell of an inheritance, some damn hookers and some furniture."

Melinda shook her head at me again and rolled her eyes. "You type dumb. You've been living with Banger all this time and don't know what he does?"

"You set me up to see what he does at that 'hiring event' last year, remember?" Her calling me dumb got under my skin, and I wasn't sure how much longer I'd be able to take it.

"Yeah, but that ain't all of it." She looked around the restaurant. Besides the person cleaning tables on the other side of the room, and the cooks behind the counter, we were the only ones there. She leaned in and whispered, "No wonder you'll listen to hoodrat ass Shanae about your man; you don't know shit about him.

"Look. I'm gonna tell you something, but there's some rules to this shit. Number one is, you can't let anyone know what I told you. Number two is, you can't let this shit go to your head. I think you might be too childish to handle this, but I'm hoping it'll inspire you to grow the fuck up."

She came around the table and sat next to me before she said, "I'm gonna put this in the simplest terms possible. Banger runs The County. The hustlers in every single city around here bow down to him. Anybody who wants to do anything illegal has to pay him first and wait for his permission. Nobody pushes weight or weed or even bootleg videotapes in the gas station parking lot without paying him a tax on it."

Disbelief made me suck my teeth. "I know I'm from the suburbs, but do you expect me to believe drug dealers are just handing over this money to my man? And where does he keep this money because I haven't seen it?"

"Everybody has to pay for letting themselves be used to tear us down," was her answer. She could read on my face that I had no idea what she meant, so she went back to what she was saying before I interrupted her. "If it gets back to him that somebody broke the rules, then I'm not even gonna talk about what happens. If he can learn to control his temper, he's gonna be Chillz's right hand. That's why the family stays mad at you. You hold him back from getting where he needs to be.

"My brother is really salty about you being with Banger, because you basically moved on to his boss. So Best has to pay him in order to sell weed and then think about you laying up with him and spending his money after. He was *tight* when he saw you in that Iceberg outfit. Please don't ever entertain my brother's bullshit again, by the way. Banger might kill him, and I'd hate to lose my brother to violence. He's an asshole, but I do love him."

I took in everything she told me. Damn. I was even better at picking them than I thought. I never knew Best sold weed. but I didn't tell Melinda that. She already called me dumb too many times.

"And Shanae's stupid ass thinks she can take my man?" I asked.

"I guess she thinks that telling him everything she sees you doing and everything you tell her will make her seem like a down ass bitch or something. She ain't even on Banger's radar, though, with her Cabbage Patch looking ass. Banger ain't never had a girl as fine as you, so why she thinks she can compete with you is an unsolved mystery."

Melinda sure did know how to gas my head up. I laughed at the Cabbage Patch comment and asked why she seemed like she hated Shanae.

"Because she don't got nothing better to do but stir up shit. She's the one who told that girl we were in the mall that day last year," Melinda said.

I gasped. "Why would she do that?"

"Because she's jealous that I never took to her like I did you. I've always stayed away from her, because her mouth runs too much, and she lives for drama."

She went back to her side of the table and thanked the waiter for bringing us our food. When I got my first bite in my mouth, she started talking again.

"You gotta stop doing dumb ass shit, Nay. I know you think you're too fine to get left, but you've fucked up the money too many times. I told you when you first asked about him, that nigga Banger is all about his money. Now, that baby might be holding y'all together, but your attitude is gonna drive you apart. Now that they know he's capable of being in a relationship, it's too many bitches in line for you to be acting like your spot is so secure. That nigga used to have hoes on rotation. He calmed that right down when you got pregnant."

My blood was boiling at her bringing up other girls with that smirk on her bow lips. It almost made me want to slice her golden face open. "You sure do know a lot about my nigga."

She laughed. "Girl, listen to me. I taught that nigga everything he does that got y'all bitches going crazy over that dick. I was his first. Rico and Trigga paid me to let Banger and Rize run a train on me for their 18th birthdays. You need to be thanking me, boo."

"Thanking you for what?" I exclaimed. "You must get a hard-on from making me look stupid. First, it was my dad. Now this. Tell me, where does my dad think you work?"

Melinda chuckled. "He used your family's light bill money to pay for a half hour with me. Why do you think your parents were sweating you so hard to pay bills? The money was disappearing while you were gone. With you home, he could put a bill on you and put his money toward who he really wanted. Think about how hard he was sweating you. Almost sounded like a crackhead, didn't he? He was in the strip club on Hyman and 105th fiendin for me, begging me to let him get into VIP on credit. He was waiting for me in the parking lot after I got off to try to cut deals with me like he used to do to get you and Kidra Buffalo Bills tickets when he drove y'all out there to games. Matter of fact, he started driving charter buses to pay for me." She watched my face drop and leaned in. "I keep telling you, little girl, you're really dumb."

I went from wanting to slice Melinda's face open to wanting to stab my father and then back to wanting to cut Melinda. She always tried to present herself as a mentor, but she really thought she had one up on me. What she said about Banger, though, told me I had to get my shit together for the thousandth time. I told Melinda to take me to get my baby and my car so I could go home and put on something skanky after NyQuest went to bed.

"Monaysia, I'm sorry I talked to you like that," Melinda said softly. When I didn't say anything or look at her, she said, "I was just talking stupid because I really care about this family."

She glanced at me, so I turned my back to her and waited for her to turn on her 5 disc changer. She usually played Monica songs for me when I rode with her. That time, she removed the face to force us into a silent ride. I huffed.

"Monaysia, you and me are more alike than you realize," she said. "It's selfish, but I let my brother know what's up with you and Banger for me."

"For you?" I asked.

She nodded her head. "I wanted to give him the chance to put his family first. It would have meant the world to me if he would have stepped up and been there for you like he was supposed to, since he wasn't there for me when I needed him.

"When I was about 16, I started messing with this nigga from West Sanford—"

"You?" I exclaimed.

She nodded her head again. "He used to push his Benz past my school every day and stop to ask me for my phone number, but I had a boyfriend."

"Trigga?" I guessed.

"Nope," she said. "Trigga was just my best friend. Me and Trigga have been like glue since birth. Aunt Lisa was my mother's best friend. This nigga from West Sanford, though, was so fly. He promised me that he'd put me through school to be a veterinarian and a zookeeper."

I wrinkled my nose. "What the hell? You need to be a model, Melinda."

"I like animals way more than I like being told what to eat and that I'm too fat and too black." She tugged at her ponytail, and said, "Anyway. He convinced me to stay with him, got me pregnant, and then beat the babies out of me after I got caught carrying drugs for him."

"What happened to him?" I asked.

"Trigga. Chillz. Unc. Banger. Everybody who sits around Chillz's table and eats except Squeak. Squeak was outside beating up his little brother, Miguel."

She and I met eyes when she mentioned my ex's name.

"My family distanced themselves from me after that. I think messing with that boy from the Chavez Projects is what made my parents get out of Nat Turner and move to Sapphire Cadre. People from across the bridge aren't supposed to lay down for people over in West Sanford, and I knew better. Best told me I deserved being told that I could never have kids again. Chillz and his family, though? They took me right back in. Aunt Lisa was mad at me, but she still crawled in the bed and held me every morning before she went to work and every night until I went to sleep. Chillz fed me three meals and two snacks a day. That family means the world to me, and I will kill for them niggas. They have always been *the* family. I get so upset watching you treat Banger the way that you do, because he's giving you way more than you deserve."

She pulled into my dad's driveway. I shot her a dirty look. "Melinda, you're full of shit. If that story had any truth to it, then you wouldn't be playing house with my dad after what he did to me, and you would've told Banger about that scene between Miguel and me that day last year."

"I was getting to that," she said.

I put my hand between our faces. "Save it. I don't care. You made up that sad story to make me feel bad about doing to my man what he's been doing to me."

While Melinda shook her head at me, I slammed her car door and went into the house to get my son.

As I sat in line to cross the bridge, Peaches paged me. I forgot all about her needing to come over to finish those outfits to take to The Green Balloon. Whoever was teaching her how to make patterns had her going way past my level. I couldn't let her know that, but I had to find out who it was just in case something happened between us to make us stop doing business together. When I called her back, I told her to bring whatever slutty lingerie she had in her little store. She brought some premium silk, satin, and fur. I changed into a tank top with some tiny shorts while we worked. Her best friend Cream sat in the corner on my computer, alternating between doing homework and cataloging our designs. Seeing the two of them together made me miss Siraya.

"Where's Mel? She told us she was coming over here to hang while we worked. Trigga must be coming over here, huh?" Peaches asked me.

I shrugged. "We just went to lunch, but she did that shit she does when she gotta talk down to you and make you feel stupid, so I told her to take her ass back up under my daddy."

"Oh," Peaches said.

"*Mel* talks down to people?" Cream asked. "That don't sound right. Mel mainly keeps to herself and don't bother nobody who ain't bothering her."

Cream used to get on my nerves because she giggled at the end of every sentence she spoke. It was like she had to make a noise to let it be her punctuation. She cut her eyes at me when she did it that time.

"Well, she might not do that to y'all, but she loves to make me look stupid about my dad and my man," I snapped over the hum of the sewing machine.

Peaches looked up at me and put down the pair of scissors and fabric she was holding. "What about your man?"

"She told me all about getting paid to let him and Rize run trains on her and all the shit she did with him," I continued to go off.

"Oh. Is that why you wanted me to bring that lingerie over here?" Peaches asked.

"Yes. That nigga can't forget who the wife is." I waved my finger in the air. "Between her ass and that bitch I had to cut over him, I'm letting every bitch in the world know who he belongs to."

"Oh." Peaches looked at Cream and then went back to cutting fabric.

Cream turned around in her seat and asked, "Did you cut Mel?"

I sucked my teeth and stopped the machine. "You know I didn't cut Melinda. I just didn't like her holding something like that over my head. She always gotta one up me, just like she did with my dad."

"Well, if you're that salty about it, then why do you hang with her?" Cream asked me.

"Because I didn't care until she told me that she fucked Banger too," I answered, and went back to sewing the sleeve back onto the jacket.

"Nay-Nay, how do you think we get these jobs if we don't get fucked to see if our coochie is good enough to make money off of?" Peaches asked, and Cream giggled.

"What?" I snapped.

"Nothing, girl. Shut up talking in Banger's house," Cream said. She and Peaches giggled at me for the rest of the night.

CHAPTER 3

*P*eaches and I worked on our costume collection from early in the evening until just before dawn every day that week. Selena told her that the people who owned The Green Balloon had high standards. They weren't ready for what we had in store for them. Formal wear and costumes were my favorite pieces to create. Peaches and I fed off of each other's creativity until we executed every single idea in our brains. Then we transitioned to denim designs and prayed the line we decided to call Giselle Deneen was worth the sleep we forfeited.

At sunrise, Banger brought me breakfast in bed and then took NyQuest with him so that I could get some sleep before my presentation that evening.

It was afternoon before I woke up to the buzzing of my pager with Siraya's number on the screen. Hoping she wanted to talk about more than if Rize asked about her, I rushed to call her back. I needed to talk to someone who thought like me.

"Hey, girlie!" I greeted her when she answered the phone.

I pictured her pulling the phone away from her ear and looking at it like I was crazy.

"Unh-uh. Not you calling me from a South Sanford number. What's the deal?"

"You haven't been to my spot yet, have you? I stay in the Medgar Evers Apartments," I told her.

"Medgar Evers?" Siraya damn near hollered in my ear. "Those are the nicest apartments in South Sanford! You making money like that at the phone company?"

"Girl, I might not even go back to the phone company after my maternity leave ends. I'm showing a collection at The Green Balloon tonight for their next show." I took my dishes to the kitchen while I talked to her. "And my paycheck doesn't have anything to do with the rent anyway. My baby daddy pays for everything."

"Yeah, I heard that."

My ears perked as I wiped down the counter. "You heard what?"

"Girl, your name is all in the streets. Your mama is still telling everybody who your baby daddy is related to and who sent gifts to your baby shower. The streets can't keep yours and your baby daddy's names off them. Everybody be asking about you whenever I go to The Opal Lounge. I haven't had to pay for a drink in there since that night you left with them, and Yolanda crashed your car!" she exclaimed. "They say your baby daddy got it! They said he be spoiling you."

I looked down at my three tier nameplate and smiled. "He tricks a little."

"Well, how is the baby? When can I see him?" she asked.

"Rize won't be here," I lied. Rize was always over there.

"Girl, please. Ain't nobody thinking about him. I got a man. I just miss chillin with you, and I finally got to quit one of those stupid jobs I was working once your mother told my mother you didn't have to work anymore because your man takes care of you. Now she's trying to marry me off to all those stupid school bus drivers she works with," Siraya said with a giggle.

"Well, come across the bridge and see me whenever. You bringing your friends with you?" I asked in a dry voice.

"What friends? You're my only friend," she said. "Me and Landa fell off over your car."

"What about the group?" I asked.

"She stopped showing up to sing in shows and took a different gig somewhere out of town," she replied.

"Why? You were always the better singer," I said.

"I know that, but she was the better songwriter, and she could play the piano. She wasn't the performer, though, so it won't last long. It don't matter. I sing at The Opal Lounge on Thursday nights at a real classy drinks and apps situation," she told me. "That's where I met my new man. He's the new owner of the club, and he's also a record producer, and he's gonna make me an album once he gets his label up and running."

I squealed with her. I loved Siraya's voice almost as much as I loved Monica's.

"What about the rest of your friends?" I asked her. "They don't be going to see you?"

Siraya sucked her teeth. "You know me and Yvette are just like you and your cousin Chrissy, except our mamas like each other. She got mad at me for leaving your baby shower with Rize. Brooke never had anything good to say about you after that whole thing went down with you and Landa. Plus, what those ladies said at your baby shower made sense. I wasn't your friend if I wasn't defending you. That whole night was foul. Your man hooked us up that night. We were like VIP ever since then. All you had to do was what you had to do to get your money. You had just bought that car."

"That's what I'm saying!" I said. "But who goes to hear you sing on Thursdays?"

"My man is there. He gets me paid. That's all that matters," was her answer.

"I should be there to see you," I said. "I'm coming tonight

after I show these pieces to these people. Maybe you can come with me to get a part in a play down there. I think it's supposed to be a musical."

"For real?" she asked.

"Yeah, girl. Let me just call my baby's grandmother and see if she can hook that up," I said.

She squealed. "Hold on!"

She left the phone for several minutes. When she came back, her voice was low with disappointment. "It's against my contract. I'm sorry I even asked." She was silent for a few moments and then asked, "When can I come see the baby?"

"I'm taking him to see my mom tomorrow, so maybe I'll slide through and see you while I'm over that way," I replied.

"Okay. Just call me."

"I'm coming to see you sing tonight," I reminded her.

"Yeah." She hung up the phone.

That conversation recharged me. I was exactly where I wanted to be without even realizing it. People weren't talking about me being a failed model. They were talking about me like I was a celebrity. I had to do something to keep my man down for me.

I took a trip across the bridge to the grocery store and got a bunch of ingredients for the only thing I knew how to cook. Before going home, I got some candles and new Monica CDs, just in case my old ones were scratched. I set out the lingerie that I planned to wear that night and called Chillz to see if he could babysit. He was happy to, of course, and didn't even mention the knife incident.

Banger and Rize came in with Peaches to load the car with our clothes, designs, and easels. She looked better than me in her black dress, and her makeup was better. I had to go change.

"Nay-Nay, hurry up and get this money!" Banger called after me.

I turned around and saw him standing behind me, looking at the lingerie sitting on the bed.

"Hope you got time to have a good time tonight. I'm in a good mood and got some plans for you," I told him and sashayed out the house.

I'd only been to The Green Balloon for fashion shows when I was signed to the Naomi Iman modeling agency and to one show that Miguel took me to. It was just a couple of blocks away from my job. That part of Downtown looked like the city planners couldn't decide if they wanted to copy a business center or Hollywood. Flashy lights and a couple of restaurants and boutiques sat in the middle of city and county government buildings, courthouses, and utility companies.

We passed the police academy, and I thought my nerves were driving me crazy. Within the class there was a tall, brown man doing push ups. I had flashbacks to him suspended over me like that and whispering in my ear in Spanish. He caught my eyes, and smirked at me. Before I got caught interacting with him, I turned my head.

Selena stood outside of a one story building in a unitard covered by a short leather jacket and waved to us when we got close. This man and this boy who looked like the high school version of him came outside with an empty rack. They were supposed to be helping us load the garments onto it. Instead, they just looked at mine and Peaches' butts while Banger and Rize did all the work.

We stopped at a receptionist's desk and got visitor tags. The two men stared at our knockers while we pasted the tags to our chests. They took us to a conference room at the end of a short hallway. Three beautiful older women sat there. Two of them looked at each other with disgust while one of them — a woman with blonde straw curls and flowing clothing — came to us with a smile on her face. She introduced herself as Tina Campavhore and then banished the men with the rack from her presence. She smiled wide at Rize with her arms extended.

"You're just as handsome as ever!" She planted a granny kiss on his cheek and then did the same to Banger. "And you're just as mean looking as ever. I heard you were a father now."

Banger immediately took out his wallet and watched Tina gush over NyQuest's pictures. The other two women ran to see them.

"That's a Gerber baby!"

"You've got to get that boy in the Jackson's catalog. Those eyes! He's meant to be a model!"

Banger pointed to me, and said, "He gets it from his mama. She's a professional model."

I introduced myself and almost laughed at how they cringed at my speaking voice.

Tina introduced the other two women as her cousins, Iris and Delilah. They were sepia skinned women who swayed around the room like it was a runway and cut their eyes at each other every time they spoke. One of them wore a full bridal set. The other wore an engagement ring whose solitaire diamond was bigger than all of the stones in the bridal set combined. That was Delilah. I remembered which one she was by how hard she flashed her ringed hand around as she spoke, and the tattoo on her neck of Daisy Duck doing something X-rated to Donald Duck.

Banger and Rize set up the easels and then told us they'd sit outside the room and wait for us. Tina had food for them. I reminded Banger not to eat too much because I had a surprise for him later. While Peaches and I made sure the visual part of our presentation was in order, a glasses-wearing girl with waist length braids stuck her head inside the room without knocking.

"Ma, Daddy said gimme your keys so I can get to class," she said.

31

"Sarita, there's a bus stop a block away. The bus runs up to campus every ten minutes," Iris said.

Sarita sucked her teeth and then huffed. "I'll just call Miguel then. He'll be done with his class soon." She stared right at me as she spoke.

I tried to keep cool when she said his name. There was no way that funny looking little girl was what Miguel moved onto after getting out of jail. Maybe she was in law school or something. Her parents had enough money to get him a good lawyer to get his drug charges dropped if they owned an entire theater. Whatever the case was, he wasn't my problem anymore. There was no reason for that girl to be staring at me through her glasses with so much disdain. Miguel probably had her doing work that Banger would never think about asking me to do. I smiled to myself, thinking that all I had to do to hook his ass was lug his baby around for nine months.

That thought carried me throughout the presentation with an air of confidence that Peaches fed off of to seal the deal.

"How comfortable are you ladies with traveling?" Delilah asked when we were done.

"We're great with it," Peaches said without a second thought.

"I'm just wondering how the new mother would feel about it," Delilah said, "because there is a theater in Paris that we partner with, and I'd love to have the costume designers and set designers go with the cast to pull this show off better than the last one."

Iris explained, "We have at least one show a year traveling to Paris, and we've scaled our business model to allow to send our own costume designers this year. You'd be responsible for styling the cast for press events as well."

"That's understood," Peaches said.

"So you have no problems with traveling?" Iris asked. She turned to me. "Your boyfriend has worked on our stages and sets before. We'd be happy to hire him so that he and the baby can travel with you."

I squealed instead of speaking. Having Banger's baby was getting me everything I wanted, just like I thought it would. Gratitude swam through my heart, and I couldn't stop patting myself on the back for being so smart. I couldn't wait to get home and tell my mother I was getting back to where I was supposed to be.

"This won't happen until next year," Tina said. "It's just something we want to make sure you're able to do before we hire you."

Everything they said circled around my head and didn't make it into my ears, because I was thinking about finally getting out of Sanford County. Peaches poked me. I perked.

"I'm sorry. I was trying to convert everything you were saying into French in my head." I laughed at that with everyone. "You have to excuse me. This is the longest I've ever been home. Working in an office for the past year has me feeling so trapped."

"We hear that a lot from Sanford County natives. We were born and raised here, but we were always taught to bring The County to the world. We've always wanted to get with like minded people who thought this was possible," Iris said. "So far, we've done a little bit with these friends of ours in Paris. We used to do something with Naomi Iman as well." She smiled hard at me.

I nodded, and said, "I did go to Tokyo after that runway show I did here in the ninth grade. I got silk from there to make a robe for my mother."

"These are the kinds of stories we want to give the people from here, especially the children. That's what our parents wanted to do. That's what we'll continue to do," Delilah said with a wide smile on her face. "So how many languages do you speak besides French?"

"Just conversational Spanish," I answered, disappointed that I'd skipped all four of the foreign languages I took in NYU to work on a line of silk dresses that were called "too urban."

"I'll help you," Peaches said. "My godmother travels internationally for her job and has taught me languages from every place she's visited."

I gave her a polite smile that masked my irritation at her trying to upstage me in front of those women. That bitch was trying to show them which one of us was more valuable.

Delilah got out of her chair and went to our star piece.

"Tell me about this platinum gown." She fingered the fabric and circled it while she inspected it. "How did the two of you collaborate?"

"I think my strength is knowing how fabrics work together and move, and Monaysia's is knowing what they should be doing. Monaysia's still teaching me about sewing and patterns. She's the encyclopedia on them," Peaches began.

I looked at her and blinked several times. That wasn't something I was used to in that setting. I was waiting for her to pop up with something that she'd seen me working on or hidden from her in my house. All she did was talk about how much we complimented each other.

"Because of the job that I have, I have to stay ahead of the trends, but Monaysia is more of a visionary. She plants the seeds to create the trends. I'm the math. She's the science," Peaches kept going.

I was so caught up in waiting for her to do something backhanded that I didn't realize she was just filling the empty space until I found room to talk. That made me think of my public speaking class, which made me remember that was where my water broke, which made me think of NyQuest. I'd never been that scatterbrained during such an important meeting. Usually, I was focused on getting to the money. I wanted to get home and snuggle against my baby, and I hated it.

"Nay, why did you say we should go for platinum instead of silver?" Peaches asked me.

I rubbed my temples, and said, "I'm sorry. This is my first time being outside the house without the baby since I had him. I didn't realize it was gonna hit me this hard."

Delilah and Iris both snickered at that.

"Think about this: he's cute now because he can't say anything. One day, he'll bust up in your job demanding keys to a car he won't even put gas in, or he'll be looking at your clients' butts and boobies when you're trying to work, and all you'll have is this day when you were actually missing him," Iris told me. She stood and came around the table. "Tell us about this dress."

I sniffled, and it irritated me. Quickly, I got my shit together and rambled about platinum being hotter than silver at the time. When I wrapped the fur stole around the neck, those three women lost their damn minds. That was the moment we knew we had the job. They even made the actress come in for a fitting. It was a little bit snug on her.

"Nyla J'adore, did we send them the correct measurements? You've been the same size for the past three or four years," Iris said.

I put a tape measure around the girl's waist and then met her eyes. There was something familiar in them. Her eyes darted around the room.

"I need to talk to you guys alone," she said in a small voice.

They said the girl was only 15, and she was pregnant. I hoped she had as good of an outcome as me.

We exited the room, leaving the Campavhores to fuss at that girl about her career plans. There were a lot more solutions than when I had that conversation with my parents. Banger and Rize came in and took the easels that held our sketches and our patterns and loaded them back onto the rack. We left the costumes there and went to the car. The older man who'd brought the racks out to the car pulled himself away from a short woman in police academy sweats. She frowned at us and turned away. He smacked her butt and then turned to us.

"You ladies sure you like thugs from South Ridge? I got a whole new life I could show you."

Peaches grabbed me by my wrist and pulled me away from him.

"Tell your mama I said hi, Jessica!"

Peaches spun on her heels and started toward the man. Opening his jacket, he exposed a sheriff's badge to stop her.

"Make sure you vote for me, girls."

I pulled Peaches away from him after I watched him lick his teeth and flicker his tongue at us. Peaches had her hand in her purse. I pulled her harder.

"What happened?" Rize called after us.

"Nothing," Peaches said, and bucked her eyes at me to keep me quiet.

"Nay ain't pulling you like nothing happened. What happened?" Rize pressed.

"Nothing. We just saw Kevin kissing Nadine, and he said something smart to us about telling Delilah not to meet with us anymore if we told," Peaches said quickly.

Banger sucked his teeth and told us to stay in the car.

"My mother got killed when I was five. He took the report. He makes sure to say something about my mother every time he sees me," she whispered. "And he refuses to say my full name. My name is Jessica Danielle."

I grimaced and then bucked my eyes. "Why the hell did we come down here then?"

"He's usually not here. Iris is his first wife, but they're getting divorced because that boy he was with is his son with Delilah. It looks like he might knock up Nadine before his and Delilah's wedding," she told me, and then giggled when she saw the way horror crumpled my face.

"What about Tina?" I asked.

"Tina has a bunch of cats because she sees how stupid bitches act over niggas," Peaches said with a giggle.

I didn't know if that was a shot at me, so I didn't giggle at that.

"Wow. DPD niggas look down on everybody else but have that kind of dirt?" I said.

"DPD has the dirtiest...dirt." She made a face and rolled her eyes around in dissatisfaction with her phrasing. "That's why it's called DPD. Deep Pockets District. They reach deep in their pockets to make sure all their secrets get kept."

"Money ain't too long if people know all that about that family in there." I looked back toward the building.

"That's minor dirt compared to the secrets that must be keeping them fighting over Kevin's ugly ass," Peaches said.

Banger and Rize loaded the last of the easels into the car and then hopped inside.

"So what up? Y'all get the job?" Banger asked.

"They in there talking about taking us to Paris next summer," Peaches replied.

Banger turned around and looked at me. "I know this was always the goal, but I don't want you to leave me. I love our little family."

What he said made my heart race, so I was quick to tell him, "I didn't really wanna get into this now, but they said you and Quest could come with me."

"If G-Ma ain't going, then something else is gonna have to get worked out," Rize commented.

I sucked my teeth. "See that's why I said I didn't want to discuss this now. Why we gotta have all these outside opinions?"

Before an argument started, Rize put his hands up. "You right. I'm outta line."

I crumpled my face while my eyes darted around the car.

Rize turned around and cracked a smile at me. "I know how to admit when I'm out of hand."

Banger pulled out of his parking space and asked, "Where we going next?"

"Well, we gotta go to The Opal Lounge first. My girl is singing."

Rize rubbed his palms together. "Me and Peachy are sticking with y'all tonight!"

"Why?" I snapped.

"Damn. You don't like us or something?" Peaches asked.

I giggled. "It's not that. Rize has that look on his face like he wants trouble tonight."

Rize smiled again. "It ain't that. I just like hearing good singing, and I heard about this one chick they be having at The Opal Lounge. They say she's pretty aight."

With my head tilted, I quizzed him, "What's her name?"

"I don't know. Something. I just heard she could sing," he said.

I shook my head while Banger drove.

CHAPTER 4

*T*he Opal Lounge had some upgrades since the last time I was there. With leather seating, leggy wait-resses wearing short black dresses and colored contacts, and a cigar section, it stopped being the beloved bar we'd been sneaking into since high school and started living up to the lounge its name claimed. When we got there, Siraya was standing at the side of a small stage. She spotted me and ran to me, shrieking my name. We clung to each other.

"You really came!" she cried.

"Of course I did. I would have been coming sooner if I knew you were down here doing your thing," I told her. "And if I didn't have the baby."

"I can't wait to see him. He's so cute in the pictures your mother brings to my mother's house," she said. She glanced to the side of me and saw Rize looking at her. She frowned. "Hello."

"What up, though? My name's Rize," he told her.

She huffed. "I know that."

"Where your boyfriend at then?" Rize asked her.

"Backstage getting my tracks ready." She turned her back to him and asked me, "You staying for the whole set?"

I stared at her. Something was wrong.

"Why your friend so mean, Nay-Nay?" Rize asked.

I cut my eyes at him and then rolled them while I kept studying Siraya. She had a bang swept over her left eye. I reached out to touch it. She backed away from me.

"I'll catch up to you after the show," she said, and dashed away.

I looked after her with concern, wondering what had changed.

Rize tapped me. "For real. Why was she so mean?"

"Probably because you fucked her twice, never called her, and now you're acting like you don't know her," I snapped at him while I watched her from afar. She swept the bang over her eye consciously.

"I did?" Rize asked.

Peaches and Banger laughed at that.

"Nah. I would've remembered her. She look good as hell," Rize said.

Peaches sucked her teeth. "She looks like every other girl you've ever fucked: crayon brown, skinny, long legs, short torso, and a little bubble for a booty, and crayon brown. How you manage to find every chick in Sanford County who looks like that is a mystery. Anyway, leave her alone before you make her man put his fist in her other eye. She can't cover both eyes with a bang."

"So I'm not going crazy?" I asked.

"Nope. What's her man's name?" Peaches asked.

"I don't know. This is some new nigga. I haven't seen her since my baby shower, and I'm starting to understand why," I said.

"We'll find out who it is," Banger assured me.

I looked at him. Not wanting to discuss anything further, he put his arms around me and kissed my cheek. Then, he and Rize went to the bar and got drinks for us.

Siraya sounded like she was trying not to cry as she sang, but her voice was still the prettiest in Sapphire Cadre. After her set, we waited for her until the lights came on to tell us to go home. There was a message on my answering machine from her when I got home, telling me she loved me and was so grateful to me for coming to her show. When I tried to call her back, her parents said she never came home.

"Don't worry about it," Banger told me. "I'm gonna go pick something up from Rico and stop at the store. You need anything?"

"For you to stay out the house for about an hour so that I can get your surprise ready," I told him.

He looked at the lingerie on the bed and cracked a half smile before he left. Once the door closed, I hurried to put on the lingerie and get dinner started for him. I was lighting the candles by the time he got back. He sniffed the air.

"Who'd you find to deliver food on this side of the bridge?" he asked.

A smile spread across my face. "I cooked for you."

"You went to find work, *and* you cooked?" he asked. He walked behind me. "What you got on?"

"An apology outfit," I told him.

"An apology outfit? What you apologizing for?" He kissed my neck and then ran his hands up my thighs, stopping where stockings met flesh.

"I'm thinking about taking my portfolio with us to Paris," I said.

"What you mean 'us'?" he asked. "You know what niggas would do to G-Ma if I left?"

"Then bring her with us, Banger, damn. I can't miss this

opportunity," I told him. I calmed myself down. I'd talk him into that before the night was over. "Let me just go back to this apology. I'm sorry I pulled that knife on you. I would never do anything to hurt you. I just got caught up with everything that was going on. I thought I could erase being stupid, but I—"

He wasn't even listening to me. His lips were all over my body. I ripped his belt off and pulled his jeans down. He put me on the table. As soon as he penetrated, Melinda's voice popped into my head, instructing him on what to do to me next. The more I tried to push her out of my mind, the louder her voice was in my head. That was the first time I didn't enjoy sex with him.

"My bad," he said when he finished faster than usual. "You had me horny as fuck since we left the house. I heard you talking about missing the baby and all that. Turned me on almost as much as you talking about them dresses and shit you made. You a wifey for real. I'm the luckiest nigga in South Sanford."

I couldn't help but smile at him. He stared back at me like he was waiting for me to say something. All I wanted to hear was how I turned him on.

"Let's see what you made for dinner, though. I ain't know you learned how to cook."

I sat him at the head seat at the table and turned on Monica. While she sang "Why I Love You So Much," I made him a plate. When I sat it in front of him, he just stared at it.

"What is the problem?" I hollered when he didn't move.

He looked up at me with the most pitiful eyes. "My bad. I know you put a lot of effort into this, but I don't eat spaghetti."

I froze and glared at him.

"Get dressed. I'll take you out to eat somewhere nice in North Sanford. I owe you an apology too."

North Sanford had a special type of five star restaurants that

I hadn't experienced since my modeling days, so I should have jumped at the chance. I had an attitude, though.

"I spent time and money on *this* meal," I snapped.

"I know, and I appreciate it, but there ain't nothing in this world you can do to make me eat spaghetti, Nay. Get dressed, and let me find a tie. I wanna take you somewhere with five forks and linen napkins."

I blinked about three times before my eyes started shooting fire at him. He pulled me down on his lap and quietly explained, "Look. When I was little, my mama left me and Marcus in the house by ourselves. For about a week, all I had to eat were raw spaghetti noodles. I haven't been able to eat spaghetti since then. Please don't be mad."

Now, I knew after hearing that pitiful story, I shouldn't have been mad, but I felt like he should have put aside his personal issues with pasta and appreciated what I did. I never cooked for anybody in my whole life. "Fuck your mama! That bitch ain't got shit to do with me and the shit I do for you, nigga!"

He looked at me like I was crazy, and I felt like I was.

"First, I can't go to Paris. Now you talking this bullshit about spaghetti that *I* cooked for you! Do you know who I am? I don't cook for niggas!"

"Nay, I ain't say you couldn't go to Paris." His voice was so even that it pissed me off.

"You don't tell me what the fuck I can and can't do!"

In the panel of mirrors that was on the dining room wall, I caught a glimpse of myself flailing around while I screamed. I wanted to stop and ask myself if I'd lost my damn mind.

"Nay, can you calm down so we can talk? What's up with you?"

"Fuck you, nigga! I gave up my whole life to carry your baby, and you don't appreciate shit that I do! I'm going to Paris whether you come or not! Fuck you!"

He got up from the chair and walked around me. Seeing his

43

back made me see red. I ran to the kitchen, took the pot of spaghetti off the stove, and hurled it at his back. Since his hair was in a jumbled fro, his neck was exposed. I heard the sizzle when the rim of the pan met his neck. He screamed and dropped to his knees. It was satisfying as fuck.

"Yo, what the fuck is wrong with you?" he screamed while he rolled into the bedroom. The lock on the bedroom door clicked. I ran after him and pounded on it. Upon hearing him dialing somebody's phone number, I went to get a knife. He begged for me to calm down while I screamed for him to come out. I wanted to fight, and we weren't going to end up on the bathroom floor unless I got to feel flesh ripped apart by a blade.

Within twenty minutes, Rize, Selena, and all four of Chillz's sisters were at the apartment. In their family, everyone had a key to everyone else's house. That pissed me off even more. I started stabbing the door with the knife. Lynn put me in a headlock while Rize grabbed me by my wrists and snatched the knife from me. Selena lifted my legs and helped her get me away from the door. I jerked myself out of their grasp while Banger fled the house. Rize ran behind him at Lynn's command. Adrianne and Renee came in to help Lynn and Selena with me.

"Who fights in lingerie?" Adrianne asked while Lynn held my head to the floor. She told her hippo of a sister to let me go. I clawed at Lynn and kicked at Selena while screaming for Banger.

"Monaysia, have you lost your mind?" Selena asked me while she clamped my legs.

Lynn let me drop and helped Renee find something to clean the spaghetti sauce out of the carpet, mumbling about Banger's security deposit when he took the baby and left me.

A voice catapulted from the core of my diaphragm, warning her, "My nigga ain't going nowhere!"

Everyone jumped between us to shield me from Lynn. Selena let go of my legs and covered my mouth. "Monaysia, this is postpartum depression making you act like this. Please relax before you back yourself into a place you can't get out of." She clenched my arms when she felt me trying to swing. "Monaysia, you're fighting in $1000 worth of lingerie. You just assaulted the only person in the world who gives a damn about you. Let me get you some help."

Lynn came from a broom closet lugging a rug shampooer that I didn't know we owned. She swung the nozzle in my direction while looking at Selena.

"You trying to rationalize with this hoe?"

Selena put her hand up for Lynn to stop talking. Lynn folded her arms and tightened her mouth.

"I've read a lot about postpartum depression, Monaysia. I didn't say anything until now, but you seem to be suffering from it," Selena said in a bedtime story voice. "Do you want me to help you find someone to talk about it with?"

"I want you to get the fuck out of my house so I can get my baby!" I screamed.

"Is everything okay in here?" I heard a woman's voice say while she knocked on the door and walked in. I hadn't seen that woman since my elevator ride with her on the day I moved into the building.

"You wait until you're invited into someone's house," Adrianne directed her.

"I understand, but I'm concerned with the amount of noise I heard coming from this apartment. We don't normally do—" She stopped speaking and looked into each of the sisters' faces, her frown going deeper the longer she looked at them. "You're the daughters of the death row inmate, Jeremiah Revolution, aren't you? With the way this city is fighting to make the rest of the county believe that he didn't orchestrate that child trafficking ring, why are you conducting yourselves like this?"

They all stared back at her without answering. Lisa pushed

that woman out of the house and slammed the door in her face. She whipped around and pointed at me.

"This is your last, bitch. If anything happens to my nephew or my great-nephew, your ass is dead. I'm not fighting you, not paying no little hood chicks, nothing. Your ass is *dead*." She stared at me long enough for what she said to sink into the walls and carpets and then turned around and ripped the door open. The woman was still standing there, so she yelled, "What the fuck do you want?"

The woman turned around. "I'm glad my husband and I are closing on our own house and buying this complex next month. I know South Ridge when I smell it, and I can't wait to get rid of your stench."

"Lisa, no! That lady is elderly!" Renee charged after her sister, who was on the hunt for that woman's blood. I heard the staircase door slam.

Adrianne said, "We gotta get out of here. This shit is about to get real bad for Shaan if that's that mouthy bitch from G-Ma's church that I think it is." She looked directly into my eyes and asked, "Are you going give me permission to check you in somewhere and get you some help that's gonna prevent you from getting your ass whooped? Because I don't give a fuck what Lisa's talking about. I'll beat your ass every single day for the rest of my life if it keeps my nephew safe from your crazy ass."

"You ain't gonna touch me!" I yelled at her.

Lisa came back into the doorway, panting. She glowered at me. Her eyes were darker than black.

"Let's go. I told that bitch what the deal is. If anything happens to Shaan or Quest, she's gonna die a slow, miserable, rotten death. That's on my mama. Now let's get out of here before that bitch calls the police."

All of the windows were closed, and we were too many floors up for it to matter if the main floor door was closed. When Lisa spoke, the wind gusted through my apartment. They all left me there like they were scared of catching the death she threatened me with.

I sat in the house, all alone, and cried about not getting to see my baby. For two days I laid in bed and wondered if I'd ever see him or Banger again.

CHAPTER 5

*O*n Saturday morning, I awoke to my mother screaming at me over the answering machine for not bringing NyQuest to see her. As I was about to turn it off, Selena's voice came through, asking if I wanted to see my baby.

I snatched the phone off the cradle. "Why are you talking to me like I need your permission to see him?"

"I see you're still acting a fool. I'll try again tomorrow." She hung up the phone.

In the quiet of the apartment, I wondered where Banger was and paged him. Lynn called me back, said she wasn't letting him come back, and slammed the phone in my ear. Selena called with another offer to bring NyQuest. By then, I was crying and mad that I was crying about it.

I stepped out into the chaos that I caused. My heart thumped while I tried to wrap my head around the fact that I was capable of the scene before me. The entire dining room was covered in spaghetti sauce. I could still hear Banger's cries from the pot hitting his skin. After being told no so many times, it felt so satisfying to be able to fight back. My hands shook. I wasn't sure if it was because I was anxious to throw

48

another pot at his head, or if I was terrified by how much I enjoyed it.

Chillz was the one who brought NyQuest. He had food and a steam cleaner. Nyir was with him. They worked on the darkest stain in the carpet while I ate in my room. I sat with NyQuest and watched him judge me through his baby eyes. My phone rang.

"The baby. I want to see the baby, Nay," Siraya said.

"And I wanna see your eye, bitch. What the hell are you doing letting a nigga punch you in your face?" I demanded.

Chillz and Nyir's heads turned in my direction from outside the room, so I closed the door in their faces.

"Nay, I don't want to hear about that right now. I'm trying to be done with him, but things are crazy. I just want to see the baby," she said.

I sucked my teeth.

"I'm under a contract with him, Nay, and I don't have a way out until I get this album." Her voice shook when she said, "Hey. At least I'm getting the album out the deal. Can I come see the baby or not?"

"Yeah. I'm getting my carpet cleaned, so I'll just head out before I'm stuck in my room, waiting for it to dry," I replied while I started to pack a diaper bag for NyQuest.

When I exited the room, Chillz grinned at me. I had no idea why it made me feel warm and fuzzy inside.

"I'll hit you on your hip later to come pick him up," he told me.

I stared at him quizzically.

"You having bad postpartum depression like they say you are, you need to get some time to yourself and some rest. You're a handful, but I know you couldn't have been feeling like you to flip out like that over some spaghetti," he explained and went into his pocket. "Banger told me to give this to you to make sure you were good if you wanted to leave the house and treat yourself to anything." He placed a wad of money in my hand and went back to scrubbing the stain out the carpet with Nyir.

My car rode much smoother than the last time I was in it. That made it easier to avoid the potholes that seemed to form overnight. Getting onto smoother surfaces once I crossed the bridge was a welcomed relief.

With the divorce finalized, Mommy needed a new theme to the rooms in her house. Siraya sat on the couch in the middle of bluebird and rose chinoiserie decorations. She had a Mickey Mouse outfit and diaper bag for NyQuest.

"I know you got everything under the sun at that baby shower, but I had to get him something." She backed up when she saw me looking at how her hair was swept over one shoulder to cover her face. "I called and broke up with him after we got off the phone. I'll figure out the contract later."

"Well, good. We can't let him kill you before you get your album out and name it after me," I said.

She giggled and asked where Banger was. I told her about the spaghetti incident. Her mouth hung open while she listened.

"Girl, he pissed me off when I tried to talk to him about working in Paris," I pleaded my case.

"Girl, can you even go to Paris after slicing that girl's face open?" she asked.

I pushed my head forward. "How do you know about that?"

She sat back on my mother's couch and said, "Girl, there is not a single day that your name goes unheard. I don't care if it's on the streets or in school. That baby daddy you got comes with a whole story, and people love to talk about your part in it. You need to write a book."

That made me tingle a little bit. Then, I remembered how much I hated him at the moment.

"So did you hear that we broke up too?" I asked.

"You did?" she exclaimed. "I heard you put him out the house over that bitch, and he's begging you to get back in."

"You're such a good publicist." I smirked at her and took the money Chillz gave me out of my purse. She zoomed in on it while I picked up NyQuest. "Let's go shopping with this guilt money he had his people drop off."

My mother dashed into the room holding a dish towel and one of her good wine glasses. She frowned at us putting on our coats.

"Where are you going with my grandson?" she demanded.

"To the mall," I replied.

She looked down at the glass and back at the kitchen. "Leave my grandbaby here. There's no telling when I'll be able to get you to get up from under that man and bring him back over here. Just be back in time for him to poop."

I tilted my head at her and crumpled my face in confusion.

"Don't look at me like I'm stupid. This baby should be on a schedule by now. What time does he poop?" She put the glass and towel on the dining room table. I noticed she'd set three places.

"I don't know," I told her with my eyes on the three place settings. "I've only had to change two diapers since he was born."

My mother grimaced. "Who's been changing them?"

"His daddy. That's what he got one for, right?" I asked her.

Mommy craned her neck backward and said, "You better hold onto that one. I've never heard of the daddy changing more diapers before in my life."

That made me miss Banger. I looked at my mother's face frowning and thought how sad her life had to be that she couldn't ask the person she kicked out of her life to come have dinner with her. Siraya and I left with our eyes still on the table.

Once we were in the driveway, Siraya made a face at my car.

51

"Let's take my mom's car," she suggested. "Even as the greatest publicist in the world, I can't work my way around this one." She shook her head at the lackluster, tan vehicle.

"Girl, I just drive this one because the cars he drives for work have the pigs all over him. This little bucket is low profile to keep unnecessary attention off of me," I explained.

"Oh! That makes perfect sense!" she exclaimed, holding onto the last word while her eyes went to me as though she remembered something.

I looked into her eyes. Before the question left her mouth, I asked, "Is Miguel a cop now?"

"Girl! I was driving to work one morning and swore I saw him working out with the police academy!"

We hurried down the street to get out of the cold, comparing notes on where we'd seen my ex.

"What did he say when you gave him his ring back?" she asked me.

I sucked my teeth. "What I look like giving a ring back? I earned that shit. It's still in a drawer in my old bedroom in case I need to pawn it one day."

We ran and jumped into her mother's Buick. I eyed her for how quickly she moved.

"My ex has been following me. I never want to be in a relationship like this again. I used to think it was so cute when Miguel would come snatch you up out The Opal Lounge."

"Miguel never gave me a reason to wear a swing bang, Siraya," I pointed out.

She took a deep breath and then started the car. Memorial Mall in North Sanford was where we usually went for shopping sprees. Siraya's self consciousness about her face took us to the Mall of East Sanford out in DPD where we didn't know too many people. That didn't matter much, because people knew who I was.

I was just minding my business, spending Banger's guilt

money, and this guy with a neck full of gold walked up to the register and asked if he could take me on a date. His friend pulled him back, eyeing me.

"You can't afford her. That's Banger's baby-mama."

"Oh shit!" the one with the gold yelled loud enough for everybody in the Guess Store to hear. "My bad. They said he was with a model. I ain't know you was working with all that. Tell your man I said I'll see him on Tax Day, and I ain't mean no disrespect."

My nose was in the air the rest of the time we walked through the mall. I was full of myself and my relationship status, even though it was questionable. Nobody else in was getting the respect I was getting. Whether they got fucked by my man in a rental or not, they didn't have the title I held. The attention entertained Siraya enough to take her mind off of her swollen eye for a moment. We went back to my mother's house with a car full of bags and my head swollen.

"Monaysia, what kind of baby did you birth?" Mommy asked when we walked back into her house. "This boy don't do nothing but make this one little fussing sound if he needs something. Otherwise, he just sits here and smiles."

Siraya peered at him. "That is the cutest baby I've ever seen, Monaysia. You gotta get him in some commercials." She squinted at him. "I should hold him, right?"

"You're his godmother. Of course you should." I draped his burp cloth over her shoulder.

She gasped. "I get to be the godmother?"

"Who else would it be? Nay-Nay doesn't like anybody else," Mommy said.

Siraya looked awkward sitting there with NyQuest. He smiled up at her.

"Nope. Don't want this. I wouldn't do anything except hold him all day," Siraya said while smiling back at him.

"You sure wouldn't want it. The first time you try to go back to work after you have one, you cry because you realize your baby ain't there," I told her. "That's what happened to me at The Green Balloon the other day."

"Nay, that sounds like them crazy ass white women on Lifetime who drown their babies in the bathtub," Mommy said.

"Why would I drown my baby in the bathtub if I miss him, Mommy?" I asked. Then, I decided I didn't want to know what was going through her head.

"Well, you've never had many maternal instincts," she continued.

"Okay. Well, I got them now," I mumbled.

"So you mean to tell me you sit up in the house all day with a baby?" Mommy questioned.

"Nope. I wake up in the morning, and my man brings me breakfast in bed and thanks me for having his baby. Then, he gets the baby dressed and takes him to his grandmother's house while I heal from having his baby," I told her.

"You were in labor for 14 minutes," she argued.

"Does it matter? I pushed the baby out with no drugs," I challenged her. "And then he comes back with fabric and orders from people wanting me to make outfits for them and money from the ones that I sold out of his aunt's store. That's how he got me that costume designing job at The Green Balloon."

Mommy's face puckered as she stood over me. "What did *you* ever do to deserve a man like that?"

"What mother doesn't deserve a partner in the father who helped her make the child?" I challenged her.

Mommy's hands went to her hips. "When you and Kidra were babies, your father didn't do even half of what you're saying. What did you do to motivate this one?"

I shrugged. "He just likes me, Mommy. He liked me from the first time we met."

Mommy raised her eyebrows and asked, "Did he like you, or did he like the coochie you were selling?"

The whole room went silent. Even NyQuest stopped cooing and turned his head toward Mommy. Siraya and I stared at her. I looked around at the figurines she'd managed to replace from her fight with my dad and thought about throwing one at her. When I didn't say anything, Siraya chuckled to break the tension.

"Nay-Nay stay with a boyfriend that wanna do everything for her."

Mommy sucked her teeth and asked, "At what cost? The first time he came over here was in a truck I saw in a rap video. Got my clients asking me questions about what he does for a living and dropping hints about the answers."

"Your clients don't pay you to ask questions about me," I told her, trying to keep my voice calm.

"Well, my clients also come in there talking about the arguments you have with your drug dealer boyfriend over dinner. Some of my clients live in your building, and it's embarrassing to me that you're making them think you're from South Ridge!" Her eyebrows knitted while her voice rose, and I wished I had another pot of spaghetti to throw.

"How are you embarrassed by what somebody who lives in an apartment has to say about me?" I hopped to my feet, pounding my chest in full defense mode. "My man works at least three jobs to keep me in that house and make sure I don't leave it without money, and not one of those jobs involved."

"I've seen his mother, Monaysia," she countered.

"And?" I shot back without taking a breath. "Don't you think his mama being a crackhead is keeping him from wanting that kind of life for our son? He works at the furniture store that his family owns, some of the clubs that his family owns; he fixes cars at the place that he gets the cars from that you're judging him for driving over here; and he's gonna own one or all of them one day. Your clients can't say nothing about what my man does when he's building the generational wealth they're paying you to tell them how to scrape to get."

"Well, what is Geno's Auto Sales? It's written on every truck he drives over here." She had a smug look on her face as though she thought she had me backed into a corner.

"It's a car dealership and a repair shop." Irritation had me shuffling my feet, and something really rude was about to come out of my mouth.

"But he can't get you anything better than that piece of junk you're driving?" she shot back.

"You know what? I've been kicking and screaming about that for months, but now I understand why. It was way better for him to just fix that hoopty." Thinking about how impossible it would be to ever get a decent car while I was with him made me groan.

My pager went off. I looked at the voicemail notification and reached for the phone.

"All those jobs, and that boyfriend can't buy you a cell-phone?" Mommy snarked.

Siraya bucked her good eye at Mommy while I listened to Banger's message.

"How long you gonna have my son out?" he asked me when I returned the call.

I answered, "I'm on my way out the door right now."

He paused and listened to my mother going off before he asked, "Did you get a chance to eat? You need some money?"

"Chillz gave me the money you sent with him," I replied and frowned at Mommy still chattering.

"I'm about to come get Quest. I don't feel like waiting for you to get across the bridge," he instructed me and hung up the phone.

When she accepted that I wasn't going to argue with her, Mommy turned away and went to dust her figurines. I took

Siraya and NyQuest upstairs and checked to make sure no one had touched my ring. Siraya gasped when I opened the box.

"I see why your mama's mad. That diamond is way bigger than her wedding ring," she whispered, and we giggled. "Then again, so are the ones in your nameplate."

We giggled again. I went into my closet to see what Kidra left that I could give to Siraya. There were some handbags left-over from a show that I did for a designer that told me my hips were too wide for her skirts. I was too happy to get them away from her.

"You just bought me clothes with your boyfriend's money. Why do you always treat me like I'm your baby?" she asked me.

"Because the last time I talked to Best, he told me something crazy about your parents making you work another job because I was working and in school," I explained. "This is just to offset some of the grief being friends with me has caused you."

"Well, bitch, gimme some luggage too if that's the case," she said, and we laughed.

"Come to my house tonight," I said. "Banger probably ain't coming home, and he'll have mad niggas with him if he does." I put my ring in a different drawer and took NyQuest downstairs just as a horn honked. Banger stood in the living room, talking to my mother about how good of a baby NyQuest was.

"That's cuz Nay's a good mother," he said. He looked at me coming down the stairs and took some money out of his pocket. "Take your friend out to dinner or something. You ain't had no time out the crib in a while."

My mother sucked her teeth. We all looked to see what her problem was.

"What kind of man treats your friend that good too? Is that included in your price?" she asked.

That time, Banger joined the number of people who looked at her like she was crazy.

Mommy kept right on: "And you got the nerve to have an attitude because he doesn't want you to go to Paris? I know you didn't get pregnant, thinking he was gonna be so in love with you that he would pay your way there as appreciation for having his baby. Wake up, honey! You had your chance at Paris, and you blew it!"

"Let's just go, girl," I said to Siraya. Whatever Mommy's problem was had nothing to do with me.

We walked out the house ahead of Banger. He caught up to us and stared at the way Siraya's hair was swept over one side of her face. She tugged at it and hurried by him. He called out to me. Lynn yelled out the car window that she needed to get back to work before I could respond. Even though I was shaking, I went to Banger and pulled the carrier from his hands so that I could kiss NyQuest. He looked up at me, cooed, and smiled. For a second, I wanted to tell Banger to come back for him the next day. Lynn barked once again that she had to get to work. Tears went down my face when I told NyQuest I loved him. Then, Siraya and I walked down the street to her house. A rose and a teddy bear were on her doorstep. She sighed and kicked them over.

We dressed to impress that night so that I could show off one of the upscale businesses Banger's family owned. We went to a cocktail lounge downtown called 90 Convent Grille. Melinda took me there for lunch once. The line of people waiting to get in that went halfway down the block made the dinner atmosphere superior. Someone taking names for tables looked at me and told "Banger's baby-mama" to come right in. Siraya couldn't stop looking around. I thought she was dazzled by the live DJ and the gold fixtures, but her eyes scanned every face in sight.

"Girl, would you calm down? There are a hundred people standing outside waiting to get in, and you're in here acting crazy," I whispered.

"I swear somebody is watching me," she said.

"Let me hurry up and get you drunk so you can tell me what this sorry ass nigga did to you," I mumbled and then smiled up at a server bringing us a bottle of wine.

Siraya snickered at it and waved it away, "Bring us your finest bottle of Taylor Port."

That made me laugh as I remembered when Best snuck us bottles of Taylor Port from his parents' liquor cabinet before school dances. Horror bulged the waiter's eyes until he realized we were joking.

The server informed us, "The gentleman who sent it thinks you'll like its full bodied flavor."

We thanked him for it and let the waiter fill our glasses halfway. Siraya looked around nervously before taking a sip.

The server returned with oysters from whoever sent the wine.

Siraya pulled me from my seat. "This has my ex's name written all over it, Nay." She pulled a taser from her purse.

"Siraya, please sit down and relax," I pleaded.

The server leaned over and pretended to be refilling her glass as he told her, "There's a gentleman sitting two tables away who will make sure nothing gets in the way of enjoying your time."

To get a discreet look at who the waiter was talking about, I took a compact out of my purse and flipped it open. I was sure the large man I saw pretending to read a menu was someone who brought kids to G-Ma's house.

"Girl, let's just enjoy ourselves," I told her and hoped she'd drink some more so I could get her story. She refused to get more than a buzz, so we prepared to leave.

"I'm sorry, Nay, but this past month has been the worst month of my life, except the night that you came to hear me sing. I'm scared to keep pursuing music—"

She stopped speaking when two men who looked like they could play defense for the Bills stood over our table. Siraya's eyes enlarged. From the side, I saw our per diem bodyguard poising himself to attack.

"Siraya, please don't be afraid of me," a brown man wearing a mink jacket said. His hands were full of gold. He cradled a long stemmed bouquet of roses.

"Tell your friend that I'm done with him. I don't care how much a lawyer costs. I'm getting out of that contract," she told him, her voice shaking.

"Allow me to buy you out of your contract." He laid the roses on the empty seat next to her.

"No!" she roared, her voice loud enough to get the attention of people at surrounding tables. "No more wining and dining, and no more shady deals."

"Siraya, I wanted to work with you first. I'm the one who took Snap down to Suite 2130 to hear you sing. We were supposed to be doing business together. He snaked me and Mike." He motioned to the larger, darker man with him. That man's eyes were on me, so I kept mine on Siraya.

"Pressure, please leave me and my friend alone. We're having a girls' night out. I need to get myself together. This week has been too much."

Pressure nodded his head and stood. "I heard what he did to you. He won't be a problem much longer. That much I can promise you. Can I make a deal with you? I got a show lined up tomorrow night in Syracuse. I want you to perform in it. If you feel comfortable with the setup, then I'd love to have you come to the studio after and sing some of the songs Mike and a producer we're working with out of Atlanta named Deuce have come up with for you. We're getting rid of Snap and joining forces with Deuce's clique. Please say yes. I'd love to take you shopping for this show."

"Nay-Nay is my stylist. Give whatever money you were gonna spend on my clothes to her," Siraya snapped at him. "And how did you know I was here anyway?"

"I followed Snap. He's been following you around all day," Pressure told her. He smiled at me and then motioned toward me with his head. "You heard the lady, Mike. Give the money for her wardrobe to her stylist."

"I'll also need a notarized statement saying that this isn't a loan against any advance that I have yet to accept and has nothing to do with my contract." Siraya's voice was stern as she pointed a finger at him that let us all know she wasn't playing any games.

"Of course. You're doing me the honor of giving this performance," Pressure said.

Mike took an envelope from his leather jacket and placed it in front of me.

"My number's in there if you run into any problems," he said to me, locking his pupils into mine.

"I won't run into any problems, so take your number out of there," I said loud enough for the bodyguard to hear.

He removed the business card from the envelope and raised both of his hands in surrender.

"Can't blame a man for trying."

I looked away from him without saying anything else. We waited for them to leave before asking the bodyguard to walk us to our car. Pressure was relentless. He drove a black GMC Yukon right next to us, the gold rims spinning even after he stopped.

"I'm looking forward to seeing you perform, Siraya. Please take a chance with me," Pressure damn near begged.

Mike called me over to the driver's side of the car. I turned my head.

Siraya's voice was firm. "I'll take a professional chance with you once I see what this show is like."

"I was hoping for more than professional, but that's a start," Pressure replied. "See you soon."

We watched his car until we could no longer see its shine

and customized license plates. The bodyguard helped us into our car.

"When you feel yourself being followed this time, it's me. I didn't like the way you were shaking while he talked to you," the bodyguard said.

Once we were safe inside of my apartment, Siraya smirked at me and said, "It's about time we went out somewhere, and I got a man to pay for our dinner and send us expensive drinks."

My apartment was completely still and smelled like lemon and pine. There was no sign of my attack on Banger. Siraya marveled at my furniture. Her eyes landed on the painting in the dining room. I hadn't looked at it in a while.

"That's so sweet that he got somebody to paint your grandmother for you," she commented while she walked closer to it.

"You think it looks like my grandma too?" I asked her.

She nodded. "Except for the brown eyes, it looks just like that woman who used to use me as the model for teaching you how to make clothes."

Turning on the TVs didn't help replace the noises I was used to hearing at home. There were no messages from Banger on the machine, so I paged him. Lynn called me back to dictate my visitation schedule for the next day. Her bark competed with the loud music. I started craving fried fish and Crown Royal.

"You can't keep my baby from me," I told her through gritted teeth.

Her voice actually softened, surprising me. "I ain't doing this to be mean. Your ass needs some help. Shaan has a second degree burn on the back of his neck, and I don't even think you realize what you did to him over some fucking spaghetti. We're giving you some time to get some help. I can't make you go get it, but I can keep that baby safe from you until you get therapy for that postpartum depression. Selena even found a group for you to go to. I'll take you my damn self."

I imagined a bunch of wack bitches sitting in a circle,

drinking apple juice while they talked about how badly they wanted to drown their babies and hung up the phone in Lynn's face. I did not have time for that bullshit.

Siraya was already curled up on my couch and snoring when I hung up the phone. I covered her with a blanket and then got into my own bed. Falling asleep came easy. At 2am, though, I woke up to feed NyQuest. Instinct made me goto the kitchen and make the bottle. Then, I took it to his room as I normally did and tried to hand it to Banger. When it hit the floor, I realized Banger wasn't there, changing his diaper as he did every night. I sat in the rocking chair in his room and cried the rest of the night.

IN THE MORNING, Selena and Chillz brought NyQuest. There was the joyous sound of NyQuest cooing, lifting the mood in my apartment. They sat in the house until G-Ma was ready to be picked up from church, and they didn't leave any money. Selena made the same offer as Lynn. While shaking my head, I closed the door behind them.

The house returned to its lifeless state. To drown out the longing for the return of my family, I went into my sewing room to get Siraya's outfit together for her show. Half of the clothes I had in there were gone. An envelope of money with an invoice from Peaches and Lynn sat on my sketching table. We were selling the hell out of those jeans.

Since the first outfit I had in mind for Siraya was gone, I went into my bedroom closet to get a group of outfits I'd been working on during my maternity leave. The phone rang while I made touches on the slip dress and sheath. The Caller ID read anonymous, so I didn't answer it until the third time it rang.

"I miss you, Nay," Banger said.

The sound of his voice melted me from the inside. I clamped my legs together.

"You don't even call me back when I page you," I snapped at him.

"I ain't call to argue with you. I just wanted to hear your voice," he said.

"So come home and hear it then," I tried to keep my voice from taking on a beggar's tone.

"Can't do that right now," he said.

"Why? You out of town at work or something?" I guessed.

He didn't answer, so I hung up the phone.

Shortly after that, my doorbell rang. I looked through the peephole and snatched the door open when I saw Squeak and Shanae standing there with their kids.

"Hey, girl! Banger told us to come get some of his stuff until he could come move the rest out!" Shanae announced, her voice louder than ever.

I blinked at her rapidly with my blood boiling.

"Tell him to turn his draws inside out until I go out of town tomorrow," I barked at her.

"Girl, where you even gonna go? Your mammy put you out, and your pappy is stuck so far up Melinda's ass that he can't breathe," Shanae quipped. "Just let us get his shit. He's letting you keep the apartment."

Siraya came to the door and softly asked, "What is it that he needs? I'll get it for you while Nay calls him to make sure you get everything."

"His Sega and his Super Nintendo," Shanae replied. "Um, five white t-shirts..."

Siraya nodded her head and asked me where the things were while I paged Banger. Lynn called back, so I hung up on her and shoved everything they asked for into a bag.

"I didn't mean to get in your business, but something about

that didn't sound right. Whatever it is, he can sort out with them."

The next time the phone rang, Siraya looked at the clock and told me to answer it even if it was a private caller.

"This is Pressure of High Pressure Records. I was told I'd be able to reach Siraya at this number. Is she available?"

"He sounds professional," I said as I passed her the phone.

She listened to him for a few seconds and then said, "I'll try to hurry, but you're a lot earlier than I thought you'd be…" She cringed and then looked down at me strapping her shoe. "Do you think it's okay for him to come upstairs and wait?"

Since Banger was obviously moving out, I shrugged and told her to tell him which apartment it was.

Neither of us expected him to bring up a whole gang of people with weed and liquor. They blasted the latest DJ Clue mixtape on my stereo while they went through the house. The guy who was with Pressure at the restaurant came into the room where I was dressing Siraya and reintroduced himself.

"My name is Mike, and I have to ask you a question. Were you in a club called The Spot last Thanksgiving?"

The tips of my ears burned when I remembered peeking at him through the glass that separated his VIP section from mine in the club the year before.

When I didn't answer him, he pressed, "Is this you?"

After taking my time sweeping blush onto Siraya's cheeks, I peeked over my shoulder at him. He was holding an old magazine ad for Lovely Tresses relaxer, my first national campaign.

"Back when I was in the 7th grade," I answered.

"My mama used to do hair in the kitchen and had this box of perm in her cabinets. You was the first Black girl with green eyes I ever saw. I've been in love with your beautiful ass since back in them days, yo."

I rolled my eyes and lined Siraya's lips.

Pressure came behind Mike and said to Siraya, "I'm so glad you took this gig. It'll be nice to be able to look at how beautiful you are without worrying about Snap going upside your head for it."

Sick of the poor attempt at sweet talk, I cleaned up my stuff and took my makeup kit back to my room. I didn't realize that Mike had followed me until he spoke, causing me to jump.

"This your baby?" he asked, holding up a picture of NyQuest.

"I told you I got a man. Get out my bedroom." When I continued past him to grab an outfit from my closet, I bumped my toe on a laundry basket. On top was the lingerie I wore during the spaghetti incident. The way Mike stared, I was sure he was waiting for a pair of panties to drop a so that he could sniff them. He was scary but also cute. I turned to him with the lingerie in my hands and held it up so that he could see the whole outfit. He let out a little moan.

"I just need a man's opinion on something. If you came home to me wearing this and cooking spaghetti, what would you do?"

"Marry your ass and eat the spaghetti off you," he rushed to answer.

That made me smile. I told him to get out of my room again and closed the door.

An hour later, a stocky man named Riley called us to leave like we were getting onto a school bus for a field trip. Mike and Pressure cracked jokes about him while Siraya sang her weird warmups all the way down the elevator.

CHAPTER 6

A limo was parked in front of my building. Hope gave Siraya's eyes a glow while Riley held the door for us. Pressure and Mike climbed with us and poured champagne into rhinestone lined glasses. I put my glass to my lips but caught Siraya's eyes to keep her from turning it upward until the men drank first. I'd seen men drop things in women's drinks in clubs I partied in during my life as a model.

Riley fidgeted as he drove. Once we crossed the bridge, he got a call and took us toward Sapphire Cadre. Even through the partition, we could hear him yelling Snap's name. Mike and Pressure chuckled at him. They tried to put their arms around us. Each time, we slipped away from them. Pressure apologized for being too forward with Siraya. Mike stared at me with a gaze so intense that I was uncomfortable. I shifted my body so that my back was to him That didn't stop him from staring.

The limo sped forth. Siraya paled. I commanded her to drink the champagne and put my hand in my purse.

"He ain't gonna touch you," I promised her, and wondered if I could go farther than slicing someone's face.

Pressure put a hand on her shoulder and said, "I'm giving

you my word that he'll never put his hands on you again." He and Mike chuckled again.

Riley charged toward The Opal Lounge. Siraya wanted to be afraid, but she was too nosey. That fool rolled down the limousine window. Immediately she dropped.

"Girl, why does that look like your baby daddy?" She squinted through the window and exclaimed, "That's him and Rize! What are they...?"

I pushed her head down before we were seen. I didn't know why I cared about being spotted in that limo by somebody who obviously didn't want to be with me anymore.

"Oh shit!" we heard Riley yell into the phone before he slammed on his breaks.

"What the hell are they doing in our spot?" I asked. "I thought he was out of town."

Siraya's eyes bucked. "I knew I forgot to tell you something! Banger came to campus looking for Best and told him he would see him for blowing up his girl's pager."

"What?" I slowly made my way back up in time to see Rashad, the bartender, tearing through a crowd with a bunch of people following him.

A BOOM split the air. The scream Siraya let out was a whisper compared to the screaming, stampeding crowd outside. Like an idiot, Riley drove closer to the scene.

"Turn around!" I commanded. My heart thumped while my eyes scanned the crowd to make sure my child's father was still alive.

A car ripped past us and through the mob. Although they were dressed in black hoodies, I made out Banger's, Rize's, and Nyir's frames before they hopped into the car. Then, people cheered for them as cars formed a barricade so the police couldn't get to them before they got out of there safely.

Riley parked the limo at the edge of the scene. I rolled up the window and sat back.

"What happens now?" Siraya whispered, climbing off the floor and straightening her dress.

"We get your beautiful ass on stage at this show," Pressure told her and then projected his voice to reach the front of the vehicle, "if Riley hurries up!"

Riley didn't move, though. About five minutes passed before the emergency responders arrived. Curiosity made us roll down the tinted windows once again to see who was carried out of the bar. I figured that Banger would be too focused on dodging the police to notice I was in the crowd, especially since I thought he was out of town.

That was when I realized his phone call wasn't about him missing me. He used me as an alibi. I was kind of turned on by him including me in something, even though we weren't in the best place. Mike touched me, causing me to dry right up. I sneered at him. Before I could tell him to stop touching me, we heard Riley scream.

"Oh shit!" he yelled. "That looks like Snap on the stretcher!"

"Good. Drive off," Pressure told him.

"What? Snap might be dead!" Riley panicked.

"Even better. Drive off," Pressure said.

Riley hesitated. Just as he turned the car, I saw Best getting escorted from the club holding a white towel around his hand, embarrassment folded into his face. Riley powered the limo toward the club.

Pressure rolled down the partition. Siraya and I begged Riley not to go closer to the club before Pressure could bark his command.

"Fuck you, Siraya. I'm going to check on my man Snap. You deserved to get your ass beat the way you were throwing your pussy at Chillz's son."

"Hold up," I cut him off. "What did you just say about my baby's grandfather?"

Riley's head craned around slowly. Pressure commanded him to stop the car. He got out and wailed on Riley.

"Make sure you thank your baby-daddy for doing my dirty work while I got the opportunity to show his lady a good time." He put his hand on my knee.

I snatched away from him. "I'm here to style my friend, not cheat on my man."

"Why you acting like you don't want me?" he asked.

I sucked my teeth. "You came from out of town knowing who my man is. What use do I have for you?"

"A challenge." He nodded his head several times. "I'm up for it. You'll see who the bigger man is one day soon."

I stopped drinking the champagne after Mike voiced his plans for me. Siraya followed suit. We should have finished the bottle. It would have made us receive the gravel parking lot of the banquet hall Riley pulled into. The four of us went through a door with streamers and a homemade banner hanging over it. The event was an anniversary party for Mike's parents. Siraya's frown touched her ankles.

"Hear me out," Pressure said as we went through the doorway. "Mike's parents are heavily connected. There are a lot of people in the music industry here with their parents. I have someone here interested in having you open for a huge group in a show at Syracuse University the week after Thanksgiving."

"I'll believe it when I see it," Siraya grumbled.

I went into an empty room with Siraya and touched up her lipstick. After making sure her hair and makeup covered her eye, I was taken to a seat at a circular table with three other women. One of them looked at me and turned her back. That was the most communication I received from her. The other two women were Samantha and her friend Courtney. Their eyes lit up as though someone brought them a new playmate for the sandbox.

"It ain't no way in Hell you fuckin with my brother!"

Samantha reminded me of a dark skinned, skinny version of Shanae in that she was loud as hell and kept looking around at the men, even though her ugly boyfriend sat right next to her, looking oblivious.

"I don't even know your brother. I'm here because I made my friend a dress to sing in. Pour me some of that champagne," I told her while I took a seat.

"I knew it. He came home telling my mother he was gonna marry the girl from the perm box. I gotta pee. Y'all coming?"

I didn't know she was talking to me until she pulled me by my hand and said, "Come on, Red."

No one had ever referred to me as a redbone before, so that confused me even further. I went with them, though, because that other girl sitting at the table had an attitude that I couldn't understand.

"Don't mind her. That's my sister. We don't wanna be here," Samantha told me when I asked what her problem was. She bombarded her way into the stall and slammed the door behind her.

Courtney turned to me and pretended to be straightening my little black dress to give herself a reason to stand close to me.

"The only men in here you want to mess with are the Greeks. Mike's dad's frat brothers and their sons have *long* money. Generational money. Stay away from anybody who says they're friends with Mike. Samantha's my girl, but her brother is all over the place," she told me.

"So you're here for the Greeks?" I asked her.

She turned to the mirror to fix one of her curls. "I need me a sugar daddy."

Samantha flushed and staggered toward the sink. "Shit! Me too. Good luck with the redbone and her fine ass friend in the house. It's all eyes on them."

"Oh. I'm not single. I don't think," I said. "I don't know if hood niggas take you back after you throw hot pots of spaghetti at them."

Samantha and Courtney cracked up and led me back to the table just in time to eat dry chicken. I missed my baby's family's food and never wanted to live without it again after choking down that dinner. The wine tasted cheap, and the bar was cash. Tacky.

Toward the end of dinner, Siraya strutted on the stage singing "Inseparable." The ladies around me all asked each other if they knew where to get a dress like hers.

"You her stylist, Red! Where'd you get the dress?" Samantha asked when Siraya was done singing.

All eyes turned to me. I was excited to answer them.

"I made it."

"Did you make the one you're wearing too?" Courtney asked.

"I sure did," I replied and started handing out business cards while Siraya continued to entertain the room with her pretty Soprano voice.

"Caramel Sundae, you ain't got no more friends you could bring up here next time?" Riley asked from the next table.

I looked at the tiny, portly man and told him, "Siraya's my only friend. Sorry."

"You ain't sorry!" Samantha yelled and then took me for a lap around the room while her man continued to drink.

Per Courtney's suggestion, I only paid attention to the men with fraternity letters as centerpieces on their tables. I wasn't really looking to cheat. The uncertainty in my relationship status left me room to take sugar daddy applications. One kept his eyes on me as I walked between Courtney and Samantha. He had grey hair. It took me back to the day I found out what Banger did for a living. Before I had the chance to get sad, a woman blocked his path to me.

"I just wanted you to know that you were very rude for walking away before taking my phone number."

The voice sounded like mine in a higher octave.

"Kidra?"

She turned to me slowly. "Nay-Nay? What are you doing here?"

"I'm Siraya's stylist." When I tried to hug her, she stiffened.

"Don't you need to be at home with your newborn?" she pressed, volume at an unnecessary decibel.

"Newborn?" The man who was approaching me stopped in his tracks.

I posed for him so that he could get a view of my profile. "Don't even look like I had one, does it?"

As Kidra came closer, I saw she was wearing a dress she took from my closet at my parents' house. I smirked at her. She stopped her tirade before I blew up her spot. My eyes traveled down to her hands, allowing me to confirm the handbag she was carrying came from my old closet too.

"Nay-Nay, you've been making clothes for Siraya your whole life. I know you're not trying to pass it off as a job so that you don't have to stay home and be a mother." She was shouting over the music, and I didn't understand why. I tried to walk away, but she grabbed my arm.

Mike ran up to her and snatched her hand from my arm.

"What's the problem here? Why are you acting like this at my parents' party?" he asked.

"I'm just wondering how my sister can be so many miles away from my nephew. That's not what a mother does," Kidra complained.

Mike walked closer to her with his eyes on me. "That's your sister, huh? Well, maybe I should make friends with you so you can talk her into leaving her man and giving me a baby."

Kidra curled her lip at him, shot me a dirty look, and then stomped away.

Mike tried to put his arm around me. "My mother wants to meet you."

"I'm good on niggas' families." I ducked under his arm and went to find Samantha and Courtney.

After the party, I waited for Siraya while Mike and Pressure spoke with a dark skinned man in a Phat Farm sweater vest and jeans who was accompanied by a bunch of men in loud suits and sunglasses. Siraya walked away from them and came to me with displeasure twisting her mouth.

"This feels so shady," she said to me in a low voice. She turned to Courtney and Samantha, putting a smile on her face while I introduced them.

"Y'all the smartest bitches them two ever brought around. Usually, bitches be getting fucked in that car and crying when Pressure and Mike don't call them back. They got plans for y'all, though. They've been talking about wifing y'all up," Samantha told us.

"Well, her mind is on her money and a record deal, and I'm already taken. What else is there to do in this town?" I asked.

"You sure you don't wanna at least have Mike on the side? He has a house in Cazenovia," Courtney told me.

I stared at her while I waited for her to explain what a Cazenovia was. She laughed at how unimpressed I was.

Samantha suggested, "Let's steal their limo and go to Liquids. Go tell Riley to pull the car up," Samantha said.

Riley was willing to do whatever Courtney said, so we left them talking to those men and hopped into the limo. Samantha went right to the champagne and dropped a pill into Courtney's cup before filling it. Siraya and I watched in horror.

"It's Benadryl," Courtney explained. "Samantha has to give this to me because car rides give me bad anxiety."

Siraya and I eyed them until Samantha filled our glasses and told Riley to turn up the music. The long drive to the casino made the night worth the aggravation. I found myself in a corner, dancing with someone who claimed to play basketball for Syracuse University.

Wouldn't you know that I ran into Kidra there too? She yelled at every man who looked at me that I had a baby at home. I didn't want to be in Syracuse anymore. It turned Kidra into an embarrassing person.

I was giving my pager number to someone who was probably lying about going to the NBA when Riley came running toward me with Mike following.

"There she is!"

I acted like I didn't know who they were. As I tried to ease out of their line of vision, gunshots rang out in the club. Siraya and I yanked Samantha and Courtney by their wrists and took off, hoping to remember where the limo was parked. My heart thudded, feet were hurting, but I couldn't die in Syracuse.

Riley, Pressure, and Mike beat us to the limo. They had scowls on their faces. We took a silent ride to the studio. If I wanted to sit in a quiet car, I would have waited for Banger to come home. I wondered if I'd ever get to take a silent ride with him again.

The studio was in a basement of some hole in the wall club in the hood. People partied above our heads while Siraya tried to sing the songs given to her. The equipment looked low budget and gave a lot of feedback. The songs sounded like bubble gum commercial jingles. The Phat Farm-wearing man and the men in the loud suits sat in a corner and made snide remarks about Siraya.

"Yo, Press, why ain't she singing?" Mr. Phat Farm wondered, pointing to me.

"She's the stylist, not the singer," Pressure replied.

"Deuce, quit looking at my girl, and put my lyrics to better beats!" Mike commanded.

Deuce straightened out his Phat Farm vest and grinned at

me, showing a mouth full of diamond encrusted gold teeth. "I ain't know you was spoken for, beautiful."

"Well, I am, just not for nobody in here," I snapped.

"Good to know." He turned back to Pressure and asked, "What the fuck I'm posed to do with this skinny ass girl? That bitch is a toothpick! What's she gonna do, Bankhead Bounce to my tracks? I need a bitch who could sell my shit. The world already got a Whitney Houston."

Hearing him criticize my friend set my insides on fire. I sprang to get Siraya from the booth, just to see tears forming in the corners of her eyes. Firmly gripping her shoulders, I whispered to her, "I know getting picked apart like this in a room that can't handle your talent hurts, but I swear to God I will slap the shit outta you if you let one tear fall. Do not let these niggas see you sweat." Then, I snatched her out of the booth and started out of the room. "Riley, get us back to The County. This whole night was a waste of time."

Samantha and Courtney giggled.

"What county y'all from?" one of the men in loud suits asked me.

I focused on his square jaw. My heart sank when his deep voice hit my ears. "Sanford."

His lips turned upward slightly. "What part? Y'all look like some Saditty Cadre hoes. You the little hooker from the perm box, ain't you?"

I cleared my throat and straightened my dress. "If you're asking if I'm a professional model, the answer is yes."

"Slumburb ass Saditty Cadre. I bet you ain't never been around no real niggas from East Ridge," he said, kicking out his alligator shoes.

"You probably owe my baby's father taxes," I shot back at him.

His smile was touched by the devil. It made a bad feeling

creep up my spine. "You got a baby by my nephew, the killer? What you doing all the way out here in a spot like this?"

"Leaving," I said, pulling Siraya with me. "It was nice to meet you, Samantha and Courtney."

"How we gonna get home, bitch?" Siraya whispered to me.

"Girl, we will figure it out," I whispered back. "Just hold your head up and let these people know that you're too good for this bullshit."

Pressure ran after Siraya, apologizing to her a thousand times for the way the night turned out. She looked at me and got powered up on courage. She didn't say anything until we were back in the limo. To keep Mike from trying to cuddle with me, I made Samantha sit between us.

Once we were on the Thruway, Siraya spoke in a voice that sounded scarily close to one I used back when I was with Miguel, and he was getting on my nerves.

"Pressure, I could have been at home watching movies and playing with my godson. You said you had a gig for me. I sang at a damn banquet and then went and sang into a My First Sony Boombox in a basement for some nigga who tried to ridicule me. I'll never do business with you. I don't even believe you have a record label. Don't call me ever again."

I was so proud of her. I wanted to clap, but I had to cover my mouth to hide my laugh at how upset Pressure looked.

"Siraya, I'm trying to build. I want you to be my first artist. I know this wasn't the best night—"

"No. This night was a complete lie. Please lose my number, and give me back my demo," she told him and turned her back to him. With her arms folded, she crossed her legs and grumbled, "Had my friend waste this bad ass dress on a damn banquet. Do you see how good I look?"

Samantha cracked up while Courtney leaned against her, fighting sleep. She lost the battle and collapsed onto Samantha's shoulder.

My beeper went off. I took it from my bag and saw that I'd missed dozens of pages and voicemails from Banger. Samantha picked up the car phone and told me to call him back in case something was wrong with the baby. Mike gave her a dirty look. She gave one right back to him.

I hit *67 before dialing his number. "Where the fuck you at? You aight?" Banger panicked into the phone.

"Like you care," I snapped.

"We got robbed, and you ain't here. Why the fuck wouldn't I care about that?" he asked.

"Robbed?" I repeated.

"Yeah! They got my video games and some of the clothes you said you made for your friend! Where you at?" he continued.

I sucked my teeth. "You play so much. Squeak and Shanae came and got that stuff like you asked them. What are you even doing there?"

"I live here," he answered.

"I can't tell."

Across from me, Siraya cackled. "I told you nothing sounded right about him sending them for your stuff. Your baby's father don't even seem like he does business like that. You just gave those people Christmas gifts."

I snorted out a laugh and then hung up the phone on Banger. Samantha poured us more champagne and then popped another bottle while Mike made his last attempts at sweet talking me. I told him to switch spots with Siraya so that the liars could be on one side of the car. Samantha cracked up at the way we handled them.

Four bottles of champagne later, Siraya and I got out of the limo and dragged each other into my building. Getting into the elevator was a challenge, but getting my key into the lock was the hardest thing I'd ever done. After five minutes of trying, I laid my head against the door and slid to the floor.

"Fuck that I apartment. We don't need it. We can sleep out here," I mumbled.

"Nay?" I heard Banger say.

"Aw shit, bitch! There's somebody in your house!" Siraya slurred, and we giggled.

Banger snatched the door open. He watched both of us crawl into the house. A hint of smile on his face.

"We made it," Siraya whispered, and we sat against the wall while we waited for the room to stop spinning.

An undetermined amount of hours later, I woke up to Banger shaking me and asking me if Siraya had to be anywhere at a certain time. The smell of bacon and cheese eggs floated into the room with him.

"How long are you letting me see my baby today?" I asked him.

He sucked his teeth. "Wait until your friend leaves before you get on that dumb shit."

I huffed and rolled over. Then, I realized Siraya and I were in my bed. She was curled into a tight ball on Banger's side. I threw a pillow at her head.

"Bitch," she mumbled and then sat up and stretched. She looked around the room and grinned. "I knew you wanted me."

"Shut up and go take your midterms," I told her with a giggle and then frowned at Banger bringing both of us breakfast.

As he left the room, Siraya whispered to me, "Why did y'all argue about spaghetti if he cooks like this, friend? You know we need a recipe for ice."

Banger had the nerve to chuckle at that from the doorway. I didn't want him to have any joy, so I told him, "I'll take Quest from 10-2 today," and rolled back over in bed.

Seconds after I closed my eyes, the phone rang until the answering machine picked it up.

"Rahshaan — I hope I'm pronouncing your name right — this is Kidra. Um...I'm just calling to make sure you and Nay-

Nay are okay. She's out here in Syracuse without NyQuest, and it's a little concerning to me. What kind of mother have you chosen for your child? She's miles away from a newborn."

Siraya jerked her head toward me while I stared at the answering machine in shock.

"You got paid to style me. Why is she making it sound like you were out there butt naked dancing on tables somewhere? You made good money," she said when she could close her agape mouth.

"Siraya, you don't have to explain shit for me," I said, watching relief soften Banger's eyes.

"No, because I just remembered how pissed I am about how our time was wasted. The limo cost more than that studio session," she fussed and continued to fuss until she was done eating.

While I waited for Siraya to get dressed, I went to NyQuest's room and watched him sleep until he opened his eyes and smiled at me. Then, I snatched him out of his head and inhaled the scents of cocoa butter and baby oil on his skin and in his hair.

"I missed you," I whispered repeatedly until Banger appeared in the doorway. Then, I got up and closed the door in his face.

When Siraya was ready, we went to Nat Turner to drop off NyQuest. I objected until Banger said Peaches was sending us to the fabric store with a list. That sounded like money, so I sat in the car and watched as Moosie loaded Squeak's and Shanae's kids into an SUV. She gave me a tiny wave. I was about to return the greeting, but Siraya pointed out Shanae coming through the door. No one ever turned on their heels faster than her.

I fidgeted with the new stereo that was in my car until the high rise door flew open and banged against the railing. All the boys on the stoop ran before they got caught in the crossfire.

"Your baby-mama sold us that shit! She said she needed to

get a bus ticket for her and her little skinny friend to get to Syracuse!" Squeak yelled at him.

I popped out of the car without caring about who was mad at me over the spaghetti incident.

"How dare you lie on me! My daddy is a bus driver! Why would I pay?" I screamed, pointing through the snow at him. "You and Shanae came over with the kids and said Banger sent you to pick up his stuff because he was moving out."

"That's a lie. When do Squeak and Shanae ever have their kids? You would've been better off saying it was Moosie," a girl walking by commented.

I felt stupid once again. How did Shanae keep getting me caught in her mess, and what did Squeak know about Syracuse?

"I'm not about to argue about y'all acting like crackheads. Give my man back his draws, so I can get out the hood and keep getting money." I waved them off and opened the car door.

"You talking about money. I know niggas who know what you were doing in The Cuse last night," Squeak argued with me.

I folded my arms and leaned against the car. "So tell him what I did. You said he's moving out, right? So I ain't got nothing to lose, right?"

Squeak's mouth shut.

"Just gimme my shit back," Banger said when he took in the size of his audience.

"Nope. I want to hear what I did, since Squeak's so thirsty to come out here talking like a little hoe." I watched Banger urge Squeak to go back into the building and screamed behind him, "Y'all so thirsty to break me and my man up. Fuck y'all! If I'm out of town, it's about getting money because I'm all about mine!" Somebody in Heaven watching over me set up the perfect scene when a girl walked by wearing a pair of Giselle Deneen jeans. I pointed at how well they hugged her hips and butt and said, "You see that? I'm all about my money, and every-body out here better recognize!"

I slammed my door. Siraya slapped me five and commented, "I was worried about you living on this side of the bridge, but you can be a good little hoodrat when you need to be, friend."

After we dropped Siraya off and went to the fabric store, I settled into the comfort of a silent ride. I closed my eyes, surprisingly thankful to be in the passenger's seat of that ugly car. He pulled into our space in the parking lot. I tried to stomp ahead of him. He put his arms around me. I snatched away, but it was just for show. Under him was where I really wanted to be.

"Get off me! You embarrassed the shit out of me, and I left your ass alone," I said.

He put his arms around me again.

"I can't believe you tried to make me explain myself in the projects. And then you let that nigga tell people that I was selling shit for money? And I can only see my child when you say I can?" My heart raced. If he didn't bend me over soon, I was going to take his head off.

"That ain't it, Nay. We were just scared of what you were gonna do. The way you flipped on me wasn't normal." He tried to be gentle with his voice, but I didn't want anything gentle from him.

"And you left me by myself when you were that concerned about me?" I snapped.

"I gotta look out for my son before anybody else, Monaysia," he explained.

"So what if I would've done something to myself because I couldn't get to you or him?" I asked.

"Listen to how you sound!" he roared. "Get some damn help! Let me get it for you! Look at all the shit you go through with your jealous ass mom and sister! Your father is trying to marry your damn friend! Postpartum depression is beating your ass!"

"Fuck you! You cry over spaghetti but got the nerve to shout my business in the middle of a parking lot!" I screamed at him, trying not to cry.

He calmed his voice again and embraced me from behind. I wanted a kiss and to be slammed against the signpost while he rammed himself into me.

"My bad. I'm just worried as fuck about you."

"Worry about yourself. My mother might be going through some things, but at least she didn't leave me in the house starving," I cracked at him.

"Nah. She just put you out when you wouldn't feed her. You and me ain't really all that different, Nay."

THAT WAS the last thing we said to each other until that Thursday, which was Thanksgiving. He gave me the choice of going to Big Grams' house or G-Ma's. I told him I was spending my Thanksgiving with my mother. Banger refused to go over there and listen to her talk stupid to me. We argued. He finally gave in.

My parents' divorce didn't hit me until I looked around the table. Only Aunt Marvine and Chrissy were there. Chrissy wouldn't stop staring at Banger. It made me happy until Mommy started with her shit.

"Chrissy, you stay in those science camps you keep going to. Don't be like these two. This is the first time I've seen them together and with their baby since the hospital," Mommy fussed.

"How could you stay away from this baby, Monaysia? He's perfect," Chrissy said, and picked him up from his swing.

I got up and snatched NyQuest from her.

"Denise, I normally let you rock, but you ain't gonna say too much more on what me and my girl do for our son," Banger told Mommy.

"Young man, don't you come up in my house talking to me like we're on the same level," Mommy said.

"Monaysia, let's go," Banger commanded. He took NyQuest from me and went to get his snowsuit.

"I'm not leaving my mother's table," I said.

"Of course you're not. Then you'd have to go home and take care of your baby," Kidra said.

Banger raised his eyebrows at me. "You ain't learned yet to get away from these people when I tell you to? They don't give a fuck about you, and the only reason she wanted you over here was to show off Quest to your aunt. Our son ain't gonna be part of that shit."

He was right, but I had an attitude about it. I was hungry too. There was a small meal on our kitchen counter when we got home. We ate in silence. He tried to offer to take me to his family's houses again, but I ignored him.

"I don't sit in the crib on Thanksgiving, and I ain't about to start this year," he said, packed up NyQuest, and left.

The phone rang an hour later. Siraya sounded terrified.

"Pressure just had a car delivered to my house. He's been having expensive stuff sent here every day. I don't know what was in my contract with Snap, but I have the feeling Pressure's gonna try to put it against the advance I never accepted," she whispered into the phone.

"Well, if you didn't sign a new contract yet, then drive that car over here. Let me see it," I told her.

"I'm scared to drive across that bridge," she told me.

"Why?" I asked. "You're pretty. Just smile and wink at the sheriffs, and you'll be fine."

An hour later, Siraya pulled into my visitor's spot in a C-class Benz. She was on a car phone.

"Pressure is in New York City. He and Mike are at a bigger studio. You wanna ride to see if he's for real?" she asked.

I looked up at my empty apartment and decided I was done crying over somebody who didn't want to be around me. Dodging Mike was much better than being dodged.

CHAPTER 7

$\mathcal{T}$he trip was another waste of time, except we got to hang out with Courtney and Samantha while Mike and Pressure camped outside of the Def Jam building. At least they gave us spending money. We went Black Friday shopping while Pressure looked really disappointed at not being able to produce results. Siraya ignored him. She was fed up, and I didn't blame her.

Something about our trip made Mike think he had a chance in Hell with me. Before we left New York City, he told me he wanted to spend New Year's Eve with me. I told him to go to Hell and went home, only to receive a bouquet of roses with hundred dollar bills rolled neatly into the blossoms the next day. Something different was delivered every day up until Christmas Eve. Banger was never there, so I put the cards and wrapping into the incinerator in the hallway, threw away the flowers, and put the money in my savings account, and enjoyed the gifts that were sent.

Christmas was a day with NyQuest I didn't want to miss. Banger was surprised when he walked into the house, and I was there wrapping the last of NyQuest's gifts. Though he was carrying shopping bags, he put his hands up.

"I don't wanna argue about shit. I'm just glad you're home for Quest's first Christmas," he said.

I stuck a bow on a present and said, "I don't wanna argue either, and I'm glad you're home too. Just don't say anything about money so that we can keep the peace."

"Your job left a message on the machine saying they're happy you're coming back after New Year's. I got nothing to say. You model for that catalog. You getting it in at The Green Balloon. Chicks from here to DPD are talking about you making jeans that look better on their asses than Levis. I can't say shit about what you do with your money."

"For real?" I asked.

He shrugged. "I mean, Christmas presents ain't gonna draw unnecessary attention unless you just completely bugged out. I hope you don't mind, but I looked through some of the pictures you took of your friend before a show she was supposed to be doing. You had her looking nice," he continued.

I rolled my eyes. "Too bad none of the shows happened. She wasted her time, and I wasted her dresses."

Then, we fell into a pleasant conversation. It was as though the past months hadn't happened. I took NyQuest from him and told him how much I missed him. Banger and I went to bed together. He laid my head on his chest, and I finally got the sex from him that I'd been craving. He made me bite a pillow while he punished me with his dick for the spaghetti incident, and I loved every second of it.

On Christmas morning, we waited to hear NyQuest coo over the baby monitor. We didn't care that he couldn't open his own gifts. We just knew those green eyes were going to sparkle while he watched us.

"I'll give you your gift first, since we ain't getting no sleep," he said.

"You bought me something?" I asked.

He wrinkled his face. "We still together, right?"

I shrugged. "I guess. It don't really feel like we are, but we're in the same house."

"Oh. It's okay if you ain't get me nothing. I just had to get something for you for giving me my baby. That's the best present I ever got. You ain't never gotta get me nothing again."

That pissed me off. Refusing to give into rage on a holiday, I shook the anger off while he gave me a bag from Jackson's. I reached in and pulled out a box that could only hold jewelry. When I ripped it open, I screamed at the diamond tennis bracelet.

"That's for me?" I asked.

He chuckled at me.

"This is just like the one Melinda has!" I exclaimed, hopping from foot to foot with my arm extended so that he could put it on me.

"You stare at it every time she comes around," he said.

"Oh. Well, everything under the tree with the silver paper is yours," I told him.

"Word?" he commented.

As soon as he got up to open his gifts, NyQuest cooed over the monitor. NyQuest's eyes glowed while he watched us open things for him. He was more interested in getting to the shiny bows than the toys and stuff that we bought him. Chillz and Selena came to the house with gifts, G-Ma, and breakfast. My dad came over with Melinda. We even went to my mom's house and gave gifts to her and Kidra, but that's, of course, where things took a turn.

"Nay-Nay, your job must really like you if they keep letting you leave early on Fridays to go to Syracuse to dress Siraya in outfits that she never gets to wear because of that shady producer she follows around," Kidra said.

"I'm going to warm up the car," Banger said.

I sighed.

"Girl, that producer wants Siraya's panties more than he wants to make her CD," Mommy said. "Siobhan drives the car he bought her all over the place."

"Did she have it checked for drugs?" Kidra asked. "The word around here is the record label he's starting is a money laundering scheme.

I sighed and asked, "Kidra, did the man that you were with when I saw you in Syracuse take you on a date somewhere nice?"

"He doesn't sell drugs, so why would he? He was too busy looking at my sister's ass in the dress she was wearing. He didn't even care about me telling him that my sister had a baby at home," she said.

I nodded my head while I put on NyQuest's snowsuit.

"So you and me can't say nice things to each other because a dog was being a dog. Okay. I'll just stay away from now on," I said.

"What's that supposed to mean?" Mommy asked.

"It means that I would like to come over here just once and have a nice conversation with both of you. Instead, I gotta come over here and let y'all throw all this dirt on my name. I'm sorry y'all are having a hard time, but I'm having the time of my life."

"Hoeing always looks fun," Kidra quipped.

I picked up my stuff and stormed out the house.

"That's probably why Dad and Melinda are so happy. I'll learn to be like them and not be miserable like the two of you," I grumbled.

"At least I don't have to open my legs to be happy!" Kidra called after me as I took NyQuest outside.

"Well, maybe you should instead of yelling about me in the middle of the yard. So ghetto." I turned to her, and said, "I had bought a treadmill at the beginning of my pregnancy because Mommy suggested it after seeing how thick I was getting. It's in the basement. You might wanna use it. I had the baby, but you're the one carrying the extra weight."

Banger looked at me like I was out of my mind. I didn't know Kidra picked up something to throw at me until he zoomed in on her and promised, "Throw something at my girl while she's carrying my baby, and I'll air this whole shit out."

Kidra took her ass in the house after that.

"We don't have to go back over there anymore. I'm listening to you from now on. I just have some stuff over here that I need to check on from time to time to make sure it's untouched. I don't want to put it in storage, but we don't have enough room for it at our house," I said.

"Oh. Is that why you always sneak upstairs when we go over there?" he asked me.

"Yeah. It's my grandmother's old sewing machine. It doesn't even work anymore, but she's the one who got me into fashion. I never want to get rid of it, and I have to make sure my mother doesn't to spite me." It wasn't a total lie, but it didn't feel good to leave out the part about Miguel's ring after Banger stood up for me. "I'll come check on it when my mother's gone. I'm not dealing with that anymore."

We drove past Siraya's house. Pressure was wheeling a Sony Wega that was larger than the one in our apartment through her picket fence. I hoped something music related came from that relationship soon, because he was making things worse for Siraya than he understood.

As Banger slowed the car, we saw her holding up a pen and paper. She fussed for him to sign it, saying that everything he delivered was a gift that she had no financial liability to.

"Merry Christmas!" I screamed.

Pressure looked at me and frowned. I rolled my eyes at him.

"Hi, friend!" Siraya shrieked. "Hold on! I bought my godson some Christmas gifts!"

Her father came through the fence and fussed about her being rude to Pressure. She continued running toward the car.

"I still haven't heard about real studio time or an actual show." She rolled her eyes before going to NyQuest's window and smiling at him.

"You can at least pretend to be excited about the TV. You didn't even get cable until the eleventh grade," I reminded her.

She rolled her eyes again. "And the bill is still in my name. Good thing I got to pay it off at a discounted rate from working at the cable company." After she grunted, she added, "It wouldn't even be so bad if he would just say he can't do what he promised and wants to focus on dating. He tells me he's taking me on business dinners, and it's just him and Mike. Then, Mike leaves. Why be so shady? He's obviously romantic as hell. Take me out to dinner. Let's go walk through the mall holding hands. I wonder if he's telling me these lies to practice for someone else. I don't want to be anyone's other woman."

"Siraya! He bought you some jewelry! Come open it!" her father called.

I frowned. "Tell Dartanion he sounds like a real hoe right now."

She giggled off her irritation and blew a kiss to NyQuest. I pulled a gift out the back seat and handed it to her. She gave the candy cane decorated bag a warm smile and told me, "There's a family gift in one of NyQuest's boxes."

We took a silent ride to North Mountains. Not talking in the car went back to irritating me during that 45 minute drive. When we got there, though, Banger's face went pale. His body shook as he stopped the car.

What the hell is wrong with you?" I asked, trying to understand what he saw in the snow that made him react that way.

"That's the meanest lady in the world," he told me.

I looked at the car parked in front of us. It was a royal blue Lexus. The driver was a skyscraper of a woman with dreads going down the back of a fly Prada trench. She pulled gifts from the back of her SUV. Then, she peered at us through the windshield and commanded, "Rahshaan Bailey, get out of the car and carry these packages for me. Half of them are for your child anyway. Bring me the baby, and you're moving too slow if I'm still standing here holding packages."

My eyes bucked at how fast he moved to obey the woman. Her accent sounded like she was from the Caribbean Islands. Her walk was more like a dance than individual steps.

"Who the hell is that?" I asked.

"I just told you she's the meanest lady in the world. Don't start no shit tonight. That lady can pull a knife faster than you can think about it."

He was scared, so I was scared and got more scared as I carried NyQuest to her.

"So you're the model?" she said. "If nothing else, that child has no lack of luck in the genetics category."

She didn't introduce herself, just took NyQuest and strolled ahead of us while barking out to Banger which rooms in her house needed to be painted.

"And if I find out that you and Rize were on my wooden floors while wearing shoes ever again…"

She kept going off on him, and he just followed behind her, confirming he would be an hour early to do whatever she said. That kept me entertained all the way up the walkway.

"Oh! How funny that the mothers who leave their kids for the daddies to raise came together!" Big Grams yelled when we walked through the door.

I hated old ladies who felt the need to make smart comments and thought they wouldn't get cussed out because they were old. G-Ma told me to ignore her sister and keep walking. I was surprised to see her there and wondered who was watching all the kids she normally watched. Banger said that was the one day of the year that he kicked them out the house without having to argue with G-Ma about it.

After making that smart remark, Big Grams hugged me, kissed me, and handed me a gift with my name on the tag. She turned me toward a stocking hanging over the fireplace and my own pile of gifts under the tree. It was like being a kid again.

The lady with the accent must have been Selena's best friend, because they had the biggest smiles on their faces while they sat together and talked. The sisters joined them, reminding me of when I had a whole clique, only they looked genuinely ecstatic about being around each other.

"You look happy today," Rize commented when we walked into the basement. He handed me a blunt and a drink. I stared at it.

"We starting over with you. Can we have some peace today, please?" Moosie asked.

I took the drink and the blunt, and said, "You sure do know how to make peace."

"Don't expect me to be your friend after how you lied on me and Squeak," Shanae said, and everyone told her to shut up. They looked at me to see if I would keep things going. What would have been the point?

"We just don't have to say anything to each other then. It's Christmas. I'm enjoying my life," I said with a shrug, and puffed the blunt twice before passing it to Banger.

We ate, and then there were more gifts. That topped any of my childhood holidays, which were filled with my mother bragging to Aunt Marvine about how much she was able to buy Kidra and me while my dad had to confront Aunt Marvine for trying to steal it. I was having a good time until we started eating dessert, and Banger had hit the weed and liquor too hard for too long. Slumped against me, his words came out in one slurred sentence.

"Y'all know it ain't no pleasing women?" he began, talking directly into my ear.

Moosie plainly stated, "I could've told you that."

Shanae spoke up, "We real easy to please when you find the right one, Banger. You just had to get the most high maintenance one out of them all."

"What's wrong with being high maintenance?" Cream asked.

Peaches added, "What is being low maintenance getting you besides pregnant again?"

I let Rize pour more liquor in my cup to keep me from speaking. While he poured, I waited to hear Shanae's answer.

"Y'all on her side today?" Shanae asked.

"Shanae, who is choosing sides? That girl ain't even thinking about you, and you're mad that you can't set her up today," Cream said.

"Don't nobody be setting Nay up. That's my girl. She does way more for me than you bitches do," Shanae argued.

"Why you always looking for somebody to do shit for you?" Moosie asked Shanae.

They started arguing.

Banger pushed himself off of me, using my shoulder to prop himself up while he stood. "I was asking a question!" He tried to hold himself up to turn to Rize and ask about pleasing a woman. Rize just shrugged and told him he'd had enough to drink.

Everyone zoomed in on him. I eased his bottle of Crown Royal out of his hand. "Baby, maybe you should put this down for a minute. We can talk about this at home later."

He snatched the bottle from me and took another swig. "When you gonna be home to tell me why you let a nigga poke my baby in the head, and why you standing on *my stoop* bragging about what another nigga's doing for you? And why you throwing spaghetti at my head when I try to take you out to dinner? And why you complain about me giving you a place to stay when your parents put you out? And why you don't like how I take care of you better than your pops did because he's too busy working three jobs so he could fuck your friend?"

That comment ejected me from my seat with my finger pointed in his face. "Watch your mouth talking about my daddy!"

Cream leaned back and crossed her legs. "She tried to be quiet. Y'all provoked the hell out of that girl."

"You gonna answer my question?" Banger questioned me.

"What is the question, Banger? I'm tired of you embarrassing me in front of your family. You dropped me off in that beauty shop so they could laugh at me about my daddy buying pussy off Hyman and Hendrix! You had the bitch with the booty shorts driving around, playing songs to let me know she fucked you! I should be asking you what you want from me!"

He grabbed me by my wrists, decided he didn't like that, and then pulled me to him and kissed wherever his lips landed on my face.

"You gave me everything I want. You know that baby up there? That's all I ever wanted. You gave me him. It's all good. I got what I wanted out of life. That's my whole life up there, and you gave me him."

"Me, Banger! What do you want from *me*?" I hollered. "I'm not just your baby's mother!"

"What's higher than that?" he asked me.

"Do you even like me?" I asked him and waited for his drunk answer. Somebody handed me a blunt, and I gratefully took it.

"Look, Shanae. You got your argument out of them, and they're still going home together. You happy now?" Cream asked to make Shanae stop smirking. "One baby locked his ass down, while you're on your way to baby number four, and Moosie does more for you or your kids."

The smile faded from Shanae's face. From across the room, a girl I'd either never seen before or didn't remember seeing

95

sucked her teeth. She was short and the same shade of brown as me with a color and cut that made me want to see what I looked like as a blonde. I was about to ask her which of the sisters did her hair, but she locked her eyes on Shanae and took a sip of something from a red Solo cup. Whatever she drank was strong enough to change her mood in a flash.

"Shanae, you really think if you try hard enough, you gonna walk up outta here with somebody's man, don't you?" she asked.

Shanae leaned toward the girl and said, "I already fucked Rakim, Subira."

Rakim, the stocky man sitting next to the girl with the blonde hair hopped up and said, "Fuck is you lying for?"

Squeak went to tower over Rakim while Rakim called out for someone to jump on Shanae for lying. Everything exploded into chaos after that. I tucked my legs under me while I shook my head and repeated that I was not the cause of that scene. Peaches and Cream picked up their glasses of Crown and Coke and sat with me.

"You got proof that you ain't the only problem, girl. Ain't you happy?" Cream squealed and then giggled.

Chillz, a man everyone called "Unc," and a man in a Sanford County Police Department hoodie thudded down the stairs and broke up the fight between the men while the sisters came downstairs to see what was happening. Lynn looked at me and drew back, surprised that I wasn't in the middle of it. I looked at her, sipped my drink, and then watched Lisa pull the girl named Subira away from Shanae. Subira was waving around a shard of glass and screaming at Shanae.

Trigga and Rize helped me pack the gifts and NyQuest into the car. Then, they dragged Banger into the back seat and took us home. The heavy holiday traffic lengthened our ride. Trigga asked me about Melinda three different times, and I told him that I'd only seen her once all three times.

Banger woke up just as we pulled into our parking space. He squinted at his surroundings.

"You aight, Chief?" Rize asked him. "You was making love to that bottle for a little bit."

He didn't answer until he got out of the car. "What the fuck did I miss?"

"You just antagonized and embarrassed the shit out of your girl, and then you missed Rakim and Squeak fighting. And Subira tried to fight Shanae. Normal Christmas stuff," Rize answered.

Banger cut his eyes at a Camry pulling into the visitor's spot and asked, "Subira ain't about to be on no bullshit over here, is she?"

Trigga shrugged. "Shanae said that she fucked Rakim, so probably yeah."

Banger huffed. I sucked my teeth at him and went into the house.

Subira kept cool for a while. She and Rakim brought their four-year-old daughter up with them. The little girl followed me into NyQuest's room and went right to sleep in the recliner. We all sparked another blunt. Banger and Rakim got up and stepped onto the balcony for a minute, and Subira watched them hard. When they were away from the door, she whispered, "How many chicks does Rakim meet over here on average?"

I shook my head. "I've never seen him before today."

"You met us last Thanksgiving at the club, and he supposedly went Black Friday shopping with y'all. Who was there? Did you bring a friend for him?"

I shook my head. "If I met y'all before, then I really don't remember. I'm sorry. Who did your hair, though?"

"This chick in the Madame CJ Walker Beauty School," she answered in a curt tone.

I wrinkled my face. "You get your hair done at the beauty school? Why don't you go to the sisters' shop?"

"Because the chick I go to does it better. What you trying to say?"

That girl just wanted to fight somebody. Shanae wanting both of our men should have bonded us, but she thought everyone was against her. I didn't know what she'd been through, and I didn't want to. All I wanted was to stop being put in positions where I had to defend myself. "I wasn't trying to say anything. Your hair looks good. Makes me want to try going blonde, and your cut is bangin. I just thought everybody in the family went to Hair Revolution."

She sat back like she was surprised I didn't have something negative to say about her. "Oh. Thank you. The girl I go to is one of their nieces. That's the only reason why I let her put any type of chemicals in my hair."

I nodded my head and watched Banger lead his company inside and then go to the bedroom. Banger came out carrying a duffle bag. I made a face at it.

"You're going to work?" I asked.

"Busiest day of the year," he said. "You remember we argued about this last year. We ain't gotta do it again today."

I tried not to say anything to that, but Subira said, "All that whining you just did about her not coming home, and you just gonna leave her in the crib?"

"I'm going to work!" Banger roared.

"Rock, tell your cousin to stop yelling at me," Subira said.

"I ain't telling him shit. What you doing in them people's business? You sounding like a shit starter like Shanae," Rakim replied.

Rize and Trigga palmed their faces.

"I knew you was fuckin that Cabbage Patch face hoe!" Subira screamed, and she and Rakim took off at a volume and vitriol higher than I ever did in front of Banger's family.

I sighed and asked Banger, "You gonna let me watch my baby, or is somebody coming to get him in the morning?"

"I'm gonna be working a few days, so Selena will come get him in the morning before she goes to work and drop him off when she gets off. You'll have the whole day to yourself," he answered.

"So I'm gonna be home by myself all weekend? What the fuck did I come home for?" I hollered. "I could've been in The City for Christmas. Siraya's probably gone by now. Fuck you, nigga! This is the last time you leave me home alone."

Banger turned to Rize and Trigga. "See what I mean? Women don't know what they want. This morning she was screaming over her gifts. Now she's mad about me working to be able to get them for her. Fuck this shit, man. I give up."

He went to NyQuest's room and kissed him goodbye, but didn't even give me a second look.

CHAPTER 8

*O*f all the gifts Mike delivered to my house, the most intriguing were a silver dress and thigh high Balenciaga boots. There was a card attached that simply said, "Wear this when the ball drops." I didn't think much about it. Siraya said that Pressure put way more effort in trying to buy her than trying to sell her to record labels. She picked up a second job to pay for her own studio time and production. I hung out in the studio with her. That's where we were headed on New Year's Eve when Riley pulled in front of my building and yelled out the window.

"Y'all ain't dressed!" he panicked. "We gotta get you to brunch and to Times Square. The train leaves in an hour!"

Siraya puckered her face. "Nay-Nay don't do trains."

I searched her face and listened to her voice for signs that she was using me as an excuse. Her face was plain as she looked back at me.

"Girl, the train is the most peaceful ride. It's way better than running through the airport," I said, determined to be the first to leave that holiday.

We turned around and ignored Banger and Rize while we

got dressed. The silver dress was dramatic, but I had something much flashier for Siraya.

"So we ain't gonna bring in the New Year together?" Banger asked.

"Don't you gotta work?" I slammed the door behind me before he could answer.

Samantha and Courtney were already on the train holding seats for us. Courtney assured Samantha that she could handle the train ride without liquor and sedatives. A bag was in the seat meant for me. I peeked inside and squealed at Monica's CDs and maxi CD singles sitting on top of a Discman with a large pack of batteries.

Siraya rolled her eyes at that. "Mike had Pressure call me all week to ask me what your favorite things were." She and I stretched the Discman headphones and let Monica serenade us all the way to The City.

Instead of Times Square, we wound up at a brownstone in Brooklyn. Parties streamed down either side of the block. We thought we saw celebrities and got excited. I weaved through the crowd and bumped into a group of male models I'd done a commercial with in high school. Mike found me and yanked me toward some rappers Pressure claimed to know. When they pushed me forward and told me to do the talking for them, we saw them for the scammers they were. Siraya and I went off on them as we stomped out of the party.

"Samantha, girl, you and Courtney call me sometime. I'll bring you to The County so you can see how we party. I'm done with these games your brother and his friend like to play!" I yelled as we stomped down the block through crowds of people. With my arm hooked in Siraya's, I said, "Whatever you do, don't stop moving."

"I'm only stopping if I find something to throw at Pressure's head. I am done!" she declared.

On the subway, Siraya grumbled to herself so much that she

blended in with the rest of the crazy that was New York normal. I hoped that I could remember my dad's co-workers' names so that we didn't have to pay for bus tickets.

"We'll figure out how to shop your demo for real when we get back to The County," I promised her.

It was so cold, and I was so pissed about how hard we had to work to stay together in the thick of the crowds. Siraya asked about just putting our money together and staying in a hotel. I had enough to do that, but I felt like the disappointment was telling me I needed to stop being petty. For as much as Banger made me wait for things, he never lied about what he was getting me. He invested in my dreams, and he went out of his way to put me in a better position.

Despite the overnight bag I carried, my arms felt light. I wanted to hold my baby. That New York City aroma turned into Johnson & Johnson's shampoo. My dress was too tight. I needed to be on the couch, looking into those smiling green eyes. Just as I approached the counter to purchase our tickets, I saw a driver coming into the station through double doors. A woman walking beside him swung a long, blonde ponytail as she switched a picnic basket between her hands. She pointed me out to the driver and then ran to me with one arm extended, calling my name.

"Nay-Nay, what are you doing in New York City?" Dad asked me while Melinda hugged Siraya and me.

I jerked my thumb toward Siraya and grumbled, "Your 'good' daughter got us stranded down here."

Daddy cracked up. "I told Dartanion to stop selling his daughter for TVs."

Siraya and I frowned at him. He ignored our distaste and told us to get on the bus. We went to the back with Melinda. I looked at the picnic basket and then at her for an explanation. She took plastic cups and Chablis from it.

"To broken dreams," she said with a forced smile.

Siraya waited until the bus rolled out of the station before she allowed herself to cry.

"You don't have to feel stupid, friend. I was the one who encouraged this trip. You stood your ground." I rubbed her back before telling Melinda the story.

"High Pressure Records?" she whispered, rolling her tongue and eyes to recall something. "We turned down work from them when Lynn did a background check and found out they weren't an established label. Banger had to fuck up one of his uncles for telling them about us.

That made Siraya and me crack up and enjoy the ride.

"I'm glad that it's early enough in the day for us to get home before midnight," I remarked and looked at the picnic basket again.

Melinda said, "This is nice. It's a romantic little trip. I didn't have to put much thought into what to wear, because Eddie will be cleaning the bus when the ball drops. It's just important that we're together."

Siraya looked from her to me. "*This* is your dad's new woman? No wonder your mama's on the warpath. I'd be mad too."

I whispered to Melinda, "Trigga keeps asking about you. He just wants to make sure that you're okay."

"Tell him it's too late for him to care," she told me.

We ran our mouths and drank wine for the rest of the trip. Melinda gave Siraya way more encouraging words than I could think of. She was the type of friend we needed.

Dad's bus pulled into the 102nd Street Station at 10:15. My heart sank. There was no way I was getting across the bridge before the ball dropped. Siraya stared at my eyeballs.

"You sure do cry a lot since you moved across the bridge," she remarked.

I sniffled. "You wanna just find out where the party's at down here?"

She sucked her teeth and linked her arm tighter in mine. "Come on, friend. We gotta find a way to get you home to that man and baby. I don't understand why you're so set on making him pay for the way Best and Miguel treated you anyway."

I sniffled again, blinked, and stepped back while I stared at her. "What did you say?"

A light flashed in my head. Until she said that, I didn't realize how wrong it was for me to waste a whole year treating somebody like shit when he jumped to give me back what strangers took from me. I had to get home and fix everything.

We walked through the crowd, snow, shiny dresses, and wind. Siraya thought she heard someone calling our names and turned her head at a honking horn. Rashad hung out of a minivan across the street. He busted a u-turn in the middle of 102nd Street to get to us.

"Rashad, what are you doing driving a cab?" I questioned him. "Don't you need to be getting to The Opal Lounge?"

"This is my job now since your baby's father got my main spot shut down," he explained.

Siraya and I exchanged looks before I whined, "Rashad, please get me across the bridge before midnight! I'll pay you what I was going to pay a cab driver to get us from The City to here."

"I was just gonna charge you five, but that's even better. Get in. Y'all looking right tonight," he said to both of us while he stared at Siraya.

She gave him a polite smile and then turned to me. "Don't cry, friend. Rashad said he's gonna get us there in time."

"Rashad's a liar," I said and then sobbed. "He said he used to talk to you."

Siraya fidgeted in the second row minivan seat. "We did. After you left. He called himself my boyfriend until the second Christmas Break after you left when he remembered he had a baby on the way."

I stared at her. A river of tears stung my face. "Why do men treat you so bad? You're such a good person, and you're so pretty, and all they do is lie to you just like I lie to Banger!"

Rashad turned around and stared at me with horror contorting his face in several different directions. "Siraya, make her stop crying! I'm sorry I didn't tell you about the baby. Why is *she* sad about it, though?"

Siraya rubbed my back and softly requested, "Please just get us across the bridge."

A sheriff walked by a grinned into the car. "When they're crying is the best time to get them, son. They're vulnerable. You got two fine ones." His smile grew when he looked into the low cut of my dress and then outlined the rest of my silhouette. "Can you handle that brick house back there, son?"

Instead of replying with something crass, Rashad balled his face while giving a sarcastic chuckle until the sheriff walked off.

"Don't worry, Nay-Nay. I'll get to The South." He turned around in his seat and solemnly said, "You can't tell nobody I took you the way I'm taking you, and you can only take this way in cases of emergencies. The pigs can't know that anybody knows about it."

I was scared, but he promised me once again that he would get me home before the ball dropped.

To get rid of all the negativity, Rashad entertained us with the story of The Opal Lounge's shutdown. "That whole night was crazy!" he exclaimed. "First, Best told security not to let Banger and Rize in with Nyir. They went to go confront him, and he tried to stab Banger."

"What?" we exclaimed in unison.

"Why would Best even act like he was calling the shots like that?" I asked.

"When you came from college, Nay, me, Ronnie, and Best had a plan to go from promoting the parties to throwing the parties, to owning the club; but that went left when that dude,

Snap, bought it. He was trying to smuggle drugs in the club and cook coke in the kitchen before Happy Hour. That shit was wild. Me and Ronnie told Best not to get hooked up with none of them niggas coming from out of town, tryna set up shop. They tried to go around paying their taxes, and that shit wasn't flying. I ain't gotta tell you that, though, Nay. You already know. Your baby daddy got the streets on lock. All we had to do was wait for Snap's bullshit to catch up with him, and we could have been 22-23 year old club owners!

"Anyway, they got in the club. Best was embarrassed because he really ain't know what he was doing with the knife. Everybody was clowning him because he called himself fighting over you, Nay, but everybody heard you're way better with a blade than him.

"Then, the nigga, Snap, came in, and Rize hopped up and asked him why he put his hands on his godson's godmother. Everybody was already mad about the way Snap was watching every single drink I poured. They were ready to get their club back, and they knew they were gonna get it when Rize approached Snap. Once Rize broke the bottle across Snap's face, Nyir went off the chain! The whole club went crazy after that. Some people said Snap ain't never gonna walk again. Others say he dead, but ain't nobody saying who killed him."

Rashad always had to add something extra to a story. His folktales kept people tipping him at the bar, so I just let him keep exaggerating as Downtown Sanford turned into East Sanford. He took us to Banneker Forest and drove up and down hills. When we exited the forest, there were stretches of desolate land littered with abandoned buildings whose signs claimed they were once hospitals and junkies.

It was a quarter to midnight when we reached South Terrace. I couldn't decide between running through The Spot and preparing to snatch a bitch off my man, or just going home and waiting for him. Siraya told me my eyeliner and mascara were running, so I chose home. When Banger got there, I would apologize to him and start afresh.

Once he pulled into my complex's parking lot, Rashad's conversation went from exaggerating whatever happened to Snap and Best to marveling at such a nice set of apartments being on that side of the bridge. My heart sank at the empty lots. Siraya giggled and pointed ahead.

"We made it just in time," she said.

Banger was pulling the baby carrier out of a truck that Rize was driving. Rico and Trigga got out the back carrying pans of food and bags of liquor. They peered at the car pulling into our visitor's spot and greeted Rashad when they recognized him. I ran to Banger and threw my arms around him. He actually returned the hug and kissed my face.

"You aight? What's all that black stuff on your cheeks?" he tilted my face upward and asked.

Rashad cackled and yelled, "She was crying over not getting to you and the baby before the ball dropped! Haaa!"

I yelled over him for Siraya to get out of the car before she wound up kissing Rashad at midnight. Rize went to the car to pay Rashad and get our bags and invited Rashad to come toast the New Year with us.

We turned toward the Downtown skyline. Where we stood appeared to be so isolated from everything else. I seemed to be the only one who minded that we were caged in and locked out at the same time. While Rico and Trigga set off firecrackers in the cold, Banger pulled me against him and kissed me like he really was relieved that I was there. His pager went off. I expected him to go pack up his clothes and go out of town, but he stayed right there with me. Rashad turned to get a kiss from Siraya. Rize slid in front of him and messed up his plans.

Later, I had to remind Rize of what her name was. Siraya, on the other hand, was ready to reward him for getting rid of her abuser.

After a night of eating, drinking, and laughing at Rico and Rize laughing at our stories about the failed out of town trips, we passed out. Chillz and Selena were in the kitchen when we finally got up. Chillz was cooking. Selena was feeding NyQuest.

Chillz smiled at me, and asked, "You know there's a rumor going around that you were in a taxi crying over your son?"

I giggled at that and sat down next to Selena. I asked her about the groups she knew about for postpartum depression, and she said that she could take me on Monday. Then, she hugged me and kissed my forehead.

I kept waiting for Banger to leave that weekend, but he said the furniture store was closed for the holiday. We took Siraya home. She looked like she was dreading it. Banger told her to get some of her stuff and come stay with us for a while.

There was a line of police cars, a furniture truck, and suited men in front of her house. Our hearts stopped as we prepared for the worst. She got out of the car and ran around the scene. I followed. My mother stood on the outside of the scene with Siraya's mother while her father yelled and threw a tantrum as he watched luxury items being carried out of the house.

Siraya's mother turned on her and fussed, "The feds are taking all the stuff that boyfriend of yours brought over here."

"He wasn't my boyfriend, and I told you not to let him put that stuff in your house," she told her.

"They're taking my big screen TV!" her father yelled.

She sighed and put her hands up while she waited for the police to cuff her too. They told her she wasn't a person of interest. In back of one of the squad cards was Pressure. His head was bent while the task force members ripped the seats from his car. A dog charged forward and sniffed out cocaine. Irritation pulled at Siraya's face when we went back to my apartment. Banger and Rize went to get us dinner. My pager went off as soon as they left. I checked the voicemail.

"This is Mike. Don't worry about where I got your number

from. I seen you with your baby's father, so I don't think I made myself clear. I told you I've been in love with you since the first time I saw your pretty ass on the perm box. Your baby-daddy can't do half the shit that I plan to do for you. One way or another, you're gonna be mine."

I asked Siraya if she gave him my number. She said that she didn't, so I went to bed while he left several more messages on my beeper, each one more unhinged than the last. Siraya was rid of Pressure, but my nightmare began the day I left Mike at that Brownstone in Brooklyn.

CHAPTER 9

*T*he new year really did give us a new start. When I went back to work, my supervisor told me Amy Ruffin, the marketing director, asked about me several times. She finally looked at the resume and portfolio I left on her desk over a year ago. I couldn't re-enroll in school quick enough to do whatever I could to get on her radar. Peaches and I continued working on our own line and with The Green Balloon.

Being that I was working so much, Banger said he was going to start working less after my birthday. He seemed excited to be getting money together to do things for me, but he also seemed sad.

In general, there was a sad cloud over his whole family. We spent a lot of Saturday nights just sitting around while they talked to the lady with the dreadlocks. I still didn't know who she was, but Banger and his cousins Shondell, Ken-Ken, and PeeWee being terrified of her was constant entertainment for me. Even Moosie, Peaches, and Cream were strangely silent in her presence. I figured she must have been their teacher at some point. She had the command of a college professor when she spoke.

My birthday came, and Banger just handed me some money and told me to make sure that I got home before 10 the next morning.

"You're not spending any part of today with me?" I wondered.

He balled up his mouth, making me wonder what I did wrong. We were in a good spot, as far as I could tell. Maybe Siraya being there was getting on his nerves, because every time he got up to feed NyQuest at night, Rize was balls deep inside of her on the pullout couch. I couldn't imagine him wanting to walk in on that every night. I was just happy that Rize finally learned her name.

After mulling over how he was going to tell me that he was going to disappoint me, he wrapped his arms around my waist and said, "The fam has been having some issues. Tomorrow is gonna be a real bad day for us, and we gotta prepare for it today. I wish it wasn't on your birthday, and I promise you I'm gonna spend the rest of the month making it up to you. For today, though, I'm taking you out to lunch, and then I'm having Squeak drive you and Siraya and some other girls Siraya said you might like having with you around to a spa that Selena and Lynn approved to get massages and some other shit. Then, I'm sending you to get your hair done. My aunties ain't gonna be there, but Lynn said Haddus is nice enough with the needle and thread to fix your weave. After that, you and your girls are getting tipsy at the spot that used to be called The Opal Lounge and pissy drunk at The Spot. I just need you to be home in the morning with Quest. Big Grams and G-Ma are gonna be taking care of this thing with the rest of the fam and won't be able to hold him down. I know this sounds fucked up, but please don't be mad."

"I'm not mad," I lied.

"'Nay, I know you're lying, but there's no other day we could do this," he said.

"Is G-Ma okay?" I panicked. "She's not going to the hospital, is she?"

He paused for a really long time. Then, his voice came out like he was trying not to cry. "Yeah. She is."

"Oh my God! Why didn't you tell me?" I exclaimed.

"Because you have a tendency to say some fucked up ass shit in the worst of times, and I don't want to have arguing with you on my head while I go through this. That's why I didn't ask you to put off your birthday. You have to wait for me to do enough," he said.

I was trying not to be pissed off, but I was back to wondering what the point was in us being together. I was even more pissed off when Siraya and I got into the car with Squeak, and Subira and Shanae were in the back seat bickering already. Anticipating the night ending badly, I got into the car and let them give me the gifts I was sure somebody either bought for them or forced them to buy me.

"I would've taken you for a Gemini," Shanae said after I introduced Siraya to them.

"How? She has friends," Subira snapped.

Shanae shot her a dirty look. "*I'm a Gemini.*"

Subira cut her eyes at her and then rolled them. Shanae's confusion about what Subira was trying to say made me laugh.

Squeak pulled into the Main Street Station. Siraya hopped out of the car and screamed at Courtney and Samantha. My smile spread across my face so far that it prevented me from acknowledging Shanae's curled lip and rolling eyes. I was touched by how much thought Banger put into the day, despite whatever he had going on.

Apparently, me being happy upset Shanae. She made little comments here and there about how a man like Banger would have to be in her sight at all times. I ignored her and enjoyed the carrot cake that he had G-Ma bake for me. All of my favorite things were included in that day.

"What did he buy you for your birthday anyway?" Shanae asked as we went to Club Morganite, the place formerly known as The Opal Lounge, for the first party.

"I guess this day," I said while we hurried through the doors.

The winter weather cut the club's numbers in half. That just gave Rashad a chance to serve us personally. He had time to sit with us and stare into Courtney's face while he made our drinks extra strong. Squeak and Rashad shot each other dirty looks before Squeak announced he'd be sitting in the car and left.

"This ain't no present. What did he buy you that he could put in a box with a bow on it? Because I saw him at Jackson's," she pushed.

"I guess he's gonna give it to me when we celebrate together," I said. "Stop spoiling my surprises anyway."

"The surprise wasn't spending your birthday alone?" she asked. "Squeak never would've had Banger driving me around all day on my birthday."

"Because Banger ain't no do-boy. What the fuck do you mean?" Subira yelled, and everybody laughed at her. "Shanae, what has Squeak ever gotten you but pregnant?"

I laughed so hard that I spat out my liquor. Siraya pinched me and pointed toward the door. I wanted to hide when I saw Best walk in, but he seemed occupied by a bunch of girls who looked like fake models. They dispersed and went to wait tables. One of them climbed on the bar, trying to get a party going. Cute. His new money maker wasn't even bringing in half the business I used to when I hosted parties for him. Maybe he'd feel so stupid that he wouldn't bother me, I remembered thinking. Then, Shanae did the craziest thing. She called out to him and flagged him over to our table. He sat in her face all night and tried to act like he didn't see the rest of us. The two of them dry humped each other on the dance floor. Bold move for someone whose boyfriend was sitting outside, but who could blame her?

"I'm glad she's gone," Samantha said. "This is nice, but what the hell is her problem?"

"She wants her boyfriend," Subira answered before I could. "Don't take that personally. She wants everybody's boyfriend."

"I like her, Nay," Samantha said, and pointed to Subira. "You should bring her to Syracuse if you ever come back to visit us."

"Syracuse?" Subira scoffed. "I better not take my ass out there. That's where my daddy lives, and I stay running into him whenever I go out there. Damn sure don't wanna see his ass. You know a nigga named Don from the East Side?"

"Don is your daddy?" Samantha exclaimed. "Yeah. I know why you don't wanna be around his ass. Two minutes in the same room with him, and everybody is going to jail to do football numbers."

"Exactly." Subira banged her shot glass on the table to get Rashad to stop looking at Courtney long enough to pour her another.

"So when you coming back out?" Samantha asked.

I shrugged. "Probably never. Siraya ain't singing out there no more, and I'm staying away from your brother."

"For what?" Subira asked. "The nigga paid somebody to babysit you all day, and you know he got Shanae watching to see if you're gonna cheat. This whole night ain't nothing but a test for both of us. Rock thinks I'm stupid."

Rashad brought us a pitcher of margaritas plus fishbowl-sized glasses. Whatever Subira was talking about was not going to stress me. Banger had gotten with my friend to plan every detail of that day and had more planned for me.

We left Shanae grinding on Best and went to the bathroom. When we came out, Best was standing there waiting for us. He was using the wall to hold himself up.

"Let me taste it," he slurred.

Subira sucked her teeth at him. "You still the corniest nigga on the planet. Get outta here before I tell your mama on you, little boy."

"I just want one taste, Nay," he begged.

Subira pulled me around him and warned him that he didn't want the trouble he was starting. I was grateful for her.

The Opal Lounge didn't pick up any, so Squeak took us to The Spot and sat in the parking lot again while we were taken to a VIP room. There was a snowstorm approaching, so it wasn't as packed as it usually was. The crowd being small didn't stop the party. Everybody knew it was "Banger's baby-mama's birthday" from the posters with some of my old modeling pictures on them. I was dancing on couches and on the bar with my girls. Shanae had gotten drunk enough to be tolerable, and everybody in the club was all over us.

The DJ played Monica's "Street Symphony." I screamed and rocked. Then, I pushed away somebody who tried to come behind me and dance while it played. Somewhere between Monica asking her man if he loved her and threatening to leave him, a pain wrestled into my heart and wouldn't go away. I didn't understand it. Banger wasn't even really in the streets. He just wasn't with me on my 21st birthday.

As the last notes of the song played, something banged. Glass shattered. We all hit the floor and tried to crawl outside. The bartenders pulled us behind the bar with them and shielded us while gunshots fired above our heads. We clung to each other and screamed.

When the gunfire stopped, and the police came in to clear us out, I wished that I'd been shot. Miguel stood over me and wished me a happy birthday with a stupid grin on his face. That was the first time I'd seen him on my birthday since I was in high school.

"Don't talk to me. I saw you get caught up in a raid, and now you're in a pig uniform. I know exactly what that means," I said.

"You don't love me anymore, Nay-Nay?" he asked me, putting his hand on my chin.

"Bitch, is this really happening?" Siraya shouted. "This nigga is really a cop?"

"Wasted all my damn high school years on a damn cop," I mumbled.

After we got out of there, Subira gave me the biggest side eye. I was never one to explain myself, but that one needed an explanation.

"I was in high school, and he drove a Lex. He disappeared on me when I went to college, then came back, bought me thousands of dollars worth of shit, and disappeared again. I saw him in a drug bust on the news and didn't hear from him again," I told her as we walked through the snow in the parking lot.

"High school? Sounds about right," she grumbled. Then, she looked around and asked, "Where the fuck is Squeak at?"

We went all through that parking lot and didn't see him. A minivan pulled up next to us. The wavy haired driver with the neck full of gold stuck his head out the window and called out to Courtney. Subira sucked her teeth.

"Tiggs, how did your little young ass even get in here?" she yelled. "And whose chain did you borrow?"

"Bi—" He stuck his head out the window to get a better look at her, and then sucked his teeth. "Aw shit."

"Aw shit my ass. Take your ass home. Was that you in there doing all that wild shit?" she asked.

Shanae jumped in front of her and asked, "Have you seen Squeak? We gotta get home!"

"What y'all even doing out here?" he asked instead of answering. "Don't y'all need to be at home praying or some shit? My mom's been at church all night. I stopped through and said a couple Hail Marys myself."

Shanae sucked her teeth and said, "They made the problem children go out so we ain't mess up their little moment."

He looked behind him, and said, "Y'all could squeeze in, and I'll drive y'all around to find Squeak."

My birthday night ended with me sitting on some high school aged boy's lap while helping Samantha make Courtney stop whimpering.

"What the hell is wrong with her?" I asked.

Samantha shrugged. "She acts like this every time she gets into a car. She can ride the bus or a train with no problem, but cars make her act like she's dying."

An ambulance fled past us. We tried to see what was happening. All we could make out as the snow fell harder were paramedics carrying a body from the club. Squeak was nowhere to be found, and the high school aged boys begged their driver to get out of the parking lot before the police approached them.

With his lip curled, Tiggs barked at them, "Quit acting like punks in front of these females."

"Nigga, fuck you! I ain't tryna get kidnapped by the pigs tonight!" the boy whose lap I was sitting on yelled.

Samantha looked around for an explanation. I had none, so I just asked the boy to get us out of the parking lot. If anyone went missing that night, I was sure I would be blamed.

We went to a townhouse in Frederick Douglass. That setting sparked a rage in me as I was reminded of the cranberry Maxima that I never received. The boy named Tiggs paged Banger and Rakim, both with 911. Subira screamed what happened when they called us back. Shanae started crying as she realized her children's father could have been the one the paramedics were carrying.

"Banger wanna talk to you," Tiggs said to me, and handed me the cordless phone.

"You don't know where that nigga at at all?" he asked.

"He disappeared," I snapped.

"Aight. Your friends are gonna have to stay with us. I'll get them home on Monday," Banger said quickly.

"We gotta go to work at 3 tomorrow!" Samantha yelled. "We ain't got niggas that care about us like you care about Nay. We gotta get home and pay bills."

Banger groaned. "Their train leaves in like 15 minutes. Fuck!"

"I can see if my dad has a bus going to Syracuse tonight," I suggested. "Otherwise, you'll have to pay them for their day off from work?"

He groaned again. "Call your pops, and then meet me at the crib.

Daddy said that he could get them on the bus if we got there in an hour. Tiggs took us to my apartment. Banger met us there and gave Tiggs money for his trouble. His eyes glowed at the amount of money Banger put in his hands. You gotta make sure your friends get home safe, so you're gonna have to take Quest with you."

"I can't take a baby on the bus!" I exclaimed.

I continued to fuss at him as I walked through the door to our apartment. He handed me NyQuest, already bundled in his snowsuit.

"Nay, I got shit to do! Just go!"

He packed a bag for NyQuest and me and pushed us out of the house after putting money in my hand. After apologizing and kissing my face a thousand times, he put us in the car with Tiggs.

Subira sighed. "Guess I'll go to Syracuse and run into my daddy."

"You don't have to come, do you?" I asked. "Can't I give this little boy some money to take you to your house?"

"Girl, I live in East Terrace. Ain't no South Ridge nigga just driving through there in the middle of the night," she said.

"Damn. I'm sorry," I said.

"Nope. It ain't your fault. I told Rock he couldn't trust

Squeak to do right. He was gonna be in his feelings about not being included," she said.

"He's that fucked up over G-Ma going to the hospital?" I asked.

Subira looked at me like I was crazy. Then, she guffawed.

"G-Ma ain't in no damn hospital. I'm surprised Banger would lie on her like that, but I guess that was the only way to shut you up." She turned her body toward mine and stated, "We are the problem children. They want our mouths as far away from them as possible. I'm fucked up about it, but shit. I know me and Shanae can't sit in the same room for too long without getting into it, and you can't sit in a room too long without being the center of attention."

"He lied to me about G-Ma?" I asked.

She sucked her teeth and rolled her eyes. "See what I mean? You can't even take your head out your ass long enough to see what's going on. It ain't like the shit ain't happening in front of your face. The Greater Sanford Area is talking about it."

I was pissed. Sleeping on the bus was impossible, because people around me kept commenting on how good NyQuest was for staying asleep. I was glad that he didn't need his diaper changed. I wasn't going in that dirty ass bathroom on the bus.

"I wish it wasn't post season," Dad said to me as we got off the bus. "I would've taken you en route with me to Buffalo and went to a Bills game. Mel got me tickets for next season, though, so plan on going to a lot of games next year. I'll see you at 7."

"Seven?" I repeated.

"Sunday shoppers' special. This is the mall bus trip. I'm gonna see if I can get Mel something special. She's been feeling kind of down about her grandmother going to the hospital."

So we'd been fed the same lie. I sighed and followed Samantha off the bus, telling my dad that I was taking the train home.

"At least let us feed you. We haven't even been to breakfast," Samantha said.

We went to Samantha's too-small apartment and walked into her children's father yelling at her. There was a three year old running around and dancing to Master P's *Make Em Say Uuuuuhhh* while a baby cried.

"I could've stayed home for this shit," Subira grumbled.

We went to IHOP for breakfast. The bus boy took a good ten minutes to clean the table next to us, humming slow jams the whole time. No one paid him attention until he introduced himself to Shanae as Don. Subira zoomed in on him. He peered back.

"Ain't you my daughter?" he asked.

She sucked her teeth. "Cut it out."

That was all they said to each other. Then, he asked Shanae for her number, and she gave it to him. That was the first time I was glad that Melinda respected me enough to fuck my daddy behind my back. I was even more glad that my dad and I had a better relationship than whatever that dry ass shit was that happened at that table.

My pager went off as we waited for our pancakes. I cut my eyes at Samantha. She grinned and shrugged.

"Your baby daddy ain't want you around."

"Well, let me get out of here before I get in trouble," I said.

"Nah! I wanna check for where the niggas is at!" Shanae called, her voice powering throughout the restaurant.

"You better worry about where your nigga is," Subira warned her.

"Just take me to the train station. I told your brother I'm not interested in cheating, and now I'm telling you so that we don't have to run into this issue anymore." I locked eyes with her to let her know how serious I was. She gave me a wry smile and mouthed a half apology.

Once we were in the train station, I sat with NyQuest and

warned him against lying to his future girlfriends and making them spend their birthdays alone. He cooed back like he understood what I was saying. Hours into our wait, Mike showed up with balloons, roses, and a gift. I trembled, though I wasn't sure if it was about him having access to my every move in Syracuse, or worried that Shanae and Subira would say something. Shanae was busy switching her booty for someone who worked at the transit station. Subira was asleep and snoring. Mike was gone by the time she woke up. She eyed the balloons and then looked across the waiting room and saw my dad waving to me. She smiled.

"That was sweet," she commented. Then, we frowned while we watched him hug and kiss a woman who wasn't Melinda.

When we got back to Sanford County, I put Subira and Shanae in cabs to get them home. Every driver wanted to give us grief about going across the bridge, so we had to split one with Shanae's loud ass. All I wanted was sleep. I paged Banger to let him know we were back home but got no response.

"It started off as a good birthday," Siraya said. "He had good intentions."

"Not if he lied!" I snapped.

She left me alone and went to bed.

Dinner came and went without Banger coming home. Mike left voicemails on my pager telling me how much he missed me. He informed me that Samantha told him about the way my birthday ended.

"It would have ended with me making love to your beautiful ass on a bed of roses."

In the middle of the night, Banger still wasn't home. Curiosity made me open Mike's gift. It was a ten inch diamond encrusted Mickey Mouse hanging from a 10 karat gold cuban link chain. I fingered it and then dumped it into my purse.

An hour later, there was another voicemail from Mike on my pager

"Let's see how many more birthday gifts I need to send you to get you out here in my bed, making a beautiful ass baby like the one you had in that train station. I'm in love with the idea of having a family with your ass," he said. His inability to hear the word no was creepier than men who couldn't hear it in the past, but at least he showed interest in me. I almost gave in until he left another message, reiterating that I was going to carry multiple children for him.

NyQuest woke up whining. He refused to eat and wouldn't stop making the noise. The only person I could call was my mother.

"What kind of a mother doesn't know what teething is?" she snapped. "Get some Orajel, and get off my phone."

Siraya volunteered to go to the store, but there was nothing open on our side of the bridge. She called her mother, who told her to get a cold washcloth and put it in the freezer. She looked in the linen closet for one and started giggling.

"Your baby daddy got everything in this little closet. There's some Orajel and some teething rings."

NyQuest went from biting my finger to biting the frozen washcloths all night. He whimpered and whined so much and couldn't get to sleep. I felt bad for him. At 3 in the morning, I knew I wasn't getting to work. I called my job and then tried to snuggle with him. He just bit me and whimpered. Not being able to do anything for him made me feel so bad that I just stayed awake and watched reruns on TV until the news came on.

I knew I wasn't supposed to be watching Channel 3, but I dozed off. I woke up just in time to see Hope Thomas' dazzling smile. It seemed brighter. I looked around, and Banger still hadn't made it home.

"Sanford County can rejoice as a demon who terrorized us for decades was put to death last night. Jeremiah Revolution was killed by lethal injection after four denials of a stay of execution. Attorney Joy Gilead fought until the end, even bringing in new evidence—"

Just as a picture of the woman with the dreadlocks who terrified Banger came on the screen, I heard the door unlock. I hurried to the TV and flipped to Channel 5. A slightly more compassionately worded report was on that channel. I left it there and watched as Banger's family sobbed over this man, screaming that he didn't take anyone's children. Channel 5 discredited all the evidence Hope Thomas brought to them in her early days as a reporter that made the jury believe that he'd been kidnapping children for decades and selling them as domestic servants to buyers throughout New York State. The reporter was bitter as she rattled off the awards Hope won that year, as well as the fact that none of the alleged purchasers of the children were ever brought to justice. I was terrified as I watched Banger holding Lynn and Lisa, crying with them.

"Turn that shit off, please," he came into the room and said through a raw throat.

I watched him while doing what he asked.

"Why didn't you tell me?" I asked.

Tears continued to fall down his face. He wouldn't speak. NyQuest wailed. Banger scrunched his face and looked down at him.

"He hasn't slept at all. I think he's teething," I said.

Banger held out his arms. I handed NyQuest to him. He curled up with the baby in the bed. Immediately, NyQuest stopped whimpering and went to sleep.

"I know what I told you about taking you out for your birthday, but I thought..."

"To hell with my birthday! Does that shit matter right now?" I yelled. I calmed my voice, and said, "Quest kept me up all night, and I was worried that I was gonna have to take him to the doctor, so I called into work today. I'll be in the other room working on my stuff. Let me know what you need when you need it, and call me to come get Quest."

He didn't say anything. I heard a sob before I closed the door behind me.

After that, there seemed to be a dark cloud over South Sanford that only sat over South Sanford. It caused Siraya to quicken her search for an apartment. She said she always felt sad when she came across the bridge. I spent my time at her apartment, because it was just too depressing to go home. Banger didn't talk to anyone outside of his family. Subira said that things were so bad between her and Rakim that he moved out. There were no out of town trips for a while, so Banger was just home, moping around the house, talking to NyQuest and ignoring me.

CHAPTER 10

I tried to do what I could to make life a little bit more peaceful for Banger, but all he did was go to work, come home, smoke a blunt, and then lay in bed with NyQuest.

All of South Sanford was on that same robotic schedule. South Ridge was an emotional graveyard. One dark cloud turned into a dark gray billow of clouds over the city. In the grocery stores and on the stoops of the Nat Turner high-rises, people worried about who was next to go to jail or be murdered for crimes they didn't commit. People told me to hold my baby close to me and rushed me to my destination with him. Even people at work asked me why I was so comfortable with staying late on days that I didn't have school. The employees from South Sanford were allowed to work half days in the office and then take their work home. My sights were set on getting that job in the marketing department, so I got there early and left late, hoping to corner the director while she was with the C-suite.

Then, the stupidest thing happened: a curfew was declared for all of South Ridge after a news report that claimed some children were pushed off of a bridge by their parents.

The news had finally found a way to suck me into one of the many lies it told about South Sanford. That morning, I watched the parents of the four boys and one girl whose faces were later flashed across the TV screen stand on the bus stop with their kids and complain about the bus being late. I walked into the corner store to order a bacon, egg, and cheese. Then, I took NyQuest to G-Ma's house. As I left her apartment building, I saw those same parents and some other people chasing after what looked like a police van, screaming for them to bring back their children. The little girl was tossed onto the sidewalk and landed at my feet. The sound of her bones shattering when she hit the ground remained in my ears for months. Between watching the police arrest those parents and waiting to see if an ambulance would ever come for the little girl, I was hours late for work. They just gave me something to hook up to my computer and phone so that I could work from home that week and turned me around at the door. I wished I had someone to talk to about how badly that disturbed me, especially when the boys on the stoop confirmed the van I saw take those children away in did, in fact, belong to the police department.

The news was enough to make my mother call me. I avoided her calls so that I could avoid having her say the wrong thing about Banger. He looked like he was falling apart. Every day before I came home from work, I tried to bring home little gifts to make him feel better, but not even matching Patrick Ewing jerseys for him and NyQuest lifted his spirits as we stood at the bus stop every morning with his little cousins, waiting with parents whose children were never getting onto or off of school buses again.

Then, the Monday morning before Valentine's Day, he looked at me as though he just noticed I was there. He told me that I looked good in my work clothes and asked me where I was taking NyQuest.

"I have to go to work," I said slowly. "I take you and him to G-Ma's house in the mornings. Been in a fog, huh?"

"I must have been. My bad. Did you enjoy your birthday?" he asked.

"Up until the shootout happened," I answered.

He scrunched his face harder. "Shootout? You aight?"

I sighed. "That night was crazy. Just forget about it. I loved the amount of thought you and Siraya put into it."

"Where she at?" he asked.

"She thought she was in the way, so she moved out," I answered.

"Oh. Well, she always got a spot to stay if she needs it. She tried to give me money for the lights and everything. Tell her don't do that. You were happy when she was here," he said. He looked at the clock. "You got a little bit of time before work. Let's go take a walk so we can talk about some shit."

We walked toward the park in our complex and found it was closed. That pissed him off. His fists were clenched.

"G-Ma said she's seeing me either dead or in jail if I stay here, so I think you should start looking into how serious the Campavhore ladies are about going to Paris. If I can get G-Ma and Marcus to move, then we out," he began.

"Marcus?" I repeated. I'd almost forgotten that Banger had a little brother. "But shouldn't he just have to come because you said?"

"I can't get him a passport without taking my mom to court for custody," he said. Then, he changed the subject quickly. "What you wanna do for Valentine's Day? I fucked up your birthday, so I gotta come with it that day."

I looked at my wrist and smiled. "You already bought me the bracelet I wanted."

"Let's go to the Poconos then," he suggested.

"For real?" I asked.

He grinned a little. "That's where you supposed to take your

127

girl, right? I'll see what I gotta do to get us a weekend out there."

You can imagine my surprise when that Friday came, and his pager went off. I saw the 911 on the screen and knew it was bad news.

"I gotta drop you off at work. I gotta make a run out to Albany to get Squeak," he said.

"He's not dead?" I yelled.

Banger scrunched his face. "Nah. He said he got knocked that night before the shooting ever happened for having weed on him, and he had a bench warrant for a charge he caught in Albany years ago." He rushed me out the house.

I skipped school that night to do a little bit of shopping downtown for the weekend. The bus got me home just before the bridge closed. 11 at night came, and Banger still wasn't home. NyQuest was still with G-Ma. I paged Banger, and he called me from a private number.

"I'm packed and ready to go," I said.

He paused. "Oh shit! Nay, my bad! I forgot I had already picked up hours at work when I said—"

I didn't even give him a chance to finish his sentence before slamming down the phone. My pager went off. I looked at the 315 area code and told myself not to return that page. Instead, I paged Banger again with no answer. The solitude had all but driven me crazy when Samantha's voice sounded on my answering machine.

"I guess your man actually did right by you today. I'll go be miserable by myself then. Fuck y'all bitches and your men that treat you right."

Giggling, I picked up the phone. Samantha convinced me to take a trip up to Central New York.

That was the one time the train was completely booked, so I had to catch a bus. My dad was driving once again, and Melinda sat in the seat behind him with another picnic basket and her legs tucked under her. No makeup was on her face. Her ponytail was wound into a bun on top of her head. She slowly looked up at me looking at her.

"Are you okay?" I asked.

She shook her head. When I peered into her eyes, I saw the same vacancy in them that had been in Banger's since my birthday weekend. It made me feel so bad for her. A familiar sigh came from my father. That sound made my head crane toward him, and I saw this look on his face that said his needs were being neglected from her not being okay. I pulled Melinda to the back of the bus with me.

"You can't be enjoying spending Valentine's Day on a damn bus," I hissed.

She shrugged. "We were supposed to get married today, but I just don't feel like doing anything after Grandpa Jerry's death."

"You were close to him like that?" I asked.

She shook her head. "It's complicated. The night they say he took those kids, he was driving my parents to the hospital so that my mother could give birth to me. He's been on Death Row since I was in junior high, but he took care of my parents before he got locked up. He really was like a grandfather to me. I spoke to this man every single weekend growing up. My daddy took me to see him in jail more than a few times. And you know how Chillz touches you with that smile the first time you meet him? Jeremiah Revolution's smile and first words to you just get embedded in your mind. And for that to be the first and last things you see on him! The man died with a smile on his face, because he knew his family never stopped fighting for him and never will. It was so spooky. We were so upset that we disappointed him, and he said that we were never going to stop making him proud."

I looked toward the front of the bus at my dad and then back to her.

"Has my dad been doing anything to help you feel better?" I whispered to her.

The speed that her mouth opened and shut with said it all. I spread out my arms for her.

"I know I haven't been there for Banger the way that somebody should be. I just don't know how. He came home and didn't talk for weeks. The only person he talks to is NyQuest," I said.

"Where is NyQuest?" she asked me.

"G-Ma's house. I had to get out of South Sanford. It's so dark over there," I said.

She nodded her understanding. "It's Valentine's Day, though."

"I know that. We were supposed to go to the Poconos, but he forgot and went to work," I said.

She sucked her teeth. "But your birthday..."

"I didn't care about that after I found out what happened," I said.

"What do you mean after you found out?" she asked.

While I told her about my birthday weekend and then watching the news the following Monday, I watched her mouth drop open, and then pull in tightly as anger went across her face. I found my own voice shaking by the end of my account of the details.

"I've never had to be there for anybody before, but I wanted to be there for him. He didn't trust me to not be a fucked up ass person in the midst of his worst moments. I didn't realize I was that bad."

She shook her head. "It's not your fault. You came up in a place where everybody wakes up to brag. The minute they can't brag about something or somebody close to them, they toss them away.

"Look at me. How many years were you and Best friends, and you never even knew I existed until last year?"

When she said that, I thought about Siraya and the competition her parents had with mine. Both of us had to do what we could to get out of our hometown. I sighed away the urge to cry, because Melinda looked like the world was crashing down on her.

"I don't understand why Squeak and Shanae weren't included, though," I said.

"They didn't come along until way after Grandpa Jerry was already locked up. He only knew Mavis, and the only reason he knew her was because he had to break up fights between her and the aunties when they were younger," she explained. She looked toward the front of the bus and then shrank against the window, pulling me with her.

"What the fuck is Shanae doing on here?" she asked.

I giggled, and said, "If I tell you, you better not say anything."

"I haven't spoken to the family since your birthday weekend. Nobody wants to hear anything I have to say," she told me.

I furrowed my brows then giggled again when she waved off that sad statement and told me to get to the good dirt.

"Shanae is talking to Subira's dad."

"Bitch, what?" Melinda asked, and then covered her mouth to keep from hollering.

"She met him on my birthday weekend. Squeak disappeared that night, so she's been messing with him on the weekends and Best during the week," I said.

"What?" she exclaimed. "What the hell?"

"She picks Best up from school in his Honda. I think he just wants to make sure that I see them, but I also don't think he knows that she's pregnant again."

Melinda covered her face. "Life is going crazy."

I put a hand on hers, and asked her, "Are you okay?"

She shook her head. "Shit has been so fucked up since they showed me and Trigga hugging each other on the news. Your

131

dad has been super jealous, but I'm not giving up my friendship with Trigga to make him feel better about himself. He might not be shit as a boyfriend, but he is my best friend, and oh well if your daddy don't like it."

I nodded my head in agreement.

"So you going to Syracuse to hang out with your crazy friend?" she asked.

"Yeah. Her baby daddy's acting up too and talking about moving out the house, so I'm going to help her throw his shit out the window," I half lied. "Must be going around, because Subira said her and Rock broke up too."

Melinda sucked her teeth. "They'll be back together in another month at the most."

"Hard not to go back to the men in that family," I said.

"I don't know, Nay. You got some shit with you, but having to give up your birthday *and* Valentine's Day is asking a lot in any relationship," she commented as she bent over and took some crackers and goat cheese from the picnic basket. "I don't know why he lied about Valentine's Day anyway. That's one of the busiest times of year. The strip clubs are always packed with lonely people. We used to have regulars whose wives died, and then the day after, we'd be with our mains who promised us the world but had to be with their own wives on Valentine's Day. Even Chillz and Unc have to go on the out of town trips the days after major holidays like that."

"So you think he was lying to me?" I asked.

"I don't want to say he was lying, because he doesn't do too much lying unless it's for a good reason. His head must be fucked up, because this is not like him at all," she said.

"Melinda, I've been watching the news tell *horrible* lies, so I can't imagine what it's like inside his head right now. But this Monday was the first time he seemed to be on the same planet as me. I didn't even need to go to the Poconos. I just wanted to feel like there was a point in me even being around. It feels like

I'm just there because I get somewhere to live for carrying NyQuest."

"Isn't that what you wanted, Nay?"

I wanted to feel offended by her question, but she was there from the beginning. Looking around at the couples and families sitting together on the bus made me realize I wanted more than that.

"Maybe I did start off as a schemer, but I've changed. I want him now. I want him to want me. Not the model, not the baby-mama. Just me."

"But do you want the same from him?" she quizzed.

"I think it might be fun to get to know what he likes," I said with a nod. "Him and Rize's friendship seems like it's like mine and Siraya's. I think it would be cool to be his friend like that. But how can I? All I do is sit up in the house waiting for him to come home. I wouldn't mind that if he wasn't telling me he'd do this and that."

"Do you think that maybe he doesn't feel like he has to follow through with things because he knows you'll mess it up before it's time for these things to happen?" she suggested.

"That's fucked up if that's what's going on," I responded.

She put a hand on her forehead, and said, "I didn't mean to piss you off all over again. One of us deserves to be happy on this day." She sighed. "Forget I said that."

"Well, I want you to start coming back around. My dad should not have you on a bus like this on Valentine's Day," she said.

"It's not gonna be all bad," she said. "We're going to Niagara Falls and staying there until Tuesday. He's just upset that I wouldn't take him with me to see Grandpa Jerry, but he had so much fucked up shit to say based on what the news said. I couldn't deal with it. Pair that with the fact that he started looking at me cross eyed after I took him down the way to show him where I grew up, and I don't even know why we're still together."

"Then why are you still together?" I asked.

"I ain't about to go back down the way with them all laughing at me for thinking I could be a regular wife. They've been laughing at me for years for thinking your daddy was gonna leave your mama. Now they're laughing at me for thinking I even wanted this life, but I do.

"I sit in East Terrace and look out the window, and no matter what the weather is, South Ridge has a dark cloud over it. I'm never gonna turn my back on that place, but I'm so scared to ever live on that side of the bridge again. You've got to be terrified to have a son right now."

"You know what, though? I'm not." I shook my head. "It feels like Banger will never let anything happen to Quest, no matter how fucked up his head is."

Melinda sighed. "Nay, please don't be naïve. You just saw what happened to the man's grandfather. Nobody is invincible."

"I know," I said. "The worst part of this is G-Ma. She seems so different."

"Grandpa Jerry and his wife were like her kids. Seeing them both get taken from the world before her is tearing her down," Melinda said.

"But she told me to bring NyQuest over there," I said.

"For peace of mind, Nay. She thinks that as long as the children are at her house, she'll be able to keep them safe. People take advantage of that." Melinda sniffled and then took some wine from the picnic basket. She poured me a glass. "You're a good Valentine's date."

"Let's start going to lunch and stuff again during the week," I suggested. "I miss you. Come over to my house while me and Peaches work on stuff."

"That's right! You two are getting ready for Paris," she said.

I sighed. "Banger changes his mind about that from hour to hour."

She pointed her finger at me. With her neck rolling, she declared, "No. You give up too much already."

"He doesn't want me to give it up. He just doesn't want to come unless he can bring G-Ma," I said.

"Banger's full of shit, bringing G-Ma into it," Melinda told me. "I'm mad he even tried to use her for that. Y'all are gonna have to just do long distance."

"But what if we break up before I get back? We have enough problems in the house together. If I'm gone, he might have another bitch raising my son. I know there's a line of them waiting for me to disappear from the scene," I said.

She wrinkled her face. "They never bothered you before." Then, she wrinkled her face even harder. "Bitch, are you in love?"

"I don't know. I know that I care about him, and I want him to feel better. And I know that I want him to not have other bitches raising my son. And I've been going to a therapy group so that I could get rid of my postpartum depression, so that people won't be scared of me being alone with my son," I told her.

"Hmm. I don't know if that's love, but that's a big turn-around from when this started," she said. "It's his turn to work on himself and step it up. He ain't never been an angel in all of this."

My time at Samantha's house was spent throwing all of her boyfriend's stuff out the window. Shortly after, I had to help her bring it back in, because she found out that she was pregnant again. I did the craziest things with her.

"Where's Courtney?" I asked her on Sunday while we left her apartment to go to IHOP again. Nobody loved IHOP more than Samantha.

"That bitch got a man, and she's up under him all the time.

Since he left his wife to be up under her, the only time I see her is at work," she answered, rolling her eyes. She squinted at an SUV powering through the snow to get to us. I cut my eyes at her.

Mike got out of the car and handed me yet another money-filled bouquet. If it had been any day but Valentine's Day, I wouldn't have put my fears of Mike aside; but I'd been blatantly lied to. We went on a double date at the casino with Samantha and her man. Samantha and I didn't win very much, and Mike didn't gamble at all, but Samantha's boyfriend was a beast at the Blackjack tables. They kept him distracted for hours, giving Mike time to take me to dinner and a Jacuzzi suite. I regretted the mediocre sex we had in that room.

"I want you to start moving out here," he stated plainly.

"I'm not going to," I told him. "I'll tell you what, though. Go ahead and build your record label. We can just kick it when we have time for each other."

Something flashed in his eyes, but he kept his voice gentle. "I see you only understand power moves, so I need you to do something for me."

"You're not the one in power if you need me to do it," I informed him, irritably sipping on champagne that did nothing to improve the situation between us.

"Something that'll get you $2500," he told me.

"What is it?" I asked.

"With Pressure gone, nobody's taking me seriously in business; so I need you to go to this bank in North Sanford on Monday and make a deposit for me," he said. "They'll take me seriously if I have somebody classy like you going in there for me."

"Mike, my man doesn't even ask me to do work. That's for ugly girls. You see what I look like. Hire an assistant," I told him, and kept going back and forth until he raised his price to my satisfaction. I didn't expect what he was doing to last very long, and he was intimidating, standing over me with his nostrils flaring while he visibly restrained himself from arguing with me. If I got caught in anything shady, I was going to tell everybody who needed to know that I was forced to do it.

THE BANK WAS in a suburb of North Sanford Abolition Town. The roads were brick, and the streets were named after white people who'd aided in ending slavery. They were lined with specialty shops. Out there, I saw biracial couples with mismatched wedding rings rushing light brown children with curly hair and light eyes into clothing and toy stores. I followed one of the secret families into a specialty shop when I heard the little lovechildren cheering about their weekly trip there and some toys in the window. The shop's staff gave me dirty looks the whole time. After a looking around at all the Black women holding white men's hands, I guessed I needed a chaperone. Once they looked into my green eyes, they were satisfied and took my money.

Going inside the three story bank made my skin crawl. While I waited in the lobby for someone to approve my presence, I looked up and saw little dark skinned children dashing above my head, singing:

"Dormir dormir
Se acerca tu largo sueño"

They ran dust rags against wooden railings and peeked over it to make sure no one saw them. When my eyes met theirs, they ducked into dark corners and went silent. I thought maybe I imagined them being there, but that was a stupid thing to hallucinate. Above me, I could hear little heels tapping on the floor. I looked up again and caught a glimpse of horrendous white patent leather shoes that reminded me of Easter Sundays during my childhood.

A glasses-wearing man peered at me as he walked into the lobby. He spent way too much time trying to recognize me from the waist down. I cleared my throat and barked that I had places to go. I just wanted to be out of that strange place.

"Did you participate in the Miss Junior Sanford pageants?" he asked me.

My face puckered at the thought of being involved in such a prissy, pretentious event. "Absolutely not."

"Naomi Iman then?" he asked.

That time, I softened my voice. "Yes, I did."

"My wife runs it. I've seen your picture a thousand times while she's up late working from home," he said.

"Well, tell her Monaysia Giles said hello." I said. "I've actually been trying to get in touch with her for a while. Can you have her call me? It's about the school she got me into."

His smile lingered on my legs when he said, "When she gets home, I will. She's been overseas for a few months on business for the modeling agency. Do you have a minute to get coffee and talk about what you've been doing?"

"I'm actually on my way back to work, and I'm up for a promotion. So I don't want to be late getting back from lunch," I said.

"Oh? Where's work? What's the position? I know a lot of people," he said.

I looked down at the marble floors and then at the David Yurman cufflinks on his suit. That high yellow man sure was dressed like someone who was connected to the right people, even though his tiny mustache said none of those people wanted to tell him anything about fashion. While I assessed his accessories, I heard the running again. The patent leather shoes tapped out an eerie rhythm. They were too big of a distraction to ignore. A woman with a black puff of hair pushed a janitor's cart behind them. Our eyes met briefly, and then she was gone. The only sign she had been there was the song she sang:

"Dormir dormir
Se acerca tu largo sueño"

"SANFORD RINGER," I told him with a slight smile, leaning in toward him. "I work in customer service now, but I'm in school to get a marketing degree. It's a little hard, though. I'm taking some time off to take care of some family issues and going to SCC in the meantime to make sure that I don't miss a beat with my education."

"That's very smart," he said, finally looking up and into my eyes. "What's the position?"

"Advertising," I answered him.

He nodded and said, "That's Amy Ruffin's department. I'll make a call." He gave me his card. "My name's Dexter Aldridge. I hope to see you again soon."

"I'll be back regularly." I knew the way I strutted out the building with my hips swaying made his day.

An hour after I got back to work, my boss called me into her office. Amy Ruffin had finally looked at my resume and portfolio. She offered me a position with the marketing team.

After Valentine's Day, I thought I would come home to an apology gift. Instead, I just came home to gloomy South Sanford. There were messages on my answering machine from my mother, telling me what she heard about what she referred to as the "third world county" I lived in. I blocked her number from being able to call my house. Hearing things like that was doing nothing for Banger's depression. My goal was to get him out of it so that we could talk seriously about Paris. That seemed impossible.

I continued to work during the week and went to see Mike in Syracuse every weekend to get more money to take to the creepy man at the creepy bank. Just as I was getting used to the arrangement, Samantha called to let me know that Mike and her boyfriend got arrested. I didn't ask why. I just told her to pass the message along that I didn't do jailbirds. The one letter he wrote was sent right back to that jail with a note to the people in charge asking them to ask him not to contact me anymore.

CHAPTER 11

*E*ven though the seasons changed, that dreary ass cloud remained over that city. Squeak ran around yelling out this conspiracy theory that there was a weather machine controlled by the police department. I wanted him to stop saying it out loud.

With the onset of spring, the curfew was lifted. That gave me more time to spend at Siraya's apartment. She was unhappy about the amount of money she had to pay for rent, but that was what she could expect when she moved to overpriced Midtown. She was paying double what Banger paid for 1/4 of the space and street parking for a used car. She was in the middle of telling me how dissatisfied she was when her doorbell rang. It surprised me to see Subira walk into the living room.

"What you doing on this side of the bridge?" she asked me as she took a seat. Her daughter followed her silently until she saw NyQuest crawling across the living room. She smiled at him and crawled across the floor with him, giggling. Seeing them together made me glad he had a cousin to play with who could go home after a while.

"Just tired of being in gloomy ass South Sanford and having to run from the car to the house," I answered her.

She frowned. "It's terrible down there and starting to spread. Rock is talking about moving to Saint Croix with his grandparents if we get back together."

I huffed. "And Banger put all talks of Paris on hold because G-Ma won't come. Ain't that about a bitch?"

"He better snatch G-Ma up and make her ass come on," Subira fussed and went into a rant that I didn't listen to. It wasn't that she was saying anything invalid. I'd just already said it all a million times. She ended her rant with, "So what y'all getting into tonight?"

"The basketball tournament," Siraya announced.

I smiled and said, "My girl pulled her a street ball player, *and* she's singing out there."

Subira smiled and asked, "Are you doing the halftime show?"

Siraya shook her head. "No. I'm singing *Lift Every Voice and Sing*. Hopefully, I can get somebody's attention. This man with a legit record label called Civil Truth is setting up shop here and looking for new talent."

"Let's go get you a record deal then," Subira encouraged her.

I was a little jealous that the two of them had started being friends behind my back. We walked to Kareem Abdul-Jabar Park and got seats on the front bleachers while Siraya spoke with the people in charge of the event.

The tournament was held annually; usually when I was out of town on business. I never got to see all the street vendors who sold food, toys, clothes, and CDs on the streets that led to the park. I bought two CDs and a doll that the vendor told me was made in Panama. The crowd was huge and full of people I didn't know who all referred to Subira and me by our children's father's names. She warned me that anybody who heard that and still stepped to us was just looking to cause trouble.

There were eight basketball courts connected. Each set of bleachers surrounding them was filled. Siraya ran through a group of pom-pom carrying girls in shiny suits and pointed to a woman sitting on the first bleacher behind them.

"She wants to ask you about my outfit. She's the president of the Sanford County Parks and Rec Department," she told me.

I'd made a denim jumper for Siraya for that day and made sure to stitch it so that it magnified her booty. Subira took NyQuest's stroller from me so that I could go talk to the woman. My plan was just to give her one of the business cards Chillz made for Peaches and me, but she was ready to set up meetings. She was a friend of the Campavhores and had already planned to reach out to me. I sat with her and showed her pictures of Siraya in the outfits that I made for her and a couple of the pieces for The Green Balloon. We talked well past Siraya singing and exchanged information. As tip-off happened, she asked me if Peaches and I would be interested in designing some uniforms for a cheerleading team. I ran to find a payphone to call Peaches and tell her to get down there immediately.

I was just praying that Peaches was in town while I fished around in my purse for change. After cussing myself out for not cleaning out my purse often enough, I finally found a quarter. Right after I inserted it in the slot and dialed the first digit in Peaches' phone number, a car zoomed past me. I'll never forget the way my heart dropped into my stomach while the tires screeched and scraped the pavement. A whistle blew on the basketball court. Half a second later, the sonic boom of a rifle ripped through the air. I dropped, screamed, and crawled back toward the basketball court. NyQuest was the only thing on my mind while I clawed the ground and broke my nails. The side-walk vendor who'd sold me the doll grabbed me. While she planted me under the table with her, I whimpered about how badly I needed to get back to my baby. People stampeded past our table while the sound of gunshots got louder. I screamed my son's name. The woman clamped down on me to make sure that I didn't move until it was safe.

It was amazing how quickly the police and ambulances arrived at that scene. The street vendor finally released me. I ran into the crowd of people, screaming my baby's name. The only thing I could think to do was to run to the place on the bleachers where I left Subira. It took forever for me to remember where she was. I found her and Siraya huddled under the bleachers, quaking while they shielded the babies with their bodies. I dove under there with them.

We sat there for hours until the police found us. The sound of that little girl's bones cracking on the streets in Nat Turner replayed in my mind. Siraya sucked her teeth when she looked into their faces. I crawled away, clutching both of the babies.

"Nay? What are you doing here?" Miguel asked me.

"Don't say my name!" I screamed. "Stay the fuck away from me!"

The man from The Green Balloon named Kevin appeared behind him. That man looked like a demonic bullfrog to me. I tried not to cry while I continued to back away from them. Both of them smiled, damn near drooling at my fear of them. I kept crawling backward until I was up against the fence. Then, I stood and took off running. The two of them charged after me. Out of nowhere, the street vendor who held me under the table came and threw something at Miguel. She yelled for me to keep running and get the babies away from him. I pumped my legs so fast that my sneakers burned holes into the pavement. Subira and Siraya charged behind me through the crowd. Rather than look back, I tried to see the route back to Siraya's house in my head and didn't stop until I got to the brick row house that held a sign that falsely advertised it as a condo.

It took about 30 minutes for me to calm myself enough to page Banger and tell him what happened. He told me not to move until he got there. No argument came from me. I couldn't do anything except sit on Siraya's couch and cry while I held NyQuest against me. He rested his head against me and let the sound of my pounding heart keep him calm.

Three hours later, the doorbell chimed. I still hadn't let go of NyQuest. Siraya opened the door and then jumped to the side while Banger and Rakim stormed inside, looking around for us. Chillz's children thudded behind them. Banger tried to take NyQuest from me, but I encapsulated him and wouldn't let him go.

"What the fuck happened?" Rico demanded.

Siraya tried to tell them the story, but she was cut off when they asked where I was while she was under the bleachers with my baby. I jumped in to explain, wanting to cut Banger when I saw the look of disbelief on his face. That would have required me to let go of NyQuest, though, and that was never happening. He watched me, holding NyQuest and shaking, and then joined me on the couch and wrapped his arms around me.

"The pigs found us under the bleachers, and I just knew they were gonna do something to my baby!" I blubbered.

"The fuck you doing out here with him anyway? There were four shootings out here this morning! The bridge is closed because they're looking to put that shit on somebody from our side of it!" Banger snapped at me. Rize was the only one who told him to relax.

"I didn't know! I just wanted to watch my girl sing wearing the outfit that I made her!" I cried.

"Then get a fuckin babysitter! You ain't got no problem leaving Quest with somebody else any other weekend. Why the fuck you got him out here at fuckin midnight?" His voice bounced off every corner of Siraya's house.

"Banger, you got to chill," Rico told him. "Look at how scared she is."

"Her ass needs to be scared!" Banger yelled. "Don't ever have

145

my son out in the streets this late again! Why the fuck did you think it was cute to take a baby to an event with the word 'Midnight' in the name?"

"You ain't even gonna ask if I'm all right?" I asked him. "I just ran six blocks with two kids in my arms."

"Where the fuck is his stroller?" Banger demanded.

"I don't know. It's gone. Who gives a fuck?"

We were the only jackasses in there arguing. Rize talked Siraya into taking him upstairs and showing him her bedroom. Rico, Trigga, and Nyir left with Shondell, Ken-Ken, and PeeWee to find somewhere to get food for us. Moosie said she was spending the night with her Midtown girl. The rest of them camped out in her house all night. While Subira and Rakim got back together, Siraya got her back blown out, and the others consoled some distressed women they found at a nearby Chinese restaurant, I sat on Siraya's couch and argued with Banger about why I wasn't with NyQuest when the first gunshots were fired. He commanded me all night to give him the baby until NyQuest cried for him. Then, I was left hugging myself while Banger soothed him.

The next morning, I awoke to a police siren screeching. More gunshots banged not too far after. We spent the morning ducking for cover. By the afternoon, Siraya had convinced Rize to get someone from Furniture Revolution to bring a moving truck. She was back at her parent's house before sundown.

CHAPTER 12

*E*very day for two weeks after that basketball tournament, there were shootings in Midtown. They never made the news, but at least twelve people died every day. We only knew that because it was discussed in Hair Revolution. Beauty shops were city information centers. In South Sanford, they mentioned police sirens being heard before the first gunshots. In the shop in East Sanford where Siraya got her hair done, people praised the police for their quick response time. It was really nuts how the location dictated the way the story was told.

Things were tense in my home. Banger remained pissed with me for having NyQuest at that basketball game. His family told him that he was being unreasonable. I was surprised that he could do any wrong, but they were doing heavy damage control over him acting like I couldn't be trusted with my child. That pissed me off, because they were the ones who fed him that thought originally. I was over them all.

He also made it known that he didn't trust Siraya anymore. His reasoning was that something bad happened every time I went somewhere with her. I hit the ceiling when he said that.

"Your friend left us in a shootout in the club, and ain't nobody said shit to him about that! His damn girlfriend is fuckin pregnant, and he just disappeared on her for weeks! But *Siraya's* the problem?" I screamed. "What's the explanation behind *that* shit?"

"Don't nobody gotta explain shit to you," he snapped.

"Yes, the fuck you do deserve some type of explanation behind almost dying on my damn birthday weekend that we never celebrated together, by the way! And then you left on Valentine's Day after lying." I folded my arms and waited for him to say something. He turned his back on me with his jaw clenched.

"You know what? Fuck you!" I yelled and took my ass to work.

I was tired of all the negativity in the county making it into our home, so I went to Nat Turner to see G-Ma for some help. First, I helped her clean up the house behind the kids. Then, I asked her to teach me how to cook Banger's favorite meal.

"You ain't got time for that. His favorite meal is my ham and Chillz's macaroni and cheese. That's something you gotta start the day before," she said.

I pursed my lips and commented, "He might have to work tomorrow, and I don't want him leaving with us being mad at each other."

"Why not?" she asked. "He the one in the wrong this time. He been wrong for months."

"Yeah, but that's because of everything the family was going through. If I'm so bad that he couldn't even tell me about it and had to have *Shanae* babysit me of all people, then I'm really buggin out, G-Ma. I just want him to feel better. All he does at home is take NyQuest into the bedroom and curl up with him. The only time we talk is to argue," I reasoned.

Eyes enlarged, she studied me and waited for me to say

something stupid. Slowly, she drew back when I didn't have any ridiculous follow up.

"You grew up since you started going to that postpartum therapy," she remarked.

I sighed. "I'm trying. Your family and my one friend are the only people who have been there for me and been real with me. I had to look at how my dad treated Mel after what you all went through to see it. I don't want Banger to feel the way she looked."

"I knew something was going on with my baby. She wouldn't tell me," G-Ma said.

"G-Ma, she spends her weekends riding a charter bus with a picnic basket," I said.

G-Ma's lip curled while she stared at me. Then, she laughed and motioned for me to follow her into the kitchen.

"Come on to this kitchen, chile. We'll fry some chicken for him," she told me.

Within an hour, I had a pan of fried chicken ready to take home. NyQuest was strapped to me in his baby carrier. I grinned as I walked out into the spring sun that finally decided to shine over South Ridge. If Banger liked the chicken, I decided that I would make him that ham. Shanae sat on the steps with her face balled. Subira's daddy and Best had both stopped answering her calls when they found out she was pregnant. That's what she was telling a girl sitting on the stoop with her.

The glasses-wearing girl swung her burgundy box braids as she stood and demanded to know, "Ain't you that fake model from Sapphire Cadre?"

Without waiting for an answer, she smacked the pan of chicken out my hands. Shanae struggled to get to her feet and warned the girl about hitting me while I was holding Banger's baby. I slapped the glasses off that bitch's face to warn her about hitting me period. Then, I reached into my purse. The boys on the stoop tried to jump in between us. Ken-Ken and PeeWee tore out of the alley to drag that bitch away from me. She screamed about fucking me up for getting pregnant by her nigga. I'd never seen that girl before, but NyQuest was eight months old. Shouldn't she have been mad about that way before then? It didn't matter at that moment, because I was trying to get somebody to hold NyQuest so that I could fuck that bitch up just like the last one who tried to act stupid over the man I shared a baby and an address with.

"Monaysia, *please* stop trippin. That bitch is crazy from a long time ago," Rize begged me, trying his hardest to keep my hands out of my purse. I struggled to get away from him.

"That wasn't no long time ago! I sucked his dick in Albany on Valentine's Day!" she screamed. "Squeak had me in the telly—"

Shanae got super strength and hauled her pregnant ass off that stoop. She ripped down the street after her. Rize locked his arms around me and told me to calm down.

"*I* was with that nigga on Valentine's Day. Wouldn't she have mentioned me being there too? Please listen to somebody with sense, Monaysia," he begged.

With Rize's arms around me, I melted and then calmed myself.

"We went to pick up Squeak from jail, and we went to work," he told me softly.

"I know you're lying to me." I tried to break away from him just so that he'd grab me again. Banger didn't feel like that when he put his arms around me. "Nigga called me from a private number when we were supposed to be in the Poconos."

"Monaysia, he wasn't with that bitch," Rize insisted, and Rico came up the stairs and tried to tell me the same.

It felt so stupid to cry after I made the mistake of looking down at the chicken. "I try so hard, and he just gives me his ass to kiss. He didn't think I was good enough to know that his grandfather was about to die. All he wants from me is this baby. He doesn't give a fuck about me."

"That's all the fuck you wanted out of him was a baby, so what the fuck you crying for?" Rico hollered, and bent over to clean up the chicken.

Rize let me go, and helped Rico pick up the chicken. He told Rico to stop criticizing me. Then, he begged me not to go home arguing. I stared down at my good efforts going to waste again.

"I'll help you make some more," Rize offered.

"You will?" I asked with a sniffle.

He looked up at me and said, "I see you trying to change if nobody else does."

This dimples in his grinning face warmed my heart, so I went to the car and let him drive. He let some things off his chest.

"You know it's only on the strength of your seed that you're still able to walk, right? I know you think the whole world is against you, and everybody else is being mean, but you're way more trouble than you're worth. That burn mark on the back of Shaan's neck was a death sentence," he said.

"Okay, so beat me up and kill me! I'm tired of hearing that I ain't shit but a baby-mama!" I cried.

"That's what I don't understand. You came to that nigga to get a baby in you. You got a baby. Now you're mad because he loves the baby?" he wondered, his tone as relaxed as if he were just asking a question in school.

"I'm mad because he doesn't love me!" I hollered.

Rize glanced at me from the driver's seat and then chuckled. "You don't want that nigga to love you; you want him to worship you. You a dime, so you're used to niggas falling at your feet to do whatever you want. Since Shaan won't, you're losing your damn mind. If he ever does, you'll get bored.

"You better recognize, though. My bro is a good dude. He's better than me. I'd've left your ass in the dirt after that spaghetti shit and just hoped Aunt Lynn ain't catch you by yourself one day. You never would've seen me or my seed again. That's word to Grandpa Jerry." Rize was never afraid to call me on my bullshit.

"You mind if I make a stop right quick?" he asked me when I didn't have a response.

Knowing where we were going, I shook my head. The ride to DPD seemed to take forever. The dark skinned girl stood behind that same tree when we got there, wearing some fly Mickey Mouse earrings and several gold chains. One of them had a Mickey Mouse medallion dangling from it that looked just like the one Mike gave me. I felt around for it at the bottom of my purse. Hers seemed shinier in the sun. She was so happy to see Rize that she didn't even notice me staring at them while they laughed and talked. He lifted NyQuest from his car seat. As she held him and smiled, NyQuest looked at her with so much admiration in his baby eyes that I was jealous. Then, she started crying when he said he had to go. They hugged for what seemed like hours. Rize got back into the car, obviously holding back tears. I watched her walk away. She was a stylish cutie pie, almost the same height as me. When she walked, she glided like Lisa and the rest of the aunties. Her hips swung from East Sanford to West.

"How old is she?" I wondered.

"About to be sixteen. Why?" he asked.

"Just wondering. She dresses real cute. Think she'll wear something if I make it?" I asked.

He sniffled and then smiled a little. "I bought her a few pairs of them jeans all the chicks in the hood be wearing that you and Peachy make. She loved them."

He watched her for a while and then pulled off when she was no longer in sight.

"How come your father doesn't just take her?" I asked him.

He looked at me like he wanted to tell me to shut up then

reconsidered. Maybe he saw something in me that I didn't know about myself yet that made him tell the truth.

"Her mother is an evil bitch," he began. "The last time my pops even tried to get visitation, she tried to kill my sister."

"What? That's crazy!" I exclaimed. "Why didn't y'all take her like you took NyQuest from me?"

"If the bitch had the power to get my grandfather sent to Death Row, then how do you think we would have kept my sister? Don't you see I gotta sneak up here to see her behind a fuckin tree?" he snapped.

I shrank back in my seat while we traveled down the winding road out of DPD.

"What?" Then, I gasped as I put two and two together. "Is that why Selena got so mad when I watched Hope Thomas on the news that one day?"

"Yeah. That evil ass bitch."

"She sits on the news and smiles about killing her child's grandfather?" I repeated. Then, I said, "But wait a minute. That bitch used to give presentations during Career Week when I was in high school. The main thing she used to tell us was not to get tied down with kids and a man. Up until I met Banger, she was my idol."

A cynical chuckle came from his mouth. "That explains a lot."

"But I could never tell a lie that would cost somebody jail time or his life. Why did she do that?" I wondered.

"I don't really understand it myself," Rize told me. "All I know is that Grandpa Jerry was in jail, and Hope did a story on it and got an award for that story, and we didn't live with Hope no more. My sister lived with us for, like, a year, and then we weren't allowed to see her anymore. I don't understand it, but I don't love anybody in this world more than I love my sister." He glanced over his shoulder at the car seat and grinned. "Maybe Quest is tied with her, but my baby sister is my heart. I don't want nothing bad to happen to her, but I can't go without seeing her." He turned to me and pointed his finger. "Don't tell my pops me and Mommy come up here to see her either. We could get him into a lot of trouble behind that. I'm deadass, Monaysia. He can't know."

"I understand," I said. "I heard him on the phone with her mother one time. He gives her money for everything that girl wants and needs. Why won't she let him see her?"

"Because she's a petty bitch," was his answer. "The crazy part was she broke up with him, talking about how he never supported her and always chose his family over her. How was he supposed to support her in what she did to his own father?"

That was when I understood why Rize took me on that trip and told me that story.

He said, "The only reason why my pops ain't married to Mommy yet is because my sister can't come to the wedding. We would never do something that big without her."

"Dang. Y'all just a whole family of good dudes, ain't y'all?" I remarked.

"Yeah, we are... Well, I ain't shit yet. I ain't ready to settle down."

We shared a laugh at that.

"Is that why you won't get serious about Siraya? She really likes you," I said.

"Who that?" he asked.

"My friend. You fucked her every night in January on my couch consistently up until Valentine's Day," I said.

He furrowed his brow and asked, "For real? Did she get me a good gift for it?"

I looked at him like he was crazy. "You really don't remember her? You moved her out of her house in Midtown the night of that shootout. She asks me about you every single day. You really don't remember who she is? You beat up the nigga that beat her up."

"Oh! The one you make the clothes for. When she coming back over? I might need to hit that again."

"You can't even remember her name!" I yelled, and we laughed again.

He took on a serious tone and said, "Mommy clung to you because she misses the hell out of my sister. She thought that you needed a mother, and that y'all could bond over that. You really hurt her."

"I'll call her and apologize then. I didn't understand all of this was going on," I said.

"It shouldn't take all this, though, Monaysia. It seems like you're in a fight to make the world kiss your ass. Nobody in my family deserves that shit. I see you trying to do better, but try harder. I ain't saying nothing to you that I ain't said to Shaan. He was fucked up for lying to you about Valentine's Day, and he was fucked up for not handling that situation with Grandpa Jerry better. But think about what kind of person you had to be to make him do that to you."

I shook my head. "I didn't deserve to be left in a shootout while his friend went to Albany with a hotel full of hoes who would jump on me later."

"That's not what happened," Rize insisted.

I didn't know how much I believed him. My mind traveled to the houses in DPD and why we called it that. We drove down a hill, past actual mansions. The grass seemed greener, sky seemed bluer, and the sun seemed more yellow out there. Those people had so much money that they could buy a miserable reality for some and make it look like it was those people's fault. I fingered my tennis bracelet. It suddenly looked like pebbles. No matter how hard Banger's name rang out in the streets, it didn't hold the power that an East Hills address held.

It was a little scary that I admired someone being able to fight off that family with one news story, but the optics were stunning. They had the capability of making someone whose name was better than money in the streets calculate how and when to spend it so that he stayed off of their radars. Chillz was father to every boy in the hood, yet Hope kept his daughter from him just by appearing in front of a camera at six in the morning. Siraya's and my parents could never brag about us again. It was insignificant compared to the currency the people of DPD used. Those people could do whatever they wanted and live fabulous, high profile lives while doing it.

My thoughts were so cloudy that I didn't realize we were at the grocery store until Rize announced it. I was over wanting to cook for Banger at that point. Being with him meant being treated like I was beneath his family, and they had to fight too many people for their humanity to be acting like that. I certainly wasn't going to spend my days in the kitchen for someone whose circumstances were curated by a bitch on the news.

Then, Rize came close to me and started instructing me on how to make the chicken. He had a cocky smile on his face as he dared to say that he could cook better than G-Ma. He showed me a couple of secrets and showed me how to fry cabbage. Banger came in and looked at us like he caught us fucking.

"Aryan jumped on her on the stoop," Rize calmly explained before I got indignant about the way Banger slightly cocked an eye at us.

Bags seemed to form under Banger's eyes in anticipation of the sleep he thought he was going to lose.

"I ain't fucked her no time this year!" he insisted. "That bitch is crazy! I fucked her back in the day when—"

To hush him, I walked up to him and hugged him.

"It's okay. I understand. We've been in a bad place. It's time that we both grow up and let these bitches know that we're together, and they can't break us up. Let's just start over. I won't mention my birthday or Valentine's Day again, and you stop being mad at me and Siraya about the basketball tournament."

He looked down at me with my arm around him and returned the embrace.

"What you was doing in the hood anyway? That crazy bitch ain't allowed to leave there. They give her crazy ass a check to stay down there."

"I wanted to surprise you with a dinner that you would actually eat, so I went to G-Ma's house to help her clean up. Then, she taught me how to fry chicken, but that bitch with the tight ass braids smacked the pan out of my hands while I had Quest strapped to me in the carrier."

Banger nodded and said, "Heh."

I had to back away from him when he said that. It wasn't even a word. It was just a sound, but I was terrified. He pulled me back to him.

"Sounds like you had a rough day. We got some bubble bath in here? Let me run one for you."

Rize went to NyQuest's walker and picked him up.

"Let me take my nephew so y'all could have peace."

I invited him to stay for dinner. That was the most peaceful one we ever had.

It was the middle of the night, and Banger had just got done putting my ankles behind my ears. I was trying to sort out the wave of feelings I had that day. There was one thing pricking my mind. I sat straight up in bed.

"You gotta gimme a minute, Nay." Banger panted.

I pushed him away from me and sprang from the bed. After I snatched the cordless phone from the hook, I went to the studio and called Peaches. It seemed to take forever for her to answer the phone. That just gave me time to get out my sketch pad and colored pencils.

"Bitch, it sound like money on this phone. What you got now?" she asked.

"Prom dresses. We gotta do that shit and quick," I said.

"You think we got time for that? You be working all the time at your high profile job," Peaches teased.

"Bitch, I want this more. Let's do this. Get your ass on this side of the bridge. Bring me fabric," I commanded her.

"Ain't nobody getting to that side of the bridge tonight. Tell Banger to bring me your sketchbook tomorrow, and I'll get to work while you're at work. I wanna look at Holmes Bridal and Jackson's to see what we're up against," she said.

"That's why I fuck with you." I hung up the phone and went back to drawing. Rize's little sister was heavily on my mind while I spiraled feverishly into an all night session. Banger came in the room and tried to fuck me on my sketch table. I drew while I threw my ass back at him. Peaches was there at sunrise. She snatched the sketchpad from me and looked at the first dress that came to mind.

"Biiiiiiiiiiiiitch!" she yelled.

"I need it to be that same exact shade of turquoise as that room on the top floor in Chillz's house, so we need paint chips so that I can match a dye to it," I told her in a rush. "Can you get actual rhinestones?"

"Is this for somebody?" she asked.

"More like for a specific body. I just saw a little girl yesterday that made me remember how hard it was to find a prom dress that didn't look crazy on my body," I told her.

The dress was shimmery turquoise with rhinestone spaghetti straps and the sides cut out. It took a very special body type to pull it off without it looking like she was selling it. I couldn't wait to show it to Rize and Selena.

It took weeks for me to finish it in between all the other things I had going on, but I dedicated all of my free time to that one and a pink one. Then, I invited Selena and Rize over by themselves to see it. Banger wouldn't let himself be left out of it, even though he had no idea what was going on.

My favorite part of inviting Rize and Selena over to see the dress was that they knew who it was for as soon as I showed it to them. Selena gasped and hugged me. That seemed to break down whatever barrier I put between us, and I had to admit that it felt good.

"Mommy, why you crying about a dress? That's what you wearing to your wedding?" Banger asked.

Selena cut her eyes at him and shook her head.

"It's perfect, Monaysia," she whispered, reaching out to touch the fabric. "Do we take it to her now?"

"Nah," Rize said, shaking his head. "We gotta figure out a way to have Daddy see her try it on." He turned to me and said, "I don't give a fuck what nobody else says about you. You good with me." He peeked out the room at Banger and said, "You might gotta start packing your shit for Paris, Chief. This talent is wasted here."

Banger walked back toward the room and looked at me, the dress, down at NyQuest trying to get up and walk, and then back at me. Disappointment was in his eyes, even though his face held a smile.

CHAPTER 13

*a*s soon as I had the three most important people on my side about going to Paris, the Campavhores confirmed that they wanted Peaches and I to go there for two separate three month stretches. I planned to stay there and try to shop my designs, or maybe even study over there. The only detail I had left to work out was whether or not Banger and NyQuest were coming with me, or if we were going to do a long distance relationship.

It didn't take me too long to decide that we were a family and needed to be together. All it actually took was watching Shanae on the stoop, begging Squeak to help her get the kids out the house every morning. He gave her his ass to kiss while she struggled to get a pregnant belly, a stroller, and multiple children out the house. Moosie always came to the rescue. Meanwhile, Banger didn't even make me get NyQuest dressed in the morning.

My only challenge was making Banger see that he was bigger than Sanford County. I knew his family thought it was their duty to take care of the whole county, but what did they get out of it besides being killed? I couldn't stand around and be bullied about that without turning into the bully myself.

G-Ma was at a point where she was damn near pushing him out of Sanford County. There were the kidnappings, and then there were her dreams. I didn't have dreams, so I didn't understand why she shook and cried as she recounted nightmares of Banger being buried in the floor of a jail cell. I knew that if he didn't stop acting as the authority over missing children, though, I could see him being buried. She told him to start learning French. He refused to go anywhere without her. At first, she said it was impossible for her to leave the other children behind. The family finally pushed back and told her that she had to start making her kids take care of their own kids. Around the middle of May, as I was telling her what Banger wanted her to cook for his birthday, she asked me what kinds of things there were for old Black ladies to do in France.

Everything was perfectly aligned. She and I were going to corner him and tell him that he had to get ready to pack up and see if he could get us out of our lease a few months early. Then, Amy Ruffin called me into her office. A portfolio I'd given her more than a year ago sat in front of her, along with a portfolio of the work I'd done for Sanford Ringer. I shook the woman's birch colored hand before taking a seat.

With her teeth gleaming an unnatural smile, she said to me, "I've been watching the work you've been doing in my department. I expected someone who was just starry eyed about getting out of the billing department, but you have a ton of fresh ideas. Your grades in school are great, and Dexter Aldridge can't stop talking about you. Tell me, how do you know my good friend Dexter?"

I'd forgotten who he even was by then. Quickly, I tried to remember why I knew that name. The white patent leather shoes tapped that eerie rhythm through my mind. Then, I told her, "I'm more familiar with his wife Dorothy than him. She was the head of a company I modeled for called Naomi Iman."

She nodded. "Dorothy is a great friend of mine. Dexter, though, raves about you every time I see him. How do you know him?"

"Completely by mistake. I was silly enough to try to go into business with an ex. It was just a small company. Mr. Aldridge did our banking. He was kind enough to advise me to get out of that partnership without charging me for that gem."

"So I take it the business was no good?" Amy asked.

"It was worse than no good." I shrugged, then added, "Can't help everybody."

"No you can't," Amy agreed with a smile on her face. "I'm in need of an assistant, and I want to offer you the position. You'll be spending a lot of time in meetings, assisting with presentations, sitting in on castings for commercials, researching competitors, that sort of thing. It'll help you to familiarize yourself with the kind of work that we do while you finish your education."

I was floating. Banger took me out to dinner at his family's five star restaurant, The Hyacinth Rose. Relief was all over his face. He falsely assumed that I was passing up Paris for that job.

Banger said that he didn't want a birthday party, so I just had G-Ma make a bunch of food and a cake for a get-together at our apartment. His people brought the Crown Royal. I planned to be on my best behavior and looking good in a short dress. Siraya and I spent half a day in Hair Revolution getting our hair, nails, and makeup done. She couldn't stop looking at herself in the mirror all the way out to Jackson's Department store. We had short dresses for the night that needed high heels, just in case Banger changed his mind and wanted to go to the club. I took NyQuest so that I could find him a matching pair of sneakers.

I spied a pair of red block heels that I wanted that would have looked good with the red and black dress I was wearing. I unzipped my garment bag that held my dress so that I could make sure they were the right shade of red for each other. I felt like someone lurking behind me, so I turned around slowly to see who had the problem. All I saw was a name tag and a black blazer my grandmother taught me how to make when I was in high school.

"I see you been avoiding me, bitch."

I glared down at Yolanda and thought about snatching her head off of her shoulders. My totaled car in the impound lot flashed before my eyes Brooke came rushing up to us. She was wearing a name tag and all black too.

"Landa, don't do this. You need this job to pay your fine," she told her.

"Listen to your friend," I commanded. I thought about reaching into my purse, but Yolanda was a drinker, not a fighter. My mind could have been playing tricks on me, but I thought she smelled like gin.

"Don't get cute. We're still gonna fuck you up," Brooke growled.

I laughed at the two girls who used to hide behind me in grade school when people picked on them. Siraya pulled me away.

"Neither one of you can fight, so stop making this scene in front of her baby," Siraya told them.

"Fuck that bastard!" Brooke yelled.

The curled lips and bucked eyes of customers turned their attention to our scene. Jackson's was too upscale a setting for it.

"Fuck my baby?" I asked, and pushed the stroller toward Siraya, who was conflicted over whether she should hold the stroller or jump into the fight. While I tried to punch Brooke in her face, Yolanda jumped on my back. Brooke didn't move until she saw me shielding my face. She figured I'd protect that part of me more than anything. I grabbed shoes from a display and launched them at them to keep them from landing any punches. Yolanda pulled my hair. Brooke tried to catch a shoe and throw it back at me. Siraya used one hand to hold the stroller and the other to push her back.

A crowd surrounded us. Some people cheered while others shook their heads. Led by mall security, the general manager broke through the swarm. Tisha Darnell gasped when she saw her employees attacking her catalog model. Mall security dragged Brooke and Yolanda away, and the police came to take a statement. I was given an appearance ticket for child endangerment. Tisha scolded the police for giving it to me. She assured me she would straighten it out for me. I tossed it out the car window on the way back to South Sanford.

Siraya and I giggled about how crazy things were every time we got together. There was a line of traffic waiting to get across the bridge, and it was dark by the time we crossed it. All of our visitor spaces were occupied, but there was no music coming from my apartment. I thought they would have done something to make Banger party on his 21st birthday.

When I opened the door, Banger's whole family was sitting around the living room and dining room. They asked where I'd been and came to take NyQuest from me. Banger zoomed in on my ripped shirt when I walked through the door.

"You was fighting around my son?" he exclaimed.

"I got jumped. Thank you. I'm fine," I snapped.

Banger pointed to Siraya, and asked, "Why the fuck is she always in some bullshit whenever you come around?"

Siraya's eyes bucked, and that made me crack up. She joined with nervous laughter.

"Ain't shit funny!" he yelled, causing everyone to turn and look at him.

"Shaan, it was a rough day. Chill out," Rize told him and got off the couch to approach us. "Y'all okay?"

"Two bitches in the shoe department at Jackson's jumped me, and I didn't even get my shoes. No, I'm not okay!" I complained.

Moosie asked, "What kind of ghetto ass shit Tisha got going on in her store, D?"

I looked toward the dining room to see who she was talking to and saw a brown man with a police department polo sitting at a table between Chillz and the man everyone called Unc, eating like it was his last meal. He waved at me as he swallowed his food. After he took a few more forkfuls of food, he asked if he could use the phone. After I gave it to him, we heard fussing from the other end of the line that was loud enough to fill the whole house.

"Monaysia! Where were the girls who jumped on you from?" D called to me from the living room.

"Sapphire Cadre. Does it matter?" I asked.

D returned to his phone call, saying, "I know people from Sapphire Cadre don't act ghetto like the people from my side of the bridge, Tish. They're all perfect, preppy, classy angels. People from South Ridge are the only ones who have ever gotten into a fight, at any point."

Chillz and Unc both cracked up at his sarcastic tone.

"Who the fuck jumped on you from Sapphire— Your friend you put in jail finally caught up to your ass, huh?" Banger guessed. He looked at Siraya and asked, "You just sat there and let her get jumped?"

"I held your baby," she said softly.

"Don't explain yourself to his ass!" I snapped and pulled her past him to the bedroom so that we could get dressed. I made a stop at the stereo to turn on some music, fussing about them just sitting there in silence.

"Shaan, your son's mother just got jumped. Shouldn't you be a little bit more compassionate?" Rize asked.

I turned up the music louder, because I refused to argue on his birthday.

"Your baby daddy is gonna beat me up, isn't he?" Siraya asked.

"Fuck that nigga. I'm trying to treat him better on his birthday than he did me on mine," I said. Then, we started laughing again about something crazy happening every time we got together.

"Do we even change our clothes?" she asked. "It doesn't look like we're going anywhere."

"Well, we can't stay in ripped clothes," I said, and we started giggling again. "I saw how Rize was looking at you. Don't leave with him tonight."

"Why?" she asked, and looked in the wall length mirror at herself. She touched her hair and said, "This ponytail ain't move. I'm gonna have to start going to your baby's aunties all the time."

"Just don't go with Rize tonight. He doesn't even call you back," I advised her.

"He still keeps coming back for more. He said he just doesn't wanna get caught up with a baby right now. I respect that, because the shit you be going through is enough for me. I thought the only thing you had to work on getting back right was your body. I didn't know it messed with your mind too, girl."

I cut my eyes at her. She apologized for speaking that thought. We walked out the room to people eyeing our dresses.

"I just wanted to be prepared in case Banger changed his mind and wanted to go out," I said. "Thank you to whoever put the food out."

"Nay-Nay, this was real thoughtful that you put this together for Banger. He ain't never been one for birthday parties, but twenty-one is a milestone. He needed to celebrate it," Unc said.

Despite Banger's scowl, I pushed a smile onto my face and

put my arms around him. "It'd be messed up if I didn't celebrate this man. Through all the crazy things we've been through, he's been consistently on my side."

Lynn dropped the piece of chicken she was eating on the floor.

"That bitch really did grow her ass up. I don't believe this shit." She shifted on the couch. "Because, keeping it one hundred percent honest, if I walked in the house after getting jumped and got talked to the way Shaan's ass just talked to her, I would've aired this whole shit out."

"She gotta grow up before they get out to Paris," Chillz said.

I looked at Banger and asked, "You're really gonna come?"

"It's only six months, right?" he asked.

"Well, at first, but it might turn into more if me and Peaches get over there and get with the right people," I answered.

He huffed.

"Baby, we don't have to talk about this right now. It's your birthday. We can take a walk around the park another day and discuss it in full detail," I said and got up. "It's your birthday, though. You should have a blunt in one hand and a drink in the other. What's really good?"

All the aunties eyed me except Lisa. There was a wall of ice where she was supposed to be whenever she and I were in the same room. I shivered as I passed it and went to the table where the liquor sat. Chillz made the comment that we needed to find a way to make more room in that dining room to put a small bar in it, and I agreed while I poured Banger a Crown and Coke.

"Besides, with this promotion I just got at work, things might change. Peaches might be the one who actually goes to Paris, and I'll just be doing work here and shipping it overseas. I don't know." I took Banger the cup. Then, I sat beside him and took a Dutch from the box on the coffee table.

Lynn didn't take her eyes off of me while I rolled Banger's blunt.

"You really have changed. After how he did you on Valentine's Day, I wouldn't have done shit for his ass," she remarked.

I shrugged. "I haven't been an angel. We all know that. But no matter what I do or go through, he's held me down. What more can anybody ask for? My father never did as much for my mother as this man does for me."

Banger stared at me. We stared at each other for so long that I thought he was going to kick everybody out and take me into the bedroom. The doorbell rang, though, so I got up to answer it. Melinda was there with two arms full of bags.

"You came!" I shrieked and hugged her before helping her bring the bags into the house.

"Marcus is hanging out by the elevator. He doesn't know if he's allowed in," she said.

Unc looked around, and said, "That sounds like something else is going on. How'd he even get on this side of the bridge this time of night? I'll be back."

I went into the kitchen and piled food onto a plate for Banger before joining him on the couch again. He relaxed and allowed me to serve him.

"Damn. I would've went out if I knew the day was gonna end this good," he said. "It definitely ain't look like it was."

The family dove into a conversation about all the bad things that happened in South Ridge that day. I couldn't wait to get away from there so that I didn't have to hear about children being snatched from parents, complaints about potholes, and rumors about tolls being charged to cross the bridge. That wasn't a birthday conversation. They needed to plan a business meeting or something. No child that was related to them by blood was in danger. Their need to take responsibility over something they could never beat made me angry.

At some point during the night, Selena tapped me and told

me to take the aunties to see the dress. It was hanging proudly over my design table covered by a sheath of plastic.

"My niece would love that dress!" Adrianne exclaimed.

"I hope turquoise and silver are still her favorite colors," Renee remarked. "Because based on the last school picture we got, that dress is perfect for her."

"Y'all don't feel a way about the sides or back being cut out?" I wondered.

Selena put down her drink and ran to the dress. "Look at the chain braided across the back!"

"How many colors are you making this in?" Lynn wondered.

I shook my head. "That one and the pink one are exclusives. I saw a girl one day and made a dress just for somebody with her body type. I know what it's like to be built with a grown woman's body at a young age and not wanting to hide it behind that same old white gown with the spaghetti straps."

"Well shit. I think we can all relate to that," Lynn said, and the aunties chuckled.

We went back out into the living room with them squealing over the dress. Siraya was sitting on Rize's lap by then and avoiding my glare. I went to sit on Banger's. Two bottles sat in front of him while he nodded into a drunken sleep. When I went to clean up the bottles, he pulled me down next to him.

"Never thought I'd meet a chick that changed me," he slurred.

I inched away from him, but he pulled me back. I wriggled away from him and suggested he opened the present I bought him.

"Why you always buying me shit? You could've just sat in that room and made me some shit. I woulda been way happier than whatever you spent money on. That's your problem. You think everything with a high price tag and a European name on it makes it better," he complained.

"First of all, I *did* make most of it. I just can't make shoes, so I bought you some Jordans," I snapped at him.

"I hate Michael Jordan." He actually pouted. "I'm strictly an Uptowns and Timbs nigga. You ain't never seen me walk through this crib with no Jordans on my feet."

I sighed and tried to keep myself calm. "Fine. I'll take your gift back then. I'm going to check on Quest and get a drink. You want some more cake?"

He didn't answer me. People scolded him as I went up the hallway. After confirming that NyQuest was laying on his back with his arms spread and snoring like he'd worked overtime at somebody's factory, I closed the door and took the monitor to the liquor table with me. I saw Selena and Chillz watching how much I poured, but they shrugged it off. I'd behaved myself most of the night.

"This the shit I be talking about right here!" Banger continued to go off. "It's always about what she wants. The shit don't never be about me. Now I gotta go get my picture taken for a passport. That's some fed shit. She wanted me to be in her life. Ain't ask me what I wanted."

"You told me what you wanted when you hit it raw four times in one night without pulling out. What do you mean?" I yelled, and then gulped down the liquor.

"I wanted my baby, so I ain't got shit to complain about there," he continued. "But now I gotta change the language I speak, the way I spend my days, gotta buy shit on birthdays. Fuck this shit."

"This is what you said you wanted to do for me, but you ain't gotta do none of that shit!" I shot back. "Just stay here and get your ass killed tryna protect kids because their parents are too pussy to do it themselves!"

Something even uglier was going to come out of my mouth after that, so I apologized, poured the rest of the liquor in the sink, and went to bed after thanking everybody for coming.

When Banger woke up in the middle of the next afternoon, we did go outside for that walk. There was no more avoiding the conversation. His drunken mind yelled out his sober thoughts, and I wasn't doing anything to be the villain.

"It's obvious that you can't stand me, so this is the perfect opportunity for us to just break apart from each other," I started as soon as we reached the middle of the parking lot.

"You gave me my baby. I got mad love for you," was his argument.

"Banger, I have done more with my life than given you a baby," I said. "At least, I'm trying to. I hope that when I get done with my first year over there that you'll see how much more I am than a model for somebody's clothes and the person who brought your baby into the world."

"There's nothing higher in my eyes, though, Nay. You don't understand the shit that I've been through in my life. The only thing that I ever ever ever wanted is a family, and you gave that to me," he said. "I'll do whatever I gotta do to keep us together."

Stopping to stare up into his eyes, I challenged him., "By forgetting every important day, yelling at my only friend, and making me the enemy even when I haven't done shit to set you off?"

"You don't think trying to take me from G-Ma is setting me off?" he countered.

"I told you to bring her with us!" I screamed. "I keep bending and making arrangements to fit your life, but everything has to be on your terms!"

"This is what you wanted!" he bellowed so loud that it shook the car windows around us. "I don't live a life that lets me toss away people that I can't brag on! My family takes care of each other for life! You see what happens when we don't. Ain't nobody about to be left in the dirt like my mom, Monaysia! That's why G-Ma won't come!"

"Well, how the fuck did she raise you to be like that but

didn't raise her own kids to not leave their kids behind for days?" I asked. "This is crazy that the thing that I want most out of life is depending on whether or not an old lady will take a free trip to somewhere that she won't be taken advantage of! She can put her feet up and see a different country for once in her life!"

He pointed at me while he pushed the stroller across the grass until we reached the concrete path leading down a hill to the park.

"That's your problem right there. You come down here and look down on people like you the only person in the world who ever did anything or went anywhere. G-Ma lived in France for two years when she was younger. The only reason why she came back here was because she got pregnant with my mother. You ain't special."

"Yes, the fuck I am!" I argued. "Because I won't never let South Ridge be my final destination. She did all that with her life just to spend the rest of it being taken advantage of, and I ain't gonna do it. I ain't gonna be like nobody in your family, letting the news throw dirt on my name and not doing shit about it."

I threw my hands up, and asked, "Y'all do all this shit for the hood. Who the fuck ever does everything for y'all? Your family got three businesses on one block. Does anybody else ever match your money and add to it, or do they keep waiting for you to do more shit? After you get home from looking for children that have been snatched by the police, does anybody knock on your door and ask if they can watch your baby so that you can get some sleep? No. I don't think so. So why would I not want to get out of this hell hole?"

We reached the playground, only to see that the fence was locked with several heavy chains binding the fence shut. There was a sign posted with someone's handwriting that announced it was too dangerous for the kids to play. I looked at Banger with raised eyebrows.

"This is what you're continuing to fight for, while these people call you a drug dealer and call you South Ridge trash? Fuck this shit. You can have it."

NyQuest struggled to get out of his stroller as I turned it to walk away from Banger. He stretched out his arms, so I picked him up and started up the hill. He wriggled out of my arms. I watched him to see what he was going to do next. Half of me expected him to climb up my leg. Instead, he balanced himself. He screamed baby babble at the locked gate. Then, he took one step. My mouth rounded and eyes watered. He looked up at me, smirked, and took another. My hands went over my mouth, and I squealed at him as he toddled toward the gate and banged on it. Banger and I dropped the argument as we jumped and squealed at NyQuest taking his first steps. There was no more argument to be had. We ran back to the house and called everyone that we knew to let them know that our baby had taken his first steps. Maybe I didn't need to miss any milestones.

CHAPTER 14

$\mathcal{I}$ wanted to kick myself for taking that long to dive deep into family life. NyQuest did something new every day. He said no less than three new words a day. He went from walking to running to jumping. Chillz built him a small jungle gym for his bedroom, so he basically never had to leave his room. He barely cried. The only complaint I had was that he said daddy and refused to say mommy.

South Sanford had turned somewhat normal by the time NyQuest's birthday came. Chillz went all out for his first grandchild. He reserved this three-story banquet hall called the Steve Biko Legion and filled it with games and balloons. There were indoor and outdoor bounce houses, and he even got a merry-go-round with turtles and alligators instead of horses. My childhood didn't include a party with a merry-go-round. Chillz was happier to be throwing that birthday party than Banger and I combined. He and Unc locked themselves to the grills and made the best hot dogs, hamburgers, ribs, chicken, and seafood. The ice cream came from ChillZone, a 50s-style ice cream parlor Banger took me the night we met. G-Ma made the cake. Big Grams made so many appetizers and side dishes that I didn't think I'd ever be able to eat again.

My mother switched her butt up to the food table, fully prepared to carry on the way she used to at Thanksgiving dinner. The spread Banger's family prepared made her little ziti and meatballs look sad. My dad and Kidra both said they were scared of being seen with Jeremiah Revolution's family by the police, so I told them it was the last time I'd be speaking to either of them for a while. Melinda carried their gifts in. Chillz looked at the Buffalo Bills wrapping paper and gave Melinda the dirtiest look. She giggled at it and pulled a roll of wrapping paper from the bag that had cartoon characters on it. Mommy threw her a dirty look, so Melinda went double time onto another floor and tried to avoid her for the rest of the party.

"You know, I find it strange that you're that close to a woman who tore your family apart," Mommy commented.

"Mommy, please. That woman has done way more for me and NyQuest than you have in the past couple of years. Just keep the peace, please? It's been forever since I've seen you. I'd like for this time to not end as terribly as the last few," I said. "Go try some of the crab dip that Big Grams made. You'll love it."

That family *showered* NyQuest with gifts and money. Some people got drunk and came back around two and three times, apologizing each time for not giving him money. NyQuest had his five teeth on display the whole time. He knew that day was all about him.

"I only bought him one gift. Was that enough?" Siraya whispered to me at one point during the party.

I giggled at her. "You being here is enough. I guess birthdays for little kids are really big in this family."

Big wasn't quite the word, though. The sun began to set, and police rode by a few too many times for the family's liking. I didn't understand the issue when the man named D was there in his Sanford County PD polo with his badge showing. Even he was quick to tear everything down and pass out goody boxes.

Most of the birthday parties I went to when I was little had goody bags. At NyQuest's party, Selena passed out wooden boxes that she said Chillz carved, and Banger painted. Under his picture on the lid was etched the phrase "Quest '98." Inside of each of them was a bunch of candy and little toys. The stars of the gift boxes, though, were the wooden carousels, also hand-carved by Chillz and hand-painted by Banger. They were miniature replicas of the one that the kids rode on all day. I saw Mommy take three of them and rolled my eyes while I thought about her waving them in Siraya's parents' faces.

"You expect me to believe that he doesn't sell drugs after all of this?" Mommy whispered to me as she followed me around while I cleaned up.

I turned around and shoved a trash bag at her. "If you're gonna run your mouth, then the least you can do is make yourself useful."

With a smirk on her face, she backed up and waved her hands. "This is payback from all those Thanksgivings you skipped out on me, my sista. This is *your* child's party. I just came to eat up all your food and leave to go on a date."

"Well, don't lie on my child's father. His aunt and uncle threw this party. They own a strip of businesses on Sundown Boulevard," I bragged.

"Well, what could some businesses on Sundown look like?" she asked.

"Look. This is my son's family. These people take better care of this side of the bridge than I've ever seen anybody take care of anything in my life. This is my last time telling you that if you don't have anything nice to say to me, then just stay away," I told her. "I love you, but you're not ever going to say anything bad about these people, no matter what."

Mommy raised her eyebrows at me. "Are you in love with this boy?"

I grimaced and frowned. "Do you see my son? He's amazing. Of course I love the man who gave him to me."

She shook her head and frowned. "I never thought you would stop being selfish long enough to feel anything for anyone besides yourself. Crazy how it's some drug dealer when you finally do."

"Bye, Mommy! I hope that you find some happiness somewhere, because I sure have. Daddy has. What do we have in common? Hmm. Getting out of your house and away from your miserable ass." I turned my back on her and thought she would leave, but G-Ma pulled her to a table to have a conversation that lasted until the building was pristine.

I thought cleaning up meant that the party was over, but Chillz, Selena, and all of their children went home with us. Siraya joined. I didn't bother telling her to stay away from Rize. I just wrote her name on a piece of paper and shoved it in his hand. I took NyQuest and put him on my lap while I curled up against Banger on the couch.

"Let's talk about Paris," he told me. "Let's just let Siraya house sit while we leave for three months, come back for three months, and then leave for the other three months. Talk to your job. If they don't let you take this opportunity, then put your notice in. I got us."

"You sound like you've been thinking about this a lot," I said.

"It's my turn to stop acting stupid. I want us to be together. Our family could be so dope, and I told you from the start that I wanted to help get you back to where you needed to be." He kissed my temple.

"What about Marcus?" I asked.

"If it's just three months at a time, I can rest easy with Chillz and Unc looking out for him," he told me.

"And what about G-Ma?" I asked.

He hesitated, before replying, "She said she would come stay for a month or two, but I'll believe it when I see it."

I pulled his face to mine and kissed him, surprised by how much heat I felt on his end.

"What you wanna do about the stuff that you have at your mother's house?" he wondered.

I wrinkled my face while I thought about it. "I just have to hope she doesn't disrespect her own mother's legacy on one of her jealous days."

MY MOTHER'S number was still blocked on my phone, so I had to receive a call from Siraya's house from her, asking about what kind of discounts I got at Furniture Revolution later into the next week. That made me unblock her house number. The last thing I needed was Siobhan or Dartanion Newby calling to ask me for anything. Whatever she got made Banger and Chillz come into the house, cussing and grumbling at me the day they delivered it. Somehow, Mommy talked them into giving her something expensive for free. I wasn't sure how that was my fault, but it sure was funny.

To my surprise, my job contested me putting in my notice and put out some enticing offers. The Campavhores kept throwing out names they were connected to in Paris. I planned to slowly build my name up until I went from Paris to Milan. Peaches and depended on each other to accomplish our goals.

Every day, we packed and shipped our stuff over to the address where the musical's stage hands were going to stay. G-Ma gave Banger lessons on how to ask where to buy weed in France. She told him he could smoke it in the streets if he caught a train to Amsterdam, so he was excited about that. We were so happy to be raising our son on two different continents. Banger warmed up to being the uncle who came into town with French gifts.

Toward the end of August as we packed, the phone rang. That woman with the dreads announced herself and then commanded me to give Banger the phone. I loved the way she pronounced every single letter in his name.

"Joy Gilead, Esquire, would like to speak to you," I said with a giggle and the phone extended.

"What the fuck do she want?" he asked.

"I want to speak with you, Rahshaan Bailey. I can hear you breathing. Come to this phone," she commanded, and I had to cover my mouth from laughing at him.

"Nyir and Shameik brought the campaign signs to my office this morning. My team was impressed and placed an order for more. I'll have Nyir and Shameik deliver them on Tuesday.

"I assume Chillz told you of the big project I have for you to do?" I heard her say.

Banger put the phone down on the coffee table and turned on the speaker.

"Does your entire household need to hear our conversation?" she asked.

"No. I just need my ear drums when I go to France," he quipped.

"You're such an ass." She sucked her teeth. "My daughter's sixteenth birthday is in a few weeks, and Ray and I are letting her renovate her room. After our summer vacation to India, she has some ideas. Chillz has the pictures. My question to you is do you know how to stain glass?"

"I can paint anything," he answered.

"Good. She's worked hard, and I want to make sure that I can give her whatever she wants. If you tell her that I said that, then I'm going to stab you. You know that though, don't you?" she challenged him.

"Can't let your kids know you love them. Got it, Coach," he said.

"You're such an ass," she repeated. "And you're okay with painting her room three different colors?"

"Joy Gilead, Esquire, why are you doubting my skills?" he asked.

"Because I want to make sure that you earn the money that I'm paying you for this job. I know that you'll need some money to hold you over in Paris," she said.

"You called here to tell me that you're gonna miss me?" he asked.

"It's a little difficult for me to know G-Ma won't have you in the house, I'll admit. Goodbye."

That was a weird conversation that Banger said resulted in a high dollar job. It caused him to get up extra early in the morning and not come home until late at night for two weeks. He and Chillz's children dragged into the house every night and fell asleep at the table. I started feeling responsible for having dinner waiting for them.

One day, while the rest of them dragged into the house, Rico was animated. The rest of them looked at him with one eye cocked and begged him to shut up, but words kept coming out of his mouth.

"She was so fine, though, fam!" he said, tapping Moosie. "You saw her, right?"

"Bro, she was aight, but she wasn't worth you talking my ear off like this," Moosie said.

I perked up, because I'd never seen Rico get excited about a girl.

"Those eyes, son. She had some pretty ass eyes," he remarked. He called out to me, "Nay-Nay, bring me your phone! I gotta see about taking a girl to Toronto!"

"Toronto?" I repeated.

"Niagara Falls. Somewhere. That ain't good enough for a first date?" he asked me.

"I didn't think y'all could move like that," I said. "Don't you have to wait some months?"

"To go to Toronto? It's fuckin Canada, not Jupiter," Rico said quickly. "Where the phone at?"

I went into the kitchen and got him the cordless phone. When I came back into the living room, he was still talking about her eyes.

"Y'all ain't never had a shorty with eyes that beautiful," he said and thanked me for the phone.

Banger scoffed and said, "My girl is standing right in front of you."

Rico sucked his teeth. "Her eyes are just a funny color. That girl's eyes were sexy. They stared inside of me. I couldn't tell her a lie if I wanted to."

That comment left me stuck in one spot, blinking rapidly. No one had ever been so dismissive about my green eyes before. He paid me no attention while he sat back on my couch and said into the phone, "Mama Joy, why you ain't tell me you were introducing me to my wife today? Let me get her digits." He paused and exclaimed, "Virginia? What's she doing living down there when her future is here?"

Rize shrieked out an ugly laugh, and the rest of them cracked up.

"She's in school to be a nurse?" He coughed. "Tell her I'm sick and need her to take care of—

"Hello? Mama Joy, I know you ain't hang up on me." The phone rang before he could hit the redial button. He answered it like he paid the bill that month. Then, he handed it to me. "Hurry up, though. I gotta call back and see can I get that girl's number before she goes back to VA."

I chuckled at him and said, "Hello?"

"Nay-Nay, I'm on my way to that furniture store, and then I'm coming to your house," Mommy told me. "I might as well eat with you since it'll take me forever to get across that bridge."

"My house is basically packed, Mommy. I'm about to leave to go to Paris," I said.

"I know." She sniffled. "Why did I have to find out about it through Siobhan at dinner?"

"Think about what's happened every time I've seen you for the past two years," I said.

"All the more reason to make room for me. I know Siraya is about to house sit, and I want to see what your house even looks like."

"Why does it matter what it looks like? There are a bunch of people over here packing it up."

She got her way. It didn't matter. I had a bunch of pans of wings and salad from Peter's Kitchen anyway. An hour passed, so I forgot about her. We had just finished putting away the last box so that Siraya would be nice and comfortable to live like she wasn't in someone else's house. I was so excited. In less than two weeks, I was going to be on a plane out of there. It wasn't too soon either, because they were threatening to bring back that curfew bullshit after kids started disappearing from the bus stops again. Nothing was going to upset me.

And then somebody knocked on the door. I hated when people did that because there was a working doorbell right under the peephole, a luxury on that side of the bridge. She kept banging like she had a problem until I got to the door and ripped it open. Chrissy and Aunt Marvine stood with her.

Something looked different about Chrissy. Her lips were puffy. Something was off. Whatever was wrong with her had me staring, trying to figure it out. I stood there for so long that the three of them started shuffling their feet. When Chrissy smiled at me, it made me feel nauseous. I cut my eyes and then stomped into the house ahead of them without showing them around.

"She started some shit with you already?" Banger asked me when he saw the frown on my face.

I took a few breaths and then picked up NyQuest and returned to my unexpected guests. Banger followed me.

"Bang- *Baby*, do you remember my aunt and my—"

"Hey, Moosie!" Chrissy yelled over me, leaping onto Moosie's lap.

Chrissy being one of Moosie's girls was quite the plot twist. Mommy bucked her eyes while Moosie's eyes darted from Chrissy to me. Feeling no warm return of feelings, she got off of Moosie and strutted around the room. That's when I saw the little pouch that her stomach had turned into. As soon as she saw that I noticed it, she put her hand on it. Every man in that room quaked. The air in the apartment became impossible to breathe. I turned off the air conditioner, turned on the fans, and slid the balcony door open.

"I got some chicken and stuff in the kitchen. Help yourselves," I told Mommy and Aunt Marvine.

Aunt Marvine turned up her nose. "You don't make people serve themselves when they're guests in your home."

"You gotta help yourselves today," I said.

"Well, we didn't come over here for no chicken no way. Denise took us to a furniture store to get some things for Chrissy's baby, and we wanted to compare it to what you have," Aunt Marvine said.

I shook my head and asked, "Why? We're getting ready to move to Paris."

I cut my eyes at Banger so that he would know that I would cut him if he corrected my lie.

The way that Chrissy turned on her heels made it look like she was demon possessed.

"Moving to Paris?" she exclaimed.

"Yes. Paris," I confirmed for her with my nose in the air. "I design costumes for The Green Balloon."

"Really? I heard that you just lay up in the house all day and spend your baby daddy's money," she said in this fiery voice like she was accusing me of something.

"Well, you heard wrong. I work in advertising at Sanford Ringer—"

"How? You dropped out of college!" she cried.

"I went back," I told her through gritted teeth.

The doorbell rang, causing a break in our argument. Moosie dragged herself to the door. When she came back, she announced that Marcus was there.

"Shit. I know what that means," Banger said under his breath and went to his brother.

Marcus had shot up so fast that he was almost the same height as Banger. He carried two duffle bags with him and looked thin.

"Go eat, and then we'll go talk," Banger told him.

Marcus nodded and then said hello to me. That was the saddest, skinniest looking child I'd ever seen.

No one else in the house moved, so I took Mommy and her plus two to NyQuest's room, watching Aunt Marvine closely. There wasn't much that she could steal, but she would find something. She couldn't help herself.

Their eyes went straight to the indoor jungle gym.

"Monaysia, you can pack that up bring that to our house now," Aunt Marvine said.

"Why would I?" I snapped. "My baby's grandfather built it for him, and it'll last until he turns at least five."

"But you won't be here, so what do you need it for?" Aunt Marvine countered. "I swear, you're just like your mother."

"I'll tell you where you can order one," I offered.

"You don't have to. We've got Chillz's number," Chrissy said.

I frowned. "You got on a first name basis with my baby's grandfather just from one trip to the furniture store?"

Chrissy bristled. "It's called being friendly. You should try it.

Maybe then your baby's father wouldn't be at work talking about how much he hates you and how much you stress him out."

She and I glowered at each other. She rubbed her hands on her little pouch. That bump in her belly made her think she was untouchable.

"Mom, I don't really care about what Monaysia has in her house. Chillz will make my baby his own things. We don't need her life. It sucks," Chrissy said.

"Let me hurry up and get you all some food so I can hurry up and get back to packing for Paris," I said.

"How many times are you going to mention Paris?" Chrissy screamed. "We get it! You have to take your baby's father to the other side of the world to get him to yourself since you don't stand a chance against his family. You don't have to mention him anymore."

"What did you say?" I asked.

She smirked at me and started humming. I glared at Mommy.

When we walked back toward the kitchen, we saw Chillz and Selena. Each of them gave the funniest looks when they saw Chrissy.

"I should have known Chillz was close by when I smelled that chicken. It smells just the way you cook it *every Friday night*," Chrissy said.

Chillz and Selena were frozen while Chrissy went straight to the kitchen and started piling food onto her plate.

"I thought I was going to have to starve while we waited to get back across the bridge. There was no way I was eating Monaysia's spaghetti," she said.

I was burning inside, wondering where Banger was.

"I think we need to pray," Chillz said, then added, "over the food. Over the food."

After watching them all squirm, I waited to see where

Chrissy would sit. She took a seat next to Nyir and quietly ate. His eyes rested on her stomach as though that was the first time he'd ever seen a pregnant woman. That was the most silent dinner I ever sat through with that family.

Halfway through, Banger cleared his throat and said, "Nay-Nay, Marcus wanted to talk to us about coming with us."

Chillz said, "Peaches said he could stay with her if y'all didn't have enough room."

"Oh. I think Marcus coming with us will be better for your peace of mind, won't it, baby?" I asked Banger. "I mean, you already have to leave G-Ma behind. You shouldn't have to give up much else."

Aunt Marvine snorted. "Being a mother taught you how to stop being selfish. Denise, if you had learned that, you might still be married."

"Don't start that shit at my table. We live peacefully on this side of the bridge," I demanded.

"You know what would bring peace? If Chillz brought one of G-Ma's cakes or Big Grams' cobblers. Do you have any, Chillz? I've been craving it for a month," Chrissy said.

I couldn't take it anymore. "How the hell do you know my baby's family?"

Chrissy smirked at me and pointed at her stomach. "My baby's family too."

"I remember you!" Marcus exclaimed, pointing at her. "You gave me a ride to Aunt Lynn's house on Valentine's Day!"

"Marcus…" Selena palmed her face.

I looked around the table and waited for an explanation.

Chrissy leaned over the table and said, "You thought you were gonna run out of here while I had this baby, and I told you that you were not."

My heart tore down the center. I watched Banger intensely.

"I keep telling you that's not my baby, and to leave me alone.

Stop showing up at my job. Stop coming to my family's houses—"

"Then stop taking me over there!" she screeched. "I could think of better places to spend my Friday nights than by the river."

"You took her to the river?" Nyir yelled about two seconds before everybody else. It should have dawned on me that was my first time hearing Nyir speak a full sentence, but I was too focused on Banger's conversation with my cousin.

"What the hell is going on?" I demanded, staring directly at Banger for an explanation.

Banger had a scowl on his face that was almost as icy as the block that surrounded him. Chrissy tried to get him to say out loud that they'd been fucking, but he wouldn't respond.

"I'm not delivering this baby by myself! You don't get to give one child this life while ignoring the other!" Chrissy screamed. When her voice reached a certain pitch, she placed her hand on her belly and hummed a nursery rhyme.

"I told you about walking around with your head so high, Monaysia," Mommy taunted me after she ate the last of her chicken. "You were walking around in this fairy tale at NyQuest's birthday party, and your man had probably stopped at your cousin's house that same morning."

"Get your miserable ass out my house, delete my number, and don't speak my name ever again. You put me out your house; put me out your miserable ass mind, too," I told her.

Selena got up from her chair and came toward me. I put my hand up to stop her.

"Call Lynn and the rest of your sisters. Y'all are gonna have to beat my ass tonight," I declared and then turned back to Mommy. "Why the fuck are you still sitting here? You did what you came to do, and your ex is still living in East Terrace with his new wife, and I'm still gonna have lunch with her tomorrow probably, and you're still gonna be by yourself."

"Monaysia, you were talking about you thought you loved that boy, and I just needed you to see that he can make another family anywhere," Mommy said. "You thought you hit the Lotto with that baby."

"You having a baby by her?" Nyir asked. He looked from Chrissy to Banger and said, "You already got a baby."

The scene was too weird. Chrissy started crying over. Aunt Marvine slapped her shoulder, trying to get her to say something else. Chillz and Selena were at Nyir's side. Banger was silent. Mommy continued to gloat about how stupid I was, and everybody else at the table was shaking. Nobody reached out for me to apologize or explain. It was the lowest I ever felt in my life.

"You muthafuckas just live to hate me," I said.

Rize was the only one who said anything to me. "She's lying, Nay."

"This is the second bitch that's come to me about Valentine's Day, so everybody knows he wasn't with me. Is Marcus lying too?" I asked.

Nothing could be said.

"Get him out of here, or get your aunts to come beat my ass, because he won't live if he stays in this house tonight," I warned. I picked up NyQuest. Banger peeked over his wall to offer to take him.

"I'm spending time with my son, because I'm taking my ass to Paris by myself. You stay here with your family and think of more ways to embarrass me, but they won't work. I am *done* with your ass. Nobody has to worry about you leaving G-Ma, because I'll be gone. I'll figure out where I'm gonna live when I get back. Fuck every single person sitting at this table, because you muthafuckas never liked me anyway. You wanted him away from me. You got it."

Banger hopped out of his seat. "Nay, I love you."

"What do you mean you love her? You don't even like her!

You stand in that furniture store all day and talk about how much you hate going home!" Chrissy yelled.

The scene got weirder as I watched Selena and Chillz tend to a seething Nyir. Moosie escorted Mommy and Aunt Marvine out of the house while Chrissy screamed about wanting her boyfriend to take care of her baby. I went into my bedroom and shut the door. Somebody knocked on it, but I yelled for them to go away. NyQuest started hollering for his daddy, and I felt even more betrayed.

Monica's singing was the only comfort I had that night.

CHAPTER 15

*M*elinda planned to take me out to lunch one last time before I left. There was no way I could leave the house. She called and told me to get dressed anyway. She fussed the whole time about how much the family changed and how she was disappointed in them for letting me fall into such a messy situation.

"Something else has to be going on," she said.

"I don't care!" I yelled.

Softly, Melinda said, "I know. Just get out here so we can go shopping or something to make you feel better."

"I don't want to go shopping. I don't want to go anywhere that I have to hear that I'm Banger's baby-mama," I said.

"Okay. I understand. I'll find something else for us to do," she told me.

The weather was as gloomy as I felt as I walked to my car. Something felt off. I stopped and stared. Somebody had stolen my license plate.

"Stupid, South Sanford, ghetto ass hoodrats," I mumbled while I circled the car to see if it had fallen. Instead, I found that my hub caps had been stolen. The driver's side window was busted out. I wondered how I went the whole night without hearing anything.

"I know this wasn't nobody but Chrissy's stupid ass." I slammed my purse against my car out of frustration. All of my stuff fell out of it. The skies drizzled while I crouched over my stuff and cried.

A car pulled into the visitor's space. Banger hopped out of the driver's side while Rize went to get NyQuest out the back.

"What the fuck happened?" Banger asked me.

"Your bitch came around here and fucked up my car," I snapped.

He didn't respond to that. Instead, he crouched and helped me pick up the stuff that fell out of my purse. His hand went to the Mickey Mouse before mine.

"New jewelry?" he asked.

"Yeah. I bought it as a birthday present to myself after you didn't buy me one, and I didn't want to hear about how much unnecessary attention wearing something this big would bring," I quickly explained, and tucked it back into my purse. There was an envelope full of money that I forgot all about depositing after Mike went to jail. I snatched that from the ground quickly before Banger asked what it was.

Rize came around to see what happened and shook his head sympathetically. I took NyQuest into the house and went to call Melinda. She was there in an hour and had Siraya with her. I took NyQuest with me before Rize could get into Siraya's face.

"How'd you get off work?" I asked Siraya while Melinda drove through South Sanford. She went to several different restaurants and picked up food, including wings and ice cream. It took more than an hour.

"My boss wants to fuck Melinda, so I can do whatever I want as long as my 'sister from Russia' comes back," she giggled.

"Why does he think she's from Russia?" I asked.

"*Potomu chto ya govoryu po russki,*" Melinda said with perfect diction.

I shook my head and chuckled at that.

"Siraya, I have bad news for you, but I promise I'll fix it," I said.

"What's that?" she asked.

"We don't need you to house sit," I answered.

"You're not going to Paris?" Siraya and Melinda exclaimed in unison.

"Yes. *I'm* going. Banger is staying here, and I'll figure out where I'm gonna stay when I get back," I told them.

"What happened?" Siraya asked. "I knew it was bad when Melinda showed up at my job and told me to clock out and ask questions later."

"Banger has another baby on the way, and it's by Chrissy," I told her.

"What?" Siraya flipped around in her seat and exclaimed. "That crazy ass bitch that has to sing nursery rhymes to herself to keep herself from having crazy attacks? What the hell?"

"Wait. Chrissy?" Melinda asked. "Skinny? Blonde tips to her hair? Eyes the same color as yours?"

"How do you know her?" I asked.

"She was a coworker for a quick minute, but that singing nursery rhymes used to turn clients off," Melinda explained. "How do you know her?"

That made me think of a comment that Cream made a long time ago. "She's my cousin." I was seething.

"Nay-Nay, to be honest with you, I wasn't really looking forward to crossing that bridge every day anyway, and I didn't want to make myself as easily accessible to Rize. He's got to decide what he wants to do, but if he moves anything like his boy, I'll just leave him alone. Nay, you must feel terrible!" Siraya said.

"Well, I know you're tired of—"

Siraya cut me off with a stern look and said, "We'll talk about that later. Tell me what happened."

Not believing I was crying again, I sobbed while I recounted the details of that dinner. It pissed me off to know that I was set up to be embarrassed like that. What made me really angry was that they had so much energy to put into a plot that devious while having nothing for the people who murdered the loved ones they cried over. Women like Melinda and me didn't belong down in South Ridge. That was the real reason why Melinda would rather deal with weekend bus rides with my daddy than go back there with her head hanging low. I wasn't going back to them either.

Melinda drove for about an hour after getting across the bridge. We went to a suburb of East Sanford that I'd never had any reason to visit called Clancy. It was a sexy little place, 12 blocks by 15 blocks of townhouses, condos and stores. Of course, Melinda drove to the biggest condos and parked at the ones with a fountain in front and covered by ivy to show that whoever lived in those brick and glass buildings was a mystery to everybody else.

"If you tell your dad this place exists, I'm never speaking to you again," Melinda declared. "I stay here when he starts getting on my nerves, and now you can stay here until it's time for you to go to Paris."

"For real?" I asked.

"Yeah. Me and your dad are in a real good spot now since your mama told Kidra about how lonely I looked at Quest's birthday party. I knew Kidra was waiting for something to tell him about me," Melinda told me while we went to the elevator.

Of course, Melinda lived in the penthouse. After riding in that dirty ass car, I was scared of what her house was going to look like. She assured me a cleaning service went in there twice a week, whether she was there or not.

"When your daddy starts talking that bullshit about the bills,

I just come out here. I've never had to argue about that before, and I ain't about to spend the rest of my life doing it. I ain't stupid. I know that men only want to split bills so that they could spend your half on the next bitch. I give him a little time to do his thing, miss me because I do it better, and then I go home," Melinda explained.

"You got the game on lock!" Siraya exclaimed, looking around at all the top of the line electronics. Of course the furniture was made by Chillz. There were paintings of her that I recognized in Banger's style.

"I can't believe Edwin Giles has the nerve to cheat on you," I said.

"Why?" Melinda exclaimed. "Nay, with the shit that you've seen me go through, the shit he took your mama through, and the shit you've been going through, you think there's a man in the world who won't cheat?"

"It's just... My dad is old and cheap. I don't know how he pulled you, but he needs to be counting his lucky stars," I said.

"He pulled a bad bitch, he's gonna look for somebody badder. That's what they do. It's the audacity in them," Melinda reasoned.

"Chrissy ain't badder than me!" I hollered.

"That's the thing. They never are," Melinda said. "Get comfortable. I'm gonna go stock my bar and go make sure I got enough trees to get you through the night." Her pager went off. She went to the phone and punched in ten digits. "Auntie, what's going on with Nyir?" I watched her tug at her ponytail while she listened to the other end. "Do you think he'll be able to have visitors tomorrow? The day after...? Well, just let me know."

If I were in the right frame of mind, I would have asked what was wrong, but I couldn't get myself to care. I loved Melinda for bringing her focus right back to me.

"I'm running out to North Sanford too to get you something

fancy. I don't know what yet. I'll be back. Make yourself at home. Take any bedroom." She stuck out her hand. "Come run some errands with Auntie, Quest."

NyQuest hopped off the couch with me and happily ran behind her. She stopped in the kitchen and grabbed him a bag of chips and an apple from a crystal bowl that sat on the island. I watched the door close behind them and laid on the couch.

"Your mother has been doing bad, but I didn't know she was doing *that* bad," Siraya commented.

"I didn't know it was possible for so many people to hate me at one time," I complained, staring at the ceiling. There was a diamond pattern painted into it in several shades of white and silver. The thought that my man was the one to do it made me sick to my stomach.

"You had to know they were gonna stick you after the spaghetti thing," Siraya said.

I shrugged. "I guess there was no making peace after that." I reached toward the other end of the couch that I sat on and got my purse. I took out the envelope and handed it to Siraya. "I'm gonna need somewhere to stay when I get back, so this week, you are going to find us an apartment."

Siraya's eyes bucked at the amount of money I gave her.

"Where did you get this?"she whispered.

"Don't worry about it. Just get us a nice spot," I said.

Siraya looked around. I giggled.

"Away from here, fool," I told her. "Aren't there some nice apartments in Sapphire Cadre?"

"The ones that you live in now are way nicer. Your mom was telling me a while ago that she was gonna get me an appointment with that realtor Bobby Jackson, but that car and a few other things that my father had Pressure put in my name messed up my credit. And I'll be damned if I go into some income-based, credit-building type shit and have everybody talking shit about me. Yvette's mouth has been running extra hard since my mother told hers that you were going to Paris with The Green Balloon."

"Where the hell has that bitch been?" I asked.

"Sitting up somewhere, still jealous of you. She calls me once a month to ask if you're still with NyQuest's daddy and then gets mad and hangs up the phone. It's so stupid, because her mother told my mother that she transferred to San U after her first year at SCC and is getting a degree in journalism. She works for the *Sanford Tribune*. I don't know what her problem is," Siraya answered.

I waved her off and then got up. "Let's look around this house and figure out where we're gonna sleep at."

She got up to follow me but then looked at her pager going off.

"It's NyQuest's dad. Should I call him back?" she asked. "Where did he even get my pager number?"

"It's on a board on the refrigerator in his kitchen," I told her. "Go ahead and call him back."

She spoke to him and then relayed a message. "Somebody clipped the wires in your car on top of everything else. They smashed up some stuff and put a snickers in your exhaust. Basically, your car is done."

"I don't need it. I'm leaving in a few weeks," I said.

Siraya sat on the phone in silence. Then, she said, "Just leave her alone. I don't know what you think you can do or say, but ain't no coming back from doing anything with Chrissy. Nothing. Goodbye." She shook her head and then walked with me to explore the condo.

Melinda came back with enough weed and cigars to last me until Paris. We feasted, smoked, drank, and then feasted some more.

"I'm moving in a month or two, but you're welcome to stay here until it's time to leave," Melinda offered. "I can arrange a time to take Quest to Banger. Just get yourself together. You quit work yet?"

"I had some vacation days left, so I'm taking those before my notice officially kicks in," I said.

"Good. One less thing you have to worry about," Melinda said. She turned to Siraya. "What about you? What you got going on? Can you stay here and take care of our girl?"

Siraya nodded. "I'm taking a few days off work to hopefully find a place to stay since house sitting isn't gonna happen."

"Girl, look around here. The apartments and townhouses are cheap and nice," Melinda told her.

"Define cheap?" Siraya asked.

"About 1/4 of what they ask for in Midtown," Melinda said. "Don't sleep on the suburbs now. There's some nice spots down there in Sapphire Cadre, too. That's one place where the people in control actually want better for the people who make them rich."

So we spent our days walking around the little town of Clancy, looking at each townhouse and apartment complex. There were two other suburbs that Melinda showed us, one called Civil, the other called Sahara. Siraya chose a cute little townhouse in Civil and looked happier than I'd ever seen her.

The day Siraya signed the lease on her townhouse, Selena showed up at Melinda's house to pick up NyQuest. I'd been feeling happy about my friend's happiness and really didn't feel like having my bubble burst. Selena stood in the living room with bags under her eyes.

"I was going to call you to say what I have to say, but I decided that I at least owed it to you to look in your eyes and speak to you," she began.

I rolled up. "You don't have to say anything to me, Selena."

"Yes, I do. What happened to you at your own damn dining room table should not have happened to you. You're a lot of things, but you have done nothing to deserve what you received that night. I want to apologize for leaving you hanging, but Nyir..."

I looked at her blankly.

"Right. Nyir's problems aren't yours," she said quietly. "I guess there's nothing that I can say except that I'm sorry that happened, and we did not know that girl was related to you."

"But you knew about her?" I asked.

"I know that I told Shaan not to bring that bullshit into my house," she told me quickly. "I don't know what you two had going on in the early parts of your relationship, but it wasn't my business. When they brought that girl to my house, I turned them around at the door. That's all I can tell you about that. I'm here to apologize to you for what happened at your dining room table only. Your mother set you up, and it had to feel even worse to feel like we were in on it. That thing wasn't even my style. In South Ridge, we fight. We don't do sneaky setups like that."

"So you knew about her?" I asked.

"I knew about her, and I knew about you screwing Lisa's godson while you were pregnant. I minded my business because you all are children to me," Selena said. "I can tell that I'm not making you feel any better by coming over here to tell you any of this, but I want you to know that you've always got a mother in me."

"You don't even like me," I told her.

She sighed and took NyQuest's hand. My heart broke as I watched her leave. She always tried with me, but it was never meant to be. I wasn't her daughter, and honestly, I was a little confused by her talking so tough on our side of the bridge yet leaving that child with a mother who tried to kill her. She needed to go up to DPD and get that little girl rather than worry about my grown ass.

Siraya and I sat in that house and looked through the Furniture Revolution catalogues that Melinda had sitting in her house. They quizzed me on my french. Peaches came over and worked on some ideas for dance team uniforms for the woman I'd met at the basketball tournament. I was at peace. Being by myself seemed like the right thing to do. My mother was crazy for spending her time being miserable instead of enjoying stillness.

I was sitting in my room at Melinda's house, sketching the differences between cheerleading uniforms versus dance team uniforms to make sure I understood what the new client wanted. Melinda knocked on the door and let NyQuest run inside. He had to take a small step stool to get onto my bed, and he loved that.

"His daddy is here and wants to speak to you quickly," she announced.

I sighed. "Can you watch NyQuest for me? I don't want to yell in your house."

She cocked an eye at me while sitting with NyQuest. I went outside with Banger. He commented on how nice the neighborhood was with all the little gardens we walked through instead of down a traditional sidewalk. I didn't say anything but looked at the violets. They reminded me of my mother's garden. I wondered who carried the most blame for her current state of unhappiness.

"I got two things I want to say before you take my head off," he said.

"I ain't wasting no more energy on you," I said. "Hopefully, something good comes out of Paris, because I'm not structuring any part of my life around you anymore."

When a satisfying period of silence settled between us, he said, "That ain't my baby that Chrissy's pregnant with. You the only chick I've ever been in raw."

"That's not my business anymore," I told him.

He blew air through his nostrils and then clenched his jaw.

199

"I got you tickets to see Monica at Madison Square Garden on Labor Day," he said.

I stopped walking. Then, I lit into him. "You sent me out with a babysitter on my birthday, and you just straight lied to me on Valentine's Day. Now you're bringing Monica into it? I should cut your face open. You're lucky I left my purse in the house. Go play with somebody else."

"I wasn't even saying I was gonna take you! I was sending you and Siraya!" he yelled. "I ain't lying to you no more! That shit that happened at the crib last week was fucked up how your mom set you up."

"My mom?" I repeated. "You had your whole family sitting at my table in on that bullshit. Since when do Chillz and Selena eat dinner with us? All of you hate me, but it's all good. I'll be gone soon."

"We don't even get down like that!" he yelled. "We wouldn't bring nobody to the place where you lay your head at."

"Did you fuck her?" I asked him point blank, my eyes locked on his.

"I ain't get her pregnant," he declared once again.

I felt my heart getting ready to leap out of my body, so I calmed myself before saying anything else.

"Banger, I asked you if you fucked her. That's all that I asked you, and that's all that I want you to answer," I said.

"Yes," he finally told me.

We started walking again. When we got to a section of short trees and topiaries, I asked him, "Why?"

"Because you threw a pot of spaghetti at me," he answered.

"Most people would leave," I pointed out.

"Most people would leave before they hated somebody so much that they threw a pot of spaghetti at them. I was so sick of muthafuckas talking to me about your postpartum depression. I tried hard as fuck to make it so that you ain't have to go through that shit, and you just kept giving me your ass to kiss," he argued.

I threw my hands up and yelled, "How? By making me spend my birthday with somebody I don't even like?"

"You don't like Shanae?" he asked.

"No! I can't fuckin stand her ass. She stays setting me up. I just hang around her because she's part of your family," I said. "I know that bitch doesn't like me because she wants you."

He looked at me like I was giving him news.

"How many times did you fuck Chrissy?" I asked.

"You think I counted?" he said.

I shrugged. "Was it just a couple of times? Was it regularly? Were you with her on Valentine's Day?"

"It happened after Thanksgiving until spring," he told me. "But I strapped up every time."

"Why do you keep telling me that? You fucked my cousin. Does wearing a condom make it better?" I asked.

He shook his head. "Who did you fuck to get that Mickey Mouse that fell out your purse the other day?"

"Nobody."

We stared at each other in silence. I rolled my neck and wagged my finger when I told him, "I made some extra money as Siraya's stylist when she was with that shady record label, so I bought myself a birthday present when you didn't. I wasn't about to listen to you telling me what I couldn't spend money on after nearly getting killed."

"You lying to me?" he asked me.

"I ain't pregnant, so I guess you'll never know." I leaned against one of the tree trunks and folded my arms while I waited for him to accuse me of something else.

"So why was somebody mailing dresses to the crib then?" he asked.

Stepping forward and waving my hand the length of my torso,

I firmly questioned him, "Nigga, do you see me? When I was in high school, niggas used to drop off sneakers at my parents' house for me just so that I would have something to wear when they took me to the movies. How you running around talking about you got a model but don't know how to handle a model?"

"How'd they get the address?" he asked.

"It don't matter. I ain't get pregnant," I said.

"And I ain't get nobody pregnant," he protested. "It's too many niggas that ran up in your cousin for her to be pinning it on me."

"But you went after her because she's my cousin, and you wanted me to suffer from that, right?" I asked.

"With all the bullshit you put me through? Hell yeah. Every time I ran up in that bitch was for every hour of work I put in for you just to get your ass to kiss when I got home. Every time she sucked my dick—"

I pushed him away from me and walked away.

THE NEXT DAY, he came back in a more peaceful manner and apologized. I didn't want to hear it, but he said to me, "I want to take you down to The City for Labor Day. You and Siraya come with me and Rize to see Monica. We're sitting in the front row."

How the hell was I supposed to stand by a no to having Monica singing *Angel of Mine* in my face? Siraya would have killed me if I passed up on a ticket for her to sit in the front row for our favorite singer of all time.

Until that Friday morning when Banger and Rize walked into the house with Siraya and then dropped us off at Hair Revolution to get sculptured and molded ponytails, I didn't believe we were going. I still practiced apologizing to Siraya in my head until they took us to lunch at 90 Convent Grille. Even as Banger helped me into the back seat of Rize's Infiniti,

I waited for his pager to go off. It never did. Instead, his hand found its way to my thigh. When we were an hour past Albany, we started kissing and didn't stop until we got to our hotel.

When got to our hotel room, he unpacked his bag and had a bunch of gifts for me. Most of them he said were from my birthday. He claimed he thought he gave them to me. Among them was the exact same Mickey Mouse as the one that Mike bought me. I sighed, put it on, and went to see my favorite singer live for the first time since junior high school.

In the front row at Madison Square Garden, while our tongues slow danced with each other, Monica sang "For You I Will" right above our hairlines. Her voice lived in my ears. After the concert, we spent the rest of the weekend making love in the hotel room. I made sure to touch him, taste him, look at him, hold onto his scent and how he felt inside of me. It was the best weekend of our relationship, and I decided to break up with him for good at the end of it.

"It ain't nothing I can do to get you to stay with me?" Banger asked.

"If Monica couldn't do it, then ain't no hope for you," Siraya remarked from the front seat of Rize's car. She shut up when Banger glowered at her.

He was walking me back to Melinda's condo before he spoke again. We were holding hands.

"I don't understand how we could never get it together," he said. "All I want is a family. Why can't we have that?"

"You fucked my cousin when we lived in the same house. Why would I expect you to be faithful to me with an ocean between us?" I asked.

"So you just gonna leave our son behind?" he asked.

"Hopefully, you'll bring him to see me. If not, I'll come back to see him, but the plan was always for me to get back to Paris," I reminded him.

"But you wanted a baby," he said. "I never would've hit you raw if I knew you could leave your baby behind like this."

"Stop making me out to be a bad guy just because I'm not letting motherhood stop me from living. Isn't there anything that you ever wanted to do? Look at your painting skills, Banger. You could go so far, but you limited yourself so bad that having a baby with a girl from the other side of the bridge is your only goal in life. I thought I loved you, but I don't even respect you anymore," I told him.

His mouth dropped open.

"I'm just being real." I shrugged. "You went through all that to make a fool out of me because that's the only piece of power that you have. I'm not gonna volunteer myself up for you to hurt me anymore just because you can't do anything to the people who killed your grandfather." I stared at him and waited for him to say something in response.

"You dropped the word love more than a few times, but you don't give a fuck about me. You've never even used my real name," was his shitty comeback.

"You should have given it to me if that's what you wanted me to call you," I countered. "Melinda calls Shameik Trigga, and I've never heard him complain."

"Melinda's the one that named him that," he told me like I was supposed to care.

"Well, that has nothing to do with you and me."

There was silence. I looked at the ground. It was crazy how we ended up after the way we spent our weekend.

"I can't believe you're gonna just walk out on our son—"

"Banger!" I screamed. "I am going to work! You sometimes go to work for weeks at a time. What is the difference between you and me doing it?"

"I don't want you to leave," he told me. "I love watching you with our son."

"And I love being with him, but I can't let this opportunity pass," I said. "So if I come home, and you've moved onto enjoying watching Chrissy with your new baby, then I just have to accept that."

"I ain't got no baby by that crazy bitch!" he yelled. "The only thing worse than you wanting me because of my name is her wanting me because you had me and her mother wanting her to be with me to make your mother mad. All of y'all need some damn help."

"You fucked her. I got the help I needed. Your ass needs to go see somebody too, because you sound crazy and stupid right now," I told him.

There was nothing else he could say to that, so he went back to Rize's car.

CHAPTER 16

There was something weighing on my brain the morning of my departure. I kept asking myself what I would do if I did come across something I designed hanging in a Parisian boutique window. On top of that, I wondered if it was right to leave my son behind over some clothes. I'd built a name for myself at home. Did I need someone in Europe to validate me further? My thoughts had me so consumed as I pulled my carry-on out of my bedroom that I didn't see Selena sitting on the couch, waiting for me to speak to her. I bypassed the urge to tell her how thankful I was for her despite everything we'd been through, and gave her the doll that street vendor had given me at the Midtown basketball game.

"Where did you get this?" she asked.

"Street vendor in Midtown," I answered. "I was going to try to start a collection like yours, but I think this will look better in your house."

"It looks just like a set that somebody gave me a long time ago," she remarked, studying the doll's silky hair. "Thank you."

"You're welcome. I didn't want you to think that I hated you," I said.

"I would understand if you did," she said.

I held onto NyQuest all the way to the airport. Suddenly, I didn't want to leave, but my mother's hatred of me pricked my mind. There was no way I was ever going to be jealous of my child. As I promised him that, Banger swerved and stopped just short of colliding with a cranberry colored Maxima. I squeezed my baby tighter.

Our goodbye didn't come until we got to the gate. I thought Banger was going to leave after Peaches and I found seats. It surprised me that he sat next to me with longing in his eyes while Quest sat on my lap. Part of me was going to miss the man that had taken care of me when no one else gave a fuck. I looked at NyQuest's face, and the way his little hands waved at me broke my heart.

"It's just three months," I told him softly and squeezed him. "Mommy's just going to work. I'm trying to get back the job that was taken from me. Then I'll be able to give you as much as Daddy does."

Banger opened his mouth, closed it, and then looked away. Peaches must have felt an argument brewing because she diffused it by chattering about where Cream was going to meet us when we got to Europe. I wondered who was taking care of her apartment while she was gone and why she even bothered coming back. Deciding to mind my own business, I made sure I had my passport somewhere easily accessible.

First class passengers were called to board the plane. My legs felt heavy, and my heart raced. Rocking from side to side, I hugged NyQuest until he wriggled out of my grasp. Then he pointed to his forehead, and I planted a kiss there. I turned to hug Banger and maybe thank him for keeping me from being homeless. Before I could speak, he cupped my face with one hand and kissed me like it was the first and last time he'd get to do it. The tips of my toes were hot from it. The only choice I had when he pulled away was to give him another kiss that made him dizzy.

Peaches cleared her throat. As soon as we moved toward the line, a stampede could be heard from across the room. We all got out of the way and stood against the wall to get out of the way of whatever was happening.

"That's her!" I heard a woman's voice shout.

Even though I hadn't done anything, my heart thumped. I watched as airport security and the police charged toward me. A short white woman with red hair led the pack with her hand on her service weapon. Everyone in the area gasped and tried to get out the way, but they had nothing to worry about. That tiny woman made her intended target known when she ripped handcuffs from her waist and stopped in front of me.

"Monaysia Giles?" she asked.

"Yes..." I eyed her then looked to Banger for help. He tucked NyQuest under one arm while trying to reach out for me.

That little lady surprised me with her strength to yank me away from him. "You need to come with me."

My eyes bucked. "What did I do?"

"Failure to respond to an appearance ticket for endangering the welfare of a child. Destruction of public property. Assault. Assault with a knife." She listed each charge deliberately while her fellow officers surrounded me, forming a barrier between Banger and me. Peaches took NyQuest from him and dove into a nearby phone booth, pulling the door closed with him in it. Banger was shouting something, but I couldn't make out words anymore. It felt like I was drowning.

The drive was too short for them to have taken me from the airport in North Midtown to the police headquarters downtown. When I was pulled from the car, I stepped onto a cobblestone road. That gave me a hint that I was close to Abolition Town. From the stairs out front, I could see a cranberry Maxima pass us. I stared at it until I was pushed forward.

The cops who escorted me had no problem using their hands on my ass to command my steps. It made me regret packaging all my gifts in a velour track suit. When I put it on that morning, I thought I'd be putting them on display for men who could afford first class seats, not the dirty pigs of Sanford County.

I didn't know what I thought happened when people got arrested, but I thought I'd go to jail with a bunch of women and yell about making a phone call. The little redhead took me to a little room to get my mugshot taken, huffing and puffing the whole time.

"Are you kidding me? This is a mugshot, not a magazine cover shoot!" she yelled at me.

"I'm sorry. I'm a model. I'm really photogenic. It's impossible for me to take a bad picture."

She cringed at the sound of my voice and commanded me to follow her. We went out into a common area with cubicles where I was cuffed to a desk.

"Miss, my baby's uncle is a cop. His name is D. Can you just let him know I'm here, please?" I asked.

She grunted. "Do you have a more specific name than 'D'? You're from the inner city. There's a whole gang of people who go by the street name D."

"I don't," I said and lowered my eyes at the condescending look she gave me. "I know that his wife works for Jackson's Department Store."

"Does this look like Jackson's Department Store?" she snapped.

"No," I answered in quiet defeat.

"Then why would I know who works there?" she asked. "Why don't you know your child's uncle's name? This is the number one problem with your people: babies having babies out of wedlock. You think that having a baby by a famous drug dealer from the hood means something anywhere besides the hood. Have I got news for you and every homegirl who thinks like you."

I wanted to slap that bitch, but only one of us was cuffed to her desk. I gave her his last name, Darnell, but she acted like she didn't hear that part.

"More than who you know, I'm curious to know why you thought you could leave the country without showing up to court?" she questioned me.

"Because I got jumped by two employees in a department store. Why would I have to go to court? That store is lucky that I don't feel like going through the process of suing them," I told her.

She wrote that down, then peeked inside of a manila folder. "Why didn't you come pick up your summons to appear in court?"

"Why would I pick up a summons? Doesn't 'summons' mean that someone has to deliver it to me?" I asked.

She looked through some other papers in that file before answering. "You have a South Sanford zip code listed on your ID. Everyone in South Sanford is fully aware of their responsibilities as it pertains to the legal system."

"First of all, I'm not even from South Sanford originally," I snapped at her.

"Nobody moves to South Sanford without knowing what they're getting into," she said to me. "Where did you move there from?"

"Sapphire Cadre," I answered her.

"Nobody moves from the suburbs into that ghetto," she declared. "And nobody from South Sanford would ever make it to Paris."

"That's kind of a weird thing to say, don't you think?" I asked.

"It's the way things work. That place is where the trash is dumped," she said.

A hole burned through my chest while she read through a stack of papers inside of it. "Oh. You got knocked up. Little girl from the suburbs needed a bad boy to fulfill your fantasy."

"Can you just put me in jail?" I asked her. "What I've done with my life has nothing to do with what you arrested me for."

"It has everything to do with what I arrested you for," she snapped. "Jackson's Department Store pressed some serious charges against you. The fact that you didn't show up looked really bad."

"I didn't show up because I didn't know about the charges!" I yelled at her.

"You were given an appearance ticket at the time of the altercation, were you not?" she yelled back.

"Yes, I was."

"Then, what were you doing getting on a plane without taking care of it?" she demanded to know.

"I didn't do anything to endanger my child. If anything, I kept him safe from people who attacked us," I defended myself.

"You should have said that in court." She flipped the papers and asked, "What about when you stabbed Jewana Marnes?"

"Who the hell is that?" I asked.

"How many people have you stabbed?" she wondered.

My butterfly knife came to the front of my mind during the pause I took. "I haven't stabbed anyone."

That brought a weird chuckle out of her. She turned to her computer and typed in a name. While a picture loaded, she turned the monitor toward me. My heart sank as I looked at the girl whose face I sliced open in Nat Turner.

"You've skipped several court appearances for what you did to this woman," she said.

"I didn't even get arrested for that," I said.

"She pressed charges," the cop said.

"How was I supposed to know that?" I asked.

She closed the folder and slammed her hands on her desk.

"Everyone in South Sanford knows how things work. No officer has the time to wait to cross that bridge. You get a ticket, then you go to the police station and get your summons."

"Me and that girl didn't even know each other's names. How would she have pressed charges against me?" I asked.

"Someone talked," she answered.

I shook my head. "I think you're lying."

"Oh really?" She went back into the manila folder and pulled out several court dockets. Jackson's Department Store was the plaintiff on each of them. They were looking for monetary compensation for a shoe display and suing me for damaging their brand's upscale reputation. I skimmed it until I saw Yolanda's and Brooke's names. The store wanted me to pay for them having to fire and rehire new employees so close to the Memorial Day holiday, an event that drove some of their highest traffic outside of the Christmas holiday season. Every time they went to court without me showing up, they tacked on more money. I thought of that envelope of money I'd given Siraya. She used it to pay rent for a year and furnish the townhouse. There was no way I could ask her to return any of it, especially since she never asked me for it.

As though reading my mind, the cop went into her drawer and pulled out another folder.

"We also have footage of your involvement with a money laundering operation in the form of a record label."

She opened it to a picture of me in a pink tweed skirt suit. My legs looked magnificent. No wonder that man couldn't stop looking at them that day.

"We still have the man you made the delivery for in custody. He's awaiting a trial," she told me.

"That has nothing to do with me," I said. "I went on a date with him when I was having problems with my boyfriend, and he asked me to go to the bank for him so that he'd be taken seriously."

"And you never stopped to ask yourself why?" she wondered.

"He followed me around and threatened to tell my boyfriend about us!" I was afraid of losing everything!" I damn near shouted, panicking.

"We have you on camera getting into limousines with him, going to Syracuse." She smirked as she showed me pictures of everything I'd done with Mike. Siraya was in some of the pictures too. She was the last person who needed to get caught up in anything I'd gotten myself into.

Tears fell from my eyes, and I started begging that woman who hadn't even told me her name to give me back my life. In turn, she put me in a cell.

For hours, I just sat there without knowing what was coming next. I waited for more people to be added to the cell, but no one was. It was dark. There was a metal toilet that couldn't be flushed. The benches were hard. No one came around for hours.

Finally, I saw a shiny badge strolling in my direction. It took three times before the short man stopped walking and paid attention to me calling him. He squinted at me.

"You look familiar," he said.

"I'm a costume designer for The Green Balloon," I reminded him.

He stopped and peered at me. "That's right. You're supposed to be on your way to Paris, aren't you?"

"I got arrested for not going to court dates that I didn't even know I had. Please call your wife or somebody and tell them what happened," I begged.

He put his hand on his crotch and grinned. "You got some-thing for me?"

My eyes bucked at him. He chuckled. "I'm just the sheriff. My job is to serve you papers. What happens after I get your signature on them is out of my control."

"You never served me any papers." Tears flowed from my eyes again.

He grunted. "Where do you live?"

"Southview," I answered. "That white lady who arrested me at the airport said that I'm not supposed to wait for a summons, but I have to go to a police department to pick it up. But why would I do that if I didn't even get arrested?"

"Now wait a minute, darling," he said gently. I can't stand for a beautiful woman to cry in front of me." He put a hand on his holster and leaned against the metal cell bar. He made a face at it and then studied the cell I was in. With a sarcastic grin on his face, he said, "I see they gave you the Presidential Palace."

"Mister, I don't know what that means. I just have to get to Paris," I whined.

"Okay. Okay. Let's slow down a little bit. You live in Southview, so the information you were given was incorrect. I deliver all the summonses to that area, but I have a backlog because I deliver them to all of East Sanford and Sahara as well," he said.

"But if there's a backlog, then how can a court date happen?" I asked him.

"Where did the incidents take place?" he asked.

"South Ridge and Jackson's Department Store," I answered.

He rocked back on his heels. "You're a rough little hoodrat, ain't you?"

"Mister, I'm not a hoodrat at all. I am from Sapphire Cadre. My son's great-grandmother lives in South Ridge, and whenever I take him to visit her I'm met with all sorts of jealousy. You see what I look like, Mister."

He grinned. "I sure do."

"And if you've ever been to South Ridge, you know what the girls down there look like. They're so jealous," I continued to whine.

"They have every reason to be," he said. "What's the name of the person you had to appear against from South Ridge?"

"I don't know!" I cried. "I don't know anything that's going on. I just have to get to Paris."

"Well, what's your name, darling? I'd love to help you out."

"Monaysia Denise Giles," I rushed to answer him.

He took a small pad and a pen from his pocket and wrote down my name. He told me he'd be back. After the third hour of waiting for him, he strolled back toward me, shaking his head.

"I deleted the charges from Jewana Marnes. The one from Jackson's is a corporate one, and you'll have to appear in court tomorrow," he said.

"Tomorrow?" I exclaimed.

"I spoke with my ex-wife, and she will be in court tomorrow as a character witness for you. Is there anyone I can call for you?" he asked.

"I haven't gotten a phone call yet," I said.

"No phone call?" he exclaimed. "What about food?"

"I don't want to eat. I just want to get out of here," I said.

"Oh, darling. You gotta eat. Let me get you out of here so that you can make your call," he said.

All I had for Siraya was a pager number, and Melinda didn't answer the phone at either of her homes. There was no way I was calling my mother. Slowly I dragged my fingers across the keypad to dial my home number. Banger answered before the first ring went all the way through.

"Nay?" he panicked into the phone.

I sobbed into the phone and tried to tell him what happened after they dragged me away, but he commanded me to not say anything on the phone until he could get a lawyer to me.

"What's your bail? They give it to you yet?" he asked.

"No. This man is saying that I won't go to court until tomorrow," I cried.

He growled and then said, "Peaches and Miss Delilah are

coming right back. They tried to see where you were getting booked, and D said that you haven't made it into the system yet."

"Why is Peaches still there?" I asked. "She has to take our stuff to Paris. I'll get there in a minute. She has to go."

"Miss Delilah is with her, though," he said. "Fuck them niggas. I'm worried about you right now. You good? Who they got you in a cell with?"

"I don't know people in jail," I whimpered.

"I ain't mean it like that. I meant, like, they from West Ridge? DPD? South Ridge?" he asked.

"Nobody. I'm in a cell by myself," I said.

"Something ain't right about that," he said.

"Nothing is right about this whole day," I fussed.

"I gotta get D to you. I'll be down there as soon as he can get me down there."

But nobody from that family ever came. That man reintroduced himself as Kevin and brought me a burger. The white woman introduced herself as Shannon Kimborough and announced that she made a personal request to be my probation officer.

"How could you make that request without me even going to court?" I asked.

"Do you have a law degree?" she asked me.

"No," I answered.

"Then don't challenge my knowledge on how the law works," she told me.

"So am I getting out of here?" I asked.

She walked away.

I stayed in that cell overnight without another person coming. In the morning, someone tossed a brown bag into the cell. It smelled like food, and I was starving. The sheriff had bought me bacon and eggs from somewhere and left a card with his number on one side. On the other side was a note promising me that he could make this all go away.

I was chained by the ankles, waist, and feet, put on a bus, and dragged into a courtroom. Several other people were there, confused by whatever happened before they got to that room. An old white man rattled off outrageous fine amounts and impossible due dates to have them paid by. The ones who asked about lawyers were sent back to jail. When my name came, my case was delayed due to no one from Jackson's showing up. After a few hours, the judge called me back to the stand.

"I'm told that you recently moved to Southview from Sapphire Cadre. I assume that means you know how to conduct yourself in public better than most people in your community." He peered over a pair of black framed glasses.

"Yes, your honor," I replied.

"Then I will see you back here on December 26th," he said.

"But, your honor, I was on my way to a job in Paris and not supposed to return until January," I whined.

"You can't leave the country with a corporation fighting against you and a money laundering case. You'll have to look into getting local work, and you'll have to keep it in order to stay out of jail. Idle hands are tools of the devil," he stated. "And if I see you in my courtroom again for any reason — even a traffic ticket — then I'm sending you directly to jail for a minimum of three years. You are dismissed."

"But, my job—"

"Miss Giles, your record states that you have been employed by Sanford Ringer for two years. Stay with the sure thing rather than chasing some little girl's fairytale." His voice bounced off the walls and booted me out of the courtroom.

After Kevin gave me my purse, I walked for blocks in rainy weather until I found a pay phone. Siraya answered the phone at my house. She told me that Banger was Downtown at the courthouse waiting for me to be brought in and had just called to see if I called. Eventually, he called back. She had to coordinate a three-way call between us so that he could find out where I was.

"Stay right there," he commanded, his voice shaking.

"It's raining, and I'm soaking," I complained.

"I'm on my way," he assured me.

I tried to duck into a small cafe next door, but it was filled with police. That was the last place I needed to be. A woman who was walking into a shop across the street frowned at my soaking clothes and took pity on me. Since her store wasn't opening for another hour, she let me stand in there and wait for my ride. Two other people who'd appeared before the same judge as me stood in there, shivering. They said they had an hour wait before they could start walking back toward the city of North Sanford for a bus. I hoped Banger could get to me in less time than that. The shop owner's cleaning crew came in wearing white patent leather shoes that tapped out a spooky rhythm while they dashed around to get the store cleaned. Some of their voices streamed from the bathroom as they cleaned it.

"Dormir dormir
Se acerca tu largo sueño"

TWENTY MINUTES LATER, Rize pulled in front of the phone booth, driving one of the Geno's Auto Sales SUVs. Melinda rode up front with him. Banger opened the second row door for me. I was pissed that my baby wasn't in the car with them. The man named D hopped out of the car and grabbed my hands.

"Get in the car. You have to show me where you were," he told me.

"Aren't you the one whose wife works at Jackson's?" I barked at him.

His voice was raw when he spoke. "Yeah. We have a lot to discuss."

"I just want to go take a shower and go to sleep," I complained.

"You ain't hungry?" Banger asked me.

"I'm never letting you feed me again," I snapped. "I did a lot of shit, but it never got you arrested or charges pressed against you."

He wouldn't say anything, so I went off.

"I have to go pee in a cup for this white bitch every week until the judge says I don't have to anymore!"

D put a gentle hand on my arm and said, "Just show us where you were. I sat at the computer all day and waited for you to get booked, but it never happened."

"I don't wanna talk about it," I said.

"Please?" D asked in a voice so tender that I had to comply.

I showed them to the entrance where I was taken and told them about being cuffed to that redhead's desk.

Confusion crumpled D's face. "They haven't detained anyone here in years. The people who live out here protested it and wanted it closed down. You said that you were in a cell by yourself?"

"Yes. The only person I saw the whole time I was there was the Campavhore ladies' husband. He was nice to me. He said he had a backlog because he had to serve too many areas, and he brought me food," I answered.

"Hmph. Let me see the paperwork they gave you from the court."

After I handed him the stack of court papers he gave me, he took a silent dive into them for the rest of the ride.

CHAPTER 17

*T*hat morning was supposed to be my last time seeing my apartment, and they respected that with a plan to take me to Big Grams's house already in place. Most of the family was there. Lynn took me into a room below the garage and took my tracks out my hair. She told me to take a bath, eat, and come back after I got done. While she waited for me, she said she was taking the tracks out back to a fire pit to burn them. I didn't have an appetite, so I soaked in a garden tub and let that family pamper me for the rest of the day. Big Grams forced me to eat eggs benedict with a side of G-Ma's ham. She made me a mimosa with a shot of Crown Royal on the side. Rico brought me a blunt and told me to follow him downstairs. There was nothing I needed more, but I had to live with the disappointment of not being able to smoke. Worry set in. Whether I smoked with them or not, there was still a lot of marijuana in my system. Jail was inevitable.

After Lynn finished giving me a fresh sew-in, NyQuest ran to me. I let Banger show me to a bed and then closed my eyes with my baby nestled against me.

Unc's mother, Sheila, knocked on the door and asked me if I

could rest, or if I needed a sedative. She gave me some tea that had me asleep for so long that it was dinner time the next time I opened my eyes. A woman's voice yelled in a high pitch. Every "t" and "ing" was pronounced during her tirade, as though she meant to establish superiority through her proper diction. I looked around and saw that NyQuest was gone, so I followed the sound of the voices.

"I don't love that you brought me to your family's house to make me the enemy once again, Derrick!" the voice yelled.

"Tish, that's not what I'm doing. I'm just trying to make sense out of what happened to NyQuest's mother," he said.

When I turned a corner that took me closer to the voices, I passed a room where a children's movie played. NyQuest sat on a toddler sized couch with three other children, two girls and one boy. All four children quietly drank juice boxes and watched the movie. One of the girls was Subira's daughter. She smiled at me and waved. Subira came down the hall carrying TV trays for them. She poked out her lip sympathetically.

"You feel any less dirty?" she asked me.

"I feel like I'm never gonna get the smell of jail off of me," I answered.

I tried to help set up the TV trays for the kids, but Subira wouldn't let me. Selena went in after her and served homemade pizza to the kids before coming to me and kissing my forehead. She felt my arms and looked at my face.

"Did they touch you at all?" she asked.

I shook my head. "Just made me feel stupid for hours." I looked over her shoulder and asked, "Who is that yelling like that?"

Selena looked at me strangely. "Don't you work for Tisha at Jackson's? Well, come on and get introduced to Tisha at home. We need you to talk to her about these charges she claims she never pressed against you."

"I spent my day going through corporate records instead of

finalizing holiday displays because you asked me to, Derrick. I reached out to the CEO, CFO, COO, and everyone else with three initials as their titles. No one pressed charges for that fight or entered a lawsuit against the customer. The security tapes would have given her cause for a huge lawsuit. No one has been to court. We were forced to drop legal action against the girls who attacked the customer after she didn't show up to court. That is it," the tiny light skinned woman declared. Her hair swung with every syllable she spoke. She stopped rolling her neck and pointing her finger and stared at me. "My star catalog model? *You're* the one this is all about?"

I sighed. "Mrs. Darnell, you told me I would take care of this. "I need to get out of here."

"Yes, you certainly do," she agreed, "but Jackson's has never taken any legal action against you. I'm not sure how to handle this."

"Just come to the police station with me and tell them that. Somehow they knew I was going to be in the airport today, and somehow they're keeping me from getting to Paris. I just want to get out of here and work," I complained. "Did D show you the papers that they gave me in the court? These are all lies that you can clear up. Please, Mrs. Darnell."

"The best that I can do is call the legal team tomorrow and have them look into it," she said. "When is your court date? I can attend that day."

"December 26th," I told her.

She recoiled. "That's the second biggest retail day of the year. We'll have to get that changed."

"Get it changed to something sooner, please. I can't stay in this place anymore," I begged her.

"Honey, there's a fraudulent lawsuit happening, and that's going to take priority over everything else so that this and any others filed like it can be tossed out," she told me. "I'm on top of this, though. You've graced the pages of my catalogs for many years. I promise that you'll get to Paris. I won't let you get trapped here."

She reached up and rubbed my arm to assure me and then turned to the table next to her and picked up a set of what looked like my court papers.

"Tisha, that's all I've been asking you to do all day. You said you couldn't help me. Why the sudden change of heart?" Derrick asked.

"Because you accused me of filing a suit against your nephew's baby-mama, Derrick. I do not come to your family's house to be backed into a corner. I have better things to do with my days than discuss baby-mamas. When you said that it was someone who had been fighting in my store, I thought you were referring to one of your play cousin boosters down there in South Ridge. You should have given more information. I will always look out for my girls from Naomi Iman. They're part of the reason I don't have to cross a bridge to to and from work."

She strutted into the kitchen and told D to fix her a plate. I loved the way she let the ugly stares from the women in the room bounce off her back.

"Derrick, whatever you're going to do to insert yourself to become the hero in all of this needs to be completed by 4:30 tomorrow afternoon. We have a dinner to attend with Jackson's investors at Nota Bene in Abolition Town, and Dexter Aldridge's wife is unable to attend. You know how much I hate sitting at a table with that creepy man," she commanded him.

"Tomorrow, we have to take Monaysia to speak with Joy so that we can settle the suit outside of court," D said to her.

"Well, you'll have to ask Joy to meet with us earlier then, won't you? I can't let whatever shady thing your job is doing consume all of my time, Derrick. I have a career to cultivate." She looked at me and said, "I understand that you do as well. You will not get sucked in by Sanford County and stuck for love or any other stupid reason. I will do everything in my power to be sure of it."

"Thank you," I said and turned to get away from that scene before I spoke my agreement with Tisha's side. Everyone else already had their faces puckered at her, obviously calling her the devil in their heads.

Banger caught me and asked if I was hungry. I shook my head and tried to find somewhere else to go.

"It stopped raining. Can we go outside and talk?" he asked me.

"What is there to say?" I asked. "A bitch you cheated on me with is keeping me from working my dream job. You tried to make me a demon for going to work, and now I can't go. You got what you wanted."

"I ain't want this for you," he said.

I nodded my head. "Yes, you did. You even tried to bribe me with jewelry and Monica tickets."

His voice rose. "That ain't what happened."

"Yes, it is," I said softly. "How did that bitch even know my name and address to press charges?"

"She probably wouldn't have had it if you hadn't been fighting in the damn mall, and you probably wouldn't have been fighting in the damn mall if you hadn't lied on your friend in the first place," he said.

"Rahshaan!" Chillz called. "You mighty hostile for somebody who just spent the whole night crying about his girl getting knocked."

It felt like if I stayed in there, I was going to be told a bunch of things that would make me feel cared about. I had no way to get out of North Sanford, so I just let him take me out of that house. We went through the back yard and down a bunch of hills. We walked across a yard that looked like it was the same size as the plantations seen in the slave movies. Halfway across, he stopped walking and put his arms around me. I thought I felt tears dripping down on me.

"Please get off of me," I whispered so that he wouldn't hear my voice wavering.

"I never wanted no shit like this to happen to you," he said.

"It doesn't seem that way," I said. "The last year feels like one big setup after another. You couldn't kill me, so you settled for getting me locked up."

"What the fuck are you talking about?" he asked. Before I could answer, he asked, "You talking about your birthday?"

"You told me it wasn't my business what happened to a person that you had driving me around on my birthday, even though he left me in a damn shootout. And not one, but two, bitches have come to me about what they were doing with you when I was sitting at home waiting for you to take me to The Poconos. Everybody is saying you were straight up lying about that trip anyway," I argued.

"I wanted to take you," he said.

"But you knew there was no way you'd be able to, right?" I asked.

"Yeah, but if Squeak wouldn't have called, then I would have gone," he said. "I just would've missed out on that money."

"See what I mean? It all leads back to that shit with Squeak. He came to your house and took your video games. The shit on my birthday. That's not your friend, yet you keep him around." I pushed him away and waved him off. "I don't even care anymore. You said it's not my business, so it's not my business."

"I don't mean it like that. It's just—"

"Stop talking about it. I don't give a fuck anymore," I stated.

"You act like you've been perfect," was his weak argument.

I went across the grass and past a small garden. It was an odd little plot of land. A circle of small, polished rocks surrounded a bench. A large stone sat next to the bench. Four stones with words painted on them sat within the circle, across from the bench. Each stone rested at the foot of its own tree. Right behind it was a small stream that separated the land from Banneker Forest. I remembered going camping in that forest with my Girls Scout troop when I was little. That made me giggle as I remembered Mommy making Kidra and me quit Girl Scouts after that camping trip.

Banger lifted me and then leapt onto a stone in the center of the stream. Then, he leapt again to the other side. When he put me down, he took my hand. We walked up a hiking path and saw birds, chipmunks, and all kinds of fairytale-esque woodland creatures. It was peaceful out there, so I didn't mind being stuck out there with him.

"What did they do to you in there?" he asked.

"Just talked to me like I was really stupid for not knowing shit that didn't make sense," I replied. Then, I asked him, "Why didn't you tell me I had to go to the police station to check to see if that bitch pressed charges against me after I cut her?"

"What?" he asked.

"The sheriff said the police don't have time to wait to get across the bridge, so it's your responsibility to go to the police station to pick up your summonses," I explained.

"I thought you said he told you that Southview was his territory, and you didn't get yours because he was backed up with work?" Banger asked me.

"Look. I don't know what the fuck the truth is. I just got harassed for hours for not knowing how things work after you cut a bitch but don't get arrested," I snapped at him.

He failed an attempt to calm his voice. "Aight. My bad. I shouldn't have come at you like that. I'm just confused now."

"What are you confused about? You fucked a bitch, and she wants me in jail for it," I said.

He threw his hands up in defeat. "Nay, I haven't seen that bitch since I fucked her that one time!"

"Yeah, because you ran up in Chrissy every time after that," I snapped. "It's funny. You spent all that time accusing Siraya of shit happening every time we went out like she was the one setting me up, and she was telling me how lucky I was to have you. Whole time, it you were the one setting me up."

"I ain't do that shit to you!" he hollered. "That ain't even my style."

"It looks real funny right now, honey," I told him. "You mean to tell me that somebody gave your hoe my full name? The only person I could think of who would do that is Shanae, but I got too much dirt on her for her to be stepping out of line like that. Plus, I don't think Shanae knows my full name. Or maybe she does. Who cares?"

He started to say something else, but I put my finger to his lips. "It's really peaceful out here. Everything you say sounds like a lie or feels like it will get me set up again. Can we just walk out here and enjoy the peace, please?"

I didn't let go of his hand. He nodded his head and walked with me past cabins and signs that announced luxury cabins being built soon. Construction trucks worked and blew dust around, so we took another path toward peaceful streams and through the mountains of North Sanford.

At sunset, we went back to Big Grams' house. I finally felt like eating. Joy Gilead stood at the kitchen counter while Chillz piled food onto a plate for her. She commanded me to make a plate and follow her. Banger offered to do it, I reiterated that I never wanted him to feed me again. He didn't realize how serious I was. After the way that we'd spent our time, I knew I'd have to show him rather than tell him. Joy stared at me so hard that they forced me to pick up my pace. I followed her, D, and Tisha into the library in the basement. Banger trailed us.

"Do you have anything of value to add to this gathering, Rahshaan?" she wondered.

"If she needs money, then I need to know how much," was his reply.

She glanced at me and asked, "Do you want him to sit in with us, or would you like me to give him an itemized list after you've spoken to me?"

"I don't care what he does. I just don't want him talking to me while he does it." I followed her through rows of books until we came to a desk and a group of chairs.

Banger sat in a chair against a shelf of law books without saying anything. D pulled out chairs for us ladies and then waited for us to sit before taking his own. Chillz and Unc came downstairs and sat on either side of Banger, I guessed to keep him quiet.

"I'm Joy Gilead. I'm the county DA until the next election," the woman with the dreads introduced herself formally.

"Oh. I remember you from Career Week in high school," I said.

She nodded her head and said, "I have a mayoral campaign to run and not a lot of time to deal with the foolishness that this police department has concocted. What you have stumbled across is an added platform for me to run on, so I need you to play along with this charade."

I scrunched my face and peered at her through squinted eyes. "Are you saying that this was all made up?"

"NYU did well by educating you," she remarked. "I can assure you that no part of these charges are legitimate. Tisha Darnell's first child was Jackson's department store. If she has no knowledge of something taking place there, then it's a fallacy."

"That's correct," Mrs. Darnell said with her arms folded.

"I was able to get a firm court date of three weeks from today. Delilah is happy to send you to Paris the minute your case is dismissed," Joy announced. "What I need from you is to stay out of whatever trouble the police department is going to throw at you from now until then. They will be desperate."

"I just won't leave the house, once I figure out where I'm staying," I told her.

"That's probably for the best. They will attack you from every possible angle," she warned me with her gray eyes locked on mine. "Derrick, this paperwork says that Shannon Kimborough has been assigned to her as a probation officer. Are you able to speak with this woman to get information?"

"As far as I know, she isn't a probation officer. I'm still trying to tap into that detail," he answered.

"Tap harder and faster, please? I'm a busy woman. As it is, your job is taking time from my campaign. I'm certain that was the plan all along," she said.

"Joy, you act like I wasn't investigating 34 homicides from the summer whose reports never got logged," he complained.

"I'm working overtime to help you. You work overtime to help me help you," she commanded him.

"If him being away from his family for the past 36 hours wasn't enough help, then maybe you have too much on your plate, Joy," Tisha suggested.

"Not my fault you married a slacker, Tisha. I still managed to make it home to my newly adopted baby and make goat for dinner, only to be called out to the mountains before I could take my first bite." Joy read through the papers and determined that she was satisfied with our meeting. "I still need you to attend these meetings with this probation officer to gather data for me. That means no smoking, just in case the drug tests are real. I'll also need you to find out to which lab the drug tests are being sent. Now, tell me more about the summons deliveries. Maybe we can block Kevin from running for sheriff."

That woman talked at me more than to me for 90 minutes. I sat there without complaining, because the underhanded comments she and Tisha made to each other more than made up for me spending a night in a cell. It came to mind that they never mentioned the charges against me in Abolition Town. I tried to find a way to ask about it without giving details that I'd have to explain later.

"They said there was another charge against me. I don't know what it was. The sheriff said that he deleted one of the charges against me," I said.

"You don't know what it was?" D asked.

I shook my head and said, "After a while, it just felt like they were making stuff up so that I could do some football numbers."

"You're probably right," D agreed.

"That's all you have to say?" I exclaimed.

"Nay-Nay, I know you're tired of hearing this, but this is what you wanted." D's voice lost the gentleness it held all day. "I'm really sorry that this happened, and that in the time that you've been together my nephew didn't let you know what was up, but this is the life you get when you get with us. We're a family that works to make things different. Out there in Sapphire Cadre, all you know is parents who give better than what they have and then brag about what their kids are gonna give as a reward. They get out there and forget about the projects they came from and all the sacrifices they had to make to get out."

"Who can blame them?" Tisha scoffed. She turned to me and said, "I bet you looked at that handsome, rugged boy and thought you were going to have a nice little life where some-body brought you jewels and gifts all the time, didn't you? Nobody told you about the constant need to be a superhero, the forgotten birthdays and holidays, did they?"

Before I could respond, D pulled a tiny planner from his pocket. "Oh shit!"

Tisha crossed her legs and pursed her lips.

"Tisha, baby, I'm so sorry. I—"

Tisha's eyes glistened while she glared at D. "We should have met at Joy's house so that after this we could have spent the rest of the night hearing about how I don't cook goat like Joy. That's always my favorite part of our wedding anniversary." She turned to me and unsuccessfully tried to push a smile onto her face. "We should have lunch so we can compare notes about how many of your days you have to spend with the women in his family as some sorry substitute for him going to work instead of taking a damn day off to celebrate with you. You'll hear year round about how much he loves you for pushing out his kids, but you'll never feel that he wants you on the days when he should be going out of his way to express it. Don't get me started on the promises for out of town trips. I've been told that we're going to Saint Croix for our next wedding anniversary every year since our first wedding anniversary."

"D, you forgot today was your anniversary?" Chillz asked incredulously.

Banger palmed his face and grumbled, "D, you got to be the most helpful unhelpful nigga in the world."

That sent Chillz and Unc into a fit of laughs. I saw where Rize and Rico got that ugly shriek before they laughed from. They pulled Banger back upstairs with them. D sat there with a stupid look on his face while Joy pulled in her lips and covered her face with a folder so that she didn't laugh. She took a deep breath and cleared her throat.

"Monaysia, I need you to adhere to the exact terms stated in this paperwork. You need to avoid even the slightest arguments at all costs. I will come to your house every day to check on you and make sure nothing out of the ordinary has happened," she said.

"I'll have to call you and tell you where I'm staying," I told her. "Do you have a card?"

Joy looked after Banger and then back at me with a frown. "You're not even going to try to work on your family?"

"I'm not going to be attached to somebody who hates me as much as he does," I told her.

Her frown deepened. She handed me a card and then apologized to Tisha for ruining her anniversary.

"You ruin every other day of my marriage just by being alive. Why wouldn't my anniversary be worse?" she asked.

Joy set her briefcase on the table in front of her and leaned forward. With a smirk on her face, she said, "And I'll continue until he has no choice but to admit what an evil little troll you are."

Tisha looked at me and said, "At least you got out before you had to spend the rest of your life defending yourself against a family who committed itself to hating you."

"Did I?" I asked. "At least he doesn't bring the women he's screwing to sit at your dinner table."

"He doesn't?" Tisha asked, staring at Joy. "No, he doesn't. Derrick isn't that crazy. He just brings his first love." She stood and started for the stairs. Before she climbed them, she said to me, "Good luck to you. You're way too beautiful to be stuck coming in second to South Ridge and dead relatives."

She switched up the stairs, calling, "DJ! Morgan! Let's go home, kids! Mommy and Daddy aren't going out after all!"

When she opened the door, I heard D begging, "Tisha, baby, I'm sorry!"

Chillz and Unc kept laughing.

Rize was getting ready to take Melinda home when I got upstairs.

"I'm going with you, Mel," I said.

"You ain't coming home?" Banger asked me, shocked.

"I'm never setting foot inside that apartment again." I paused, trying to keep my tone even, but I couldn't. "I guess I should thank you for buying it for me, but fucking with you just fucks me up more and more."

Joy's eyebrows shot up when she looked at me. I buttoned my lips and went to get NyQuest.

"The cleaning people should be out of there by now,"

Melinda remarked. "If they aren't, just keep the door closed to let them know you don't want them to come in there."

I kissed and hugged NyQuest quickly and then got into Rize's car. Banger brought NyQuest and his carseat without saying anything to me. Melinda let me know that my luggage was at Banger's apartment, and that she would bring it to me the next day.

"Does my dad know that I got arrested?" I asked.

Melinda changed whatever she was going to say after licking her lips and replied, "He took an out of town job."

"With a school bus?" I asked.

"The school sports started, and he's been driving teams to Albany every single night for the past week," she said.

I nodded my head and didn't force her to tell any more uncomfortable lies.

When we got to Melinda's condo, the cleaning service's trucks were blocking the entrance. We sat there while the employees boarded the trucks and waited. When the last of the people got onto the last truck, I kissed NyQuest and leapt from the car. A woman stopped in front of me. I immediately leapt backward and put my hands over my chest.

"I'm sorry," she said in a squeaky voice. "I just wanted to let your driver know that one of his taillights just blew."

I squinted at her. "Aren't you the lady who sold me the doll at the basketball tournament?"

She smiled, showing a chipped tooth. "Yes. Who did you give it to?"

I tilted my head and furrowed my brows. "How did you know I gave it to somebody?"

"They're meant to be given as gifts of protection," she said.

"Oh. I gave it to my baby's grandmother. She had some more that looked just like it, so I wanted to add them to her collection," I said.

She smiled. "That's so nice."

Rize poked his head out the window and asked, "You aight, Nay?" Immediately, he drew back when he saw the woman. She grinned at him and waved.

"I was just letting her know that your taillight is out. I didn't want to just walk up to the car and scare you," she said.

His face paled at the sound of her voice. He froze. I got uncomfortable and went into the lobby to catch the elevator.

At about 2 or 3 in the morning, my stomach started growling. I went to the refrigerator to get one of the plates of food that Big Grams sent me home with. When my feet hit the floor, I heard somebody singing in Spanish. The song's rhythm brought to mind white patent leather shoes tapping across a floor. The high pitch was pretty but creepy in the dark, since I couldn't see anyone.

"Dormir dormir
Se acerca tu largo sueño"

"MELINDA?" I called.

"No, it's housekeeping," a squeaky voice said.

I walked into the kitchen and saw the silhouette of a woman with a huge puff of hair on top of her head. It scared the shit out of me to see her turn her head toward me and smile. Her eyes were almost black, but I could still see them and that chipped tooth in the dark.

"You haven't come to the bank in months. I always liked to see what you were going to wear when you came with that big envelope of money," she said.

I turned on the light to look at her while she spoke. Seeing how hard she was scrubbing made me not want to mess up anything. I decided that I would wait until the morning to eat.

"You're a pretty girl. Where is your husband?" she asked.

"I don't have one. I don't even have a boyfriend. Men lie too much." I dismissed her question with a wave of my hand.

She nodded and went back to singing in Spanish. Then, she looked back at me and said, "They're not the only ones."

I turned around and went back to the bedroom. She turned off the lights behind me. I was too terrified to go back to sleep. That woman's singing, though it was pretty, crept up the back of my neck into my ears and stayed there. My skin crawled every time I heard her footsteps. She made that same rhythm when she walked as the patent leather shoes in the bank. Even after I heard the door shut and lock, I stared at the ceiling all night and trembled while I tried to get that song out of my head.

"Dormir dormir
Se acerca tu largo sueño"

CHAPTER 18

J paged Siraya at sunrise the next day. She tried to ask a thousand questions, but I just wanted her to shut up.

"I know I said we wouldn't be roommates until I got back from Paris, but I need to come stay with you for about three weeks," I told her in the middle of the third time she asked me if I was okay.

"Really? NyQuest's daddy called me last night and told me we couldn't go anywhere or do anything together because we have to keep you completely out of trouble," she said.

"He said that shit to you?" I asked, my tone rising to an indignant tone.

"See? You're already about to get in trouble," she said with a giggle.

I couldn't help but giggle too.

"So here's the thing," she said. "My parents went running their mouths about my new spot, and Yvette needed a place to stay..."

"Does she want to fight me?" I asked.

"Nope. Yolanda and Brooke aren't speaking to her because

she told them they were wrong for jumping on us when we had the baby with us," Siraya said.

"Then I don't care. I can go three weeks without speaking to her," I declared.

"You're really not gonna try to work it out with NyQuest's daddy?" Siraya asked. "I'm only asking because the way he was crying over you made me think he might really love you."

I guffawed. "He's just scared of the child support he thinks I'm gonna hit him with."

"Nay-Nay, be for real. That man has done a lot of wrong, but he ain't never done wrong by that baby. He's probably the type to pay your rent for the rest of your life just because your baby sleeps there on Wednesday nights," Siraya protested. "But I understand how you feel and why. Ain't no turning back from what he did. I'll leave it alone..." Several seconds later, she mumbled, "He was crying hard as hell over your ass, though, talking about what he was gonna do different when you came home."

"Too bad I ain't going there," I said.

"Okay, Nay. I got you. Your key's gonna be under the sunflower pot. Have my dinner cooked, and my slippers by the door when I get home," she told me and giggled.

"Bye, nut."

Yvette was mad that I wanted the bedroom that was supposed to be reserved for me. I surprised her by telling her she could have it until I returned. The recliner in NyQuest's bedroom was made by Chillz, so it was sturdy and comfortable. Polite greetings were all I gave Yvette to avoid arguing over anything else she felt entitled to. She watched me intensely while she pretended to be typing on Siraya's computer in the living room. This went on the whole time that I stayed there. The upside to that was that she was only there for a very small amount of time. She had to catch a cab to get Downtown to the *Sanford Tribune* by four in the morning, and she had to catch a bus to get home at night. The bus stop was a seven block walk away, because everyone in that suburb had at least two cars. I was usually asleep by the time she got home.

The third day I was there, she was glued to Siraya's computer while she worked on an article. She and Siraya were arguing about that, because Siraya had papers to write. I knew that the tension between them was going to spill over to me, so I prepared to go back to the creepy housekeeper at Melinda's house. Subira came over with a lot of gasoline to add to the fiery argument.

"I'm saying though, Ray-Ray. She's at your house, not paying rent, telling you when you can use your own shit?" Subira called from the kitchen.

Quietly I requested, "Subira, please don't start a fight between the two of them. I can't be around any type of trouble."

"They ain't gonna fight. The only reason Siraya ever fights is because you do, and the high yellow one ain't gonna bust a grape in a food fight." Subira folded her arms and stared directly at Yvette.

"Girl, ain't you from DPD? Why are you so tough all the damn time?" I asked, and she laughed.

The phone rang, causing her to stop instigating long enough to pick up the phone.

"Because Siraya's busy getting punked for her own computer in her own house. Now what do you want?" Subira snapped into the phone. I wondered when she and Siraya got cool enough for her to answer Siraya's phone.

"Bitch, I work and go to a real school! That's why I need your computer, hoe! You and Monaysia have always been the two smartest out the crew and too stupid to do anything but lay up with some niggas. How did both of you graduate with Honors Society sashes, but ended up in community college?" Yvette asked.

Subira yelled, "Bitch, what are you getting out of pulling Nay-Nay into your shit?"

Yvette's face snapped in Subira's direction, and she froze. After watching Yvette's face go from yellow to scarlet, Subira gave me the phone.

"That don't sound good," Banger commented. "I just called to check on you."

I paused and absorbed the urgency in his voice. "What's wrong with you?"

"Mel said you moved out of her spot because of her cleaning lady. Rize has been having nightmares about that lady singing this song in Spanish," he explained.

I grunted. "What?"

"I don't know. The shit just sounded spooky as hell. That's why I called," he said.

I wanted to dive deeper into it, but I decided that much of a civil conversation was enough for one day. "Can I speak to NyQuest, please?"

"Of course."

I expected NyQuest to babble, but his words came across the phone lines clear and crisp. "Hi, Mommy. I love you. I miss you."

My heart melted. "I love and miss you too, baby."

That made me want to at least go home to see him, but I was too angry with his father to be alone in his presence. Since Yvette and Siraya couldn't stop arguing, I went outside for a walk. The children in that area played free of worry, and no police driving around. NyQuest could be happy living there part of the week.

When I returned hours later, Yvette was gone. Subira and Siraya stood over the computer. Both frowned at the monitor. Their heads turned toward me. They didn't speak.

"What?" I asked.

"I put her out, but..." Siraya's voice trailed as she turned the monitor toward me.

I looked at the words on the screen and then gasped as I read, "*Dethroning a Suburban Princess: A Cautionary Tale about Bad Boys and Big Dollars.*"

The first sentence was about young girls dating older guys with expensive cars. The second was about how those girls grow into women who have babies to use as bargaining chips. Yvette mashed up the details of two of my romantic relationships and made up one jealous article about me. She deserved to have a reason to be another plaintiff on Yolanda's and Brooke's case. She sat at that computer in hopes that she'd get to eavesdrop on any of my conversations with Banger. With nowhere else to go, I made Subira give me a ride across the bridge, hating every minute of the one hour and 45 minutes it took to cross it. I hated I had to go crawling back to a man who lived to embarrass me.

Ringing the doorbell to a house with my name on the lease felt stupid until Banger opened the door. NyQuest squealed and ran across the threshold to hug my legs. Having that tiny person pressed against me with all that cheer in his voice microwaved my insides. Then, Banger slowly wrapped one arm around my back and guided me to him. The other pulled my head against his shoulder.

"I'm never gonna do you wrong again," he whispered.

I didn't feel like arguing, so I just listened to how his heart thumped until he let me go.

"I don't know how much worse things are gonna get, but a girl I used to be friends with works for the newspaper," I told him after I put my suitcases in the bedroom. "She was writing an article about me living as a drug dealer's wife. I think Subira destroyed the disk, but there's no telling if she has it saved somewhere else."

He didn't say anything. Rize came out of the kitchen with a frown on his face.

"You don't think the friend you were staying with set you up?" he asked.

I shook my head. "That's my only friend in the world. I think that the girl got a lot of information from my mother arguing with her mother."

"Your mother ain't tell them how she got put out your crib?" he asked.

"They'll never admit things like that. Yvette's mother begged Siraya's mother to make Siraya open up her house to her. By the time she went to lunch with the other mothers, she changed the story to Yvette and Siraya buying a condo together," I explained.

"Damn," Rize remarked. "We coulda used a hookup somewhere in the media."

I gave him a weird look. He went back into the kitchen without responding.

"Did you see what she wrote?" Banger asked me.

I nodded my head.

"We both going to jail if it gets printed?" he asked.

"Probably just me," I said. "She didn't even get your name right. She made up a bunch of shit about me carrying stuff for my boyfriend and him putting me out the house when I got caught."

He rubbed my shoulders. "You hungry?"

After shaking my head, I picked up NyQuest. I took him into his room and read him a few books from the football shaped shelf that Chillz built him. NyQuest got hungry, so I sent him to the kitchen to eat with Banger and Rize. Banger tried to make me eat, but I stuck to my guns about never letting him feed me again. His head and shoulders dropped. Not wanting to feel sympathy, I shut the door and cleaned NyQuest's room that didn't need cleaning. After that, I tipped into my design room to look at the prom dresses I left behind. The ones for Rize's sister still hung proudly over the table. My sewing machine was still there. I only had remnants of fabric left and didn't feel like driving across the bridge to buy more, so I picked up my knitting needles and yarn.

When NyQuest got done eating, he knocked on the door and sat in the chair Peaches normally used when we worked together. He watched me with a smile on his face, so I explained what I was doing and went over the colors with him. After he got bored with that, I gave him a piece of paper and the few colored pencils that I didn't send to Paris. He sat there and drew while I knitted. I stopped knitting and taught him how to write his name and draw shapes. He snatched the pencil from me and shook his head.

"Daddy does this."

He drew a hexagon. I studied what he'd done. He counted the sides for me and put up six fingers. I blinked at him. He drew a pentagon and then threw up five fingers. Excited, I ran out of the room to find my camera. My good one was overseas, but I had a couple of disposable ones in my luggage. I took a picture of him with his shapes and counting the sides. Then, I taped the pictures to the wall. I had to tell somebody about my baby.

"Siraya, girl, are babies supposed to know how to count? Because my baby can count and draw all his shapes, and write his name!" I announced.

"You're surprised that he's smart? You're smart, Nay," she said.

I grinned. "I am, ain't I?"

She didn't have kids, so she didn't care as much as I wanted her to. My mother would have eaten that up and spread it all over Sapphire Cadre, but I decided at that moment that I didn't want my baby's name in her mouth. I didn't want him living to compete for her to have the most bragging rights at dinner at a table in Red Lobster on a Friday night.

I waited to see if Banger and Rize would leave. Both

remained in the apartment. Banger said that he wasn't going out of town for work anymore until Joy got my case dismissed. I loved the confidence but wished that meant Rize would go home at some point. He laid on the couch at night, so I stayed in my design room, knitting all night.

CHAPTER 19

$\mathcal{M}$y vacation time was dwindling. I had to have a job before my first check-in with my probation officer. My heart sank as I dialed my job's telephone number and waited to be connected to my boss.

"Hello, Amy. This is Monaysia Giles—"

She cut me off. "And you've come to your senses and decided that you wanted to stay here and be my assistant instead of chasing a Parisian pipe dream?"

Though the excitement in her rushed speaking irritated me, I said, "Let's go with that."

Amy paused. "Wait. Is that really why you called?"

I sighed. "In so many words, yes."

"You're really passing up Paris to work with me?" she asked. Without waiting for an answer, she said, "Stick with me from here on out. I'll take you as far as you want to go with this company."

That phone call was too odd for me to feel relief. I did feel hungry for the first time in nearly a week. Banger was at work. Not wanting to bother anyone with having to come across the bridge to take me anywhere, I walked a few blocks up to Chill-

Zone. The menu had grown since Banger took me there the night we met. The ice cream was hand churned, and they were open 24/7. They made the best ham and egg sandwich I ever had in my life.

"Banger's baby's mother, right?" the person behind the counter asked me when I went to pay.

"Yes," I said in a flat voice.

"Quest's mama doesn't pay in here ever," he said.

I blinked a few times. Then, I saw Chillz coming from the back, carrying a tub of fresh ice cream. He put it in the case and then came from behind the counter and hugged me. "How you feeling today?"

"Numb," I replied.

"That's a different feeling than I would have guessed," he said.

"I was scared for so long that I don't have it left in me anymore," I told him.

He nodded and then walked outside with me.

"I know you don't want to hear this, but I wanted to apologize to you for what happened at dinner that night. It looked real bad, but it wasn't what it looked like. I thought that girl liked Nyir. I didn't know she was on the Shanae Plan."

That pulled a giggle out of the pit of my belly that surprised me. He grinned wide at hearing me express a sign of happiness.

"I don't understand these girls' thought processes. You gonna fuck the employee to get at the boss?" he remarked.

"It worked for her," I said.

"I really don't think it did. I can't get an answer that makes sense out of any of them, but there ain't no good way to spin it after what happened to you anyway. That never should have made it to your doorstep or past your door." He looked back inside and offered, "You want some ice cream? I can't leave yet, but I wanna talk to you for a minute while you're not pissed off with all of us."

"Who says I'm not?" I asked.

"You don't have fire beams shooting from your eyes like you did the last few times I saw you," He smiled when I giggled again.

That man's smile was like sunshine. I went back inside with him and ordered a brownie a la mode, even though I'd just had breakfast food. I was not disappointed at all.

"I want to tell you a story about when I fucked up. And I'm telling you this story, because I think that you think higher of me than you do Rahshaan. You should," he began.

I couldn't stop giggling at him. He made me feel the way my dad made me feel when I was little.

"You know how we keep calling Hope Thomas evil?" he began.

"Yeah…" I said slowly.

"Well, I cheated on Selena with her," he said. "She used to 'make' me fuck her when I wanted to see my daughter, so I slid out the bed, took a dollhouse I'd made over there, and fucked her to see my daughter. Selena was putting duvets on her bed and hanging curtains while I did it."

My mouth dropped open. "Not you! Chillz, you were my last hope that there were men somewhere in the world that didn't cheat."

He shrugged and looked at the floor with this longing glazing his eyes. It told me he wished he could take back what he did. In a soft voice, he said, "I told myself at the time that it wasn't cheating. My kids mean everything to me, but my daughter? I was locked up when she was born. The first time I got to see her, it was like looking at my mother being given back to me. All my kids loved her that same way and would do anything to see her. I just thought I was doing what I had to do. Her mama knew what she was doing when she put me in jail for trying to see her regularly."

"I don't understand, Chillz. How can she do that?" I asked.

He raised his eyebrows at me. "With everything that you've been through in the past week, you don't understand how she could do that?"

I shrugged and told him, "I don't understand anything that's happened to you over the past year at all." I took one of the cherries from atop the mound of whipped cream that sat on my brownie and bit into it. That was the best damn cherry I ever ate in my life, tart in a sweet syrup.

"Let's talk about it then." He finished the last of his ice cream.

"Well, ever since the day that I met you, people have talked about you like you're God. There's nothing that you can't do. Everybody goes to you for everything. I've seen people's kids get snatched from them right on the streets. None of yours get touched, and you bring as many back as you can. And yet, I have watched life whoop your family's ass since my birthday. They talked about your father like he was the devil on the news the day after his execution. Why can't the people over here just say that he didn't take those kids?" Waving my spoon as I spoke, I looked around and lowered my voice.

"Because my mother got killed for it by the person who was doing it," was his answer.

"And that's what I don't understand. Why didn't you move after that happened?" I wondered.

"Because if we leave, then somebody else is always going to be the target. We ain't about to leave people defenseless. Do you know what would happen to this place?" he asked.

"Why do you care, though, Chillz? I don't understand why you give a damn! Do you get a prize if you defeat the big, bad police department?" I exclaimed.

"Depends on what you call a prize," he replied. "After meeting your people, I see that you find value in things you can brag on. If I were a bragging man, Banger would be it. He was eight years old when Darlene left him in that house by himself

KIMANI LAUREN

with Marcus. I don't know what happened to him during that time, but I know it put up an ice wall around him. Know when that wall melted? The day Quest was born.

"But between that day that Darlene left and today, I've seen a survivor that will do whatever he has to do for his family."

"Even if he can't stand part of that family," I said softly, looking down at my ice cream. I looked back up and said, "You started by telling me that you're not perfect. I'd like to hear more about that, because it's a shock to me."

He chuckled. "Yeah, so in my mind, I had to tell myself for three or four months before I even called Hope that I wasn't cheating on Selena. That was just what I had to do if I wanted to see my baby girl, and I needed her to meet Selena. That was the mother I should have given her. The smiles on their faces had me telling myself that it was all worth it until we took my daughter back to Hope's house, and her and Selena got into a fight. Selena went to jail, and you know who got to tell her about what I did?"

"Hope?" I asked.

"Nope. The police with Hope standing behind them, telling them what to say," he corrected me.

I blinked twice and then screwed my face. "How can one bitch with a short skirt and a microphone have all that power?"

"She doesn't," he corrected me. "She's convinced herself that she does because of the consequences of her words, but she ain't nothing but a puppet for the police. They'll use her until somebody more lethal comes along, and then they'll throw her away and shut her up one way or another."

I thought of Yvette. She didn't have what Hope Thomas had, in my opinion. That's why she worked for the junior newspaper writing after school special content.

"The way Selena's face looked when she asked me if it was true made me feel like I never deserved her. I wanted her to understand why I did what I did so bad, but I knew that I didn't deserve her understanding," he continued. "I never wanted to see that look again, but I saw it on your face at dinner that night. No matter what you and him did to each other, you didn't deserve to have that look on your face at your own dinner table."

I couldn't look at him. "Thank you for saying that."

"So I understand this place that you're at where you're through with Rahshaan. I talked to you when you were pregnant about peace, and the money, and all that, but you've been losing way more than him this year. You've been growing the hell up. I just want to offer my help wherever I can, because we still have to keep NyQuest's best interest in mind through all of this. What's gonna happen with him when you and Banger split up for good?"

I tried to think of a sound plan but came up blank.

"I'm not taking Quest from him. That boy lives for his daddy, and I've never seen a more amazing father than Banger," I said. "I just don't want to think about what I'd have to do if I didn't get to go to Paris. Right now, I'm still holding onto hope that I get to go, but I'm gonna keep it real. I'm gonna be resentful as hell if I don't get to go, especially if it's because he cheated."

Chillz nodded. "Well, I got a spot I can put you up in if you decide you gotta go."

"I don't want to stay on this side of the bridge if I don't have the respect of being Banger's girl anymore. That'll just have me in this same situation over and over and over again. Plus, I'm just not the crusader that you guys are. I'm sorry. I really can't care about people who don't even check on me when I'm going through something." I ate another scoop of the ice cream. That brownie stayed hot, the ice cream stayed cold, and they tasted like my childhood fantasies when mixed together.

Chillz nodded his understanding. "Mama Sheila says that same thing. That's why she hasn't come across the bridge since the 80s. Mont's and D's fathers both got killed, and nobody went to see her or even called her after their funerals."

My heart sank. "This is what I'm talking about, Chillz. These people don't even say thank you to you, and the police just target and harass you. It never ends. And for as much as everyone likes to throw out that this is what I asked for, somebody could have told me I'd have a bullseye on my back from having a boyfriend."

"You ain't gonna get an argument out of me about that," Chillz stated.

"And I can't deal with having to fight with somebody in his family every time we get together. I'll never forget the first time I sat down with all your sisters. They couldn't wait to embarrass me about my dad," I said.

"You're right about that too," Chillz agreed with a nod. "There was a better way for them to approach you, but your father's kind of arrogant for somebody who moves the way that he does."

"Are you talking about his relationship with Melinda?" I asked.

Chillz shook his head. "Nah. I'm talking about his relationship with you. How can he justify making his wife and daughter split the bills so that he could have money for the titty bars? He's a fraud, Monaysia. He met Melinda at the club we own on Hyman but couldn't afford to talk to her until he recognized her at a county employee protest against getting their funds cut to give the bulk to the police department. He made himself out to be someone who cared about somebody besides himself. Soon as that protest no longer served him, he caved and took a slightly higher salary for himself and said fuck everybody else. Same thing he did at home. I hate to throw dirt on a grown man's name, but I've been in my feelings since he did you the way that he did."

"I don't want people feeling sorry for me, though," I said.

"I know you don't, but it's more about me than it is about you. Your father has two beautiful, smart, successful daughters that he just threw from the nest on their eighteenth birthdays and turned his back when he couldn't brag about them flying. I hate that shit," he grumbled. "That's why I wanna make sure you're good no matter what you decide going forward."

"But I'm not your daughter," I needlessly pointed out.

"Eh. You live on this side of the bridge, you become my child whether you realize it or not. You ever sleep in the buildings in Nat Turner, you're more than likely in my heart forever. But you being the mother of my first grandchild is in a whole different league," he said.

"What happens when one of your blood sons has a child?" I wondered.

"Then my second grandchild is born. Why? What up?" he asked.

I shrugged.

"Blood ain't the only thing that connects you, Nay-Nay," he said.

"Yeah. Sometimes it's pity. I don't want to be pitied." I ate another cherry.

He frowned. "So living without having to hear about what bills you need to pay all the time isn't helpful to you?"

"Chillz, all Banger talks about is money," I said. "You know that. We've had this conversation."

"Yeah, but I thought he was gonna relax with that. He just can't rest without making sure that his family is straight," Chillz said. "I talked to him about that one night when you were out with your girls, and he called you to talk about health insurance. Shit fucked my head up because I thought he told me you were at the club when he was yelling into the phone about it."

I cracked up at that.

"It's good to see you laughing," he said.

I took a breath and then looked around. "It's good to be

understood."

We let silence carry us through finishing our ice cream before we resumed our conversation. During that time, the aromas changed from breakfast foods to oils heating in fryers, freshly cut vegetables, and bread baking.

"How many restaurants do you own?" I asked when I finished eating.

"Just a few right now. I'm looking at a couple more," he said. "I'm gonna slow down for a minute so that I can help Lynn grow her spa and buy a couple more buildings on Sundown Boulevard.

"That's another reason I was asking about your backup plan. Those jeans you and Peaches make have turned type legendary. Joy's daughter said that somebody wore them to school one day, and everybody was going crazy trying to figure out where she got them from. A bunch of little girls in Nat Turner and Frederick Douglass think it's crazy that Rahshaan's girlfriend is the girl from the relaxer box. They want to be just like you."

"For real?" I giggled.

"You haven't heard about them begging him to bring you down there with your books of modeling pictures? He took them down there a couple of times to show them," he told me.

I screwed my face. "He did?"

"I understand why you don't go down there too much, but there's a bunch of little girls down there who look up to you. You could start a modeling school since Naomi Iman doesn't accept girls from this side of the bridge. You could teach classes on how to make clothes, open up a store, and hire some of the girls to work in there after school. Shit doesn't have to be terrible for you."

I thought of that reception compared to the days when I was told my jeans were too urban. They were said to discriminate against people who didn't have curves, but they just weren't meant for the people who scoffed at them.

252

Chillz leaned back and rested a finger on one of his temples.

"You know what? I've enjoyed this conversation with you, but I can't keep putting up this front like I don't have something deeper I want to talk to you about. Come get in the car with me, and let's take a ride. I haven't even been paying attention to who's been coming in and out of here."

I looked around at children coming in from school and realized that I hadn't either. Chillz scooped ice cream for them and told them to take out their homework. He told a few of them to stay there until some of his employees got off of work so that they could take them home. He made sure that everyone's parents would be home when they got there before motioning over his shoulder for me to follow him.

Every person we passed while we walked through the parking lot knew Chillz by name and had to have a discussion with him. There were no quick greetings with that man, because even just being on the receiving end of the word hello from him was like an affirmation of the good things that were to happen in your life. One man in particular — a man who was an inch shorter than me and firmly gripped the hands of two little boys — came to Chillz and only let go of one of the boy's hands long enough to slap palms with Chillz and then gripped the little boy's hand even tighter.

"Mazzi! What's the deal? How you feeling?" Chillz asked. He crouched to get a high five from both of the little boys. "I see the family's doing good. The boys are getting big."

Mazzi grinned down at the two brown boys and said, "We're doing just fine. Just came from closing on that house in the valley. Zora's out buying curtains. Women always wanna buy curtains first."

Chillz grinned at him. "Is that right? Congratulations, man!"

"Another year or two, I'll put that baby girl in Zora. By then, I'll hopefully be approving your fourth community center."

"I hope so, but for now, can you just make sure the kids in

there all got rides home?" Chillz asked.

"Of course. That's what I came down here for. I'll be seeing you soon," Mazzi said.

Chillz concluded the conversation with, "I appreciate you for helping out. Congratulations again. You know to call me or stop by the furniture store if you need any help moving."

Chillz drove a red BMW that was so beautiful it was sickening. On the dashboard was a picture of Selena draped over the hood in mesh lingerie. That cinnamon skinned woman was breathtaking. From the way her eyes bore through the camera and lured it to come fuck her through the lens, I knew Chillz was the one who took the picture.

"You've got a good eye." I pointed at her face.

"I only take good pictures of her," he said meekly.

I looked closer at the picture. "I don't know. That looks professional grade to me."

It wasn't until I looked around that I realized we were out of the parking lot. That's how smooth that thing rode. I wondered why Banger didn't have his own car. That reminded me of the Jeep he said he was saving up for at the beginning of my pregnancy. It was like he was scared to have nice things.

"I'm gonna start this off by telling you this one thing: With Joy as your attorney, you'll never go to jail." He took his hand off the steering wheel to point a finger at me.

"I already went to jail," I reminded him.

"That wasn't jail. That was a holding cell that might not even be a part of the actual justice department," Chillz corrected me.

"What?" I asked.

"They're gonna try to use you, Shorty. Your resume backs you up. You're supremely beautiful. You make great bait, and you live by tit for tat. Nobody is gonna hurt you and get away with it, and I understand that, but that makes you a great asset to them pigs. They started with the scare tactics, using phoney cases. Now that they got you shook, they can manipulate you to do whatever they need. And I know that you're hurt and embarrassed, but I'm begging you not to let them get to you. No matter what they throw at you. I need you to stand tall. I'll do whatever you want and need. I will take care of you for the rest of my life, Monaysia."

The pools forming in his eyes confused me.

"What did I do to make you so upset?" I asked softly.

"Nothing yet. I just saw this look in your eyes at dinner that night that made me believe that you're going to destroy Rahshaan for the way that he hurt you, and I don't believe in coincidences. You got arrested for a bunch of fake cases, and Kevin was there, and I just got this feeling that something is brewing. It's keeping me up at night. I know you don't owe me shit, but I'm begging you not to get the pigs involved with whatever you decide to do to get back at him. I will do whatever you want for the rest of your life."

He pulled over to the side of the road and stared at me while he waited for me to state my terms. I was confused. Never in life had a grown man been so open as to cry and beg me for anything.

"Monaysia, I don't dispute that Rahshaan should have done a lot more things better by you. You've grown up a whole lot more since the beginning of the year than he has. You sat in the house and didn't go to a single fight that you were invited to, and Shanae has been asking you to wait outside of her delivery room and beat her ass just because that's the only time you can guarantee that she ain't pregnant. I still don't know how you didn't flip that table on everybody in there. But you've been focused, and you've been hustling, and you've been really doing your thing out here. Your man's been asking me what love feels like, and he liked coming home to you before that dinner."

"Chillz, I really want you to stop crying and begging me to do something I haven't even thought about doing. I don't even know what you're talking about," I told him.

"Keep it real with me, Monaysia. If there was a way for you to make Rahshaan feel the way that you did that night without retaliation, would you do it?" he asked.

I thought about the way my heart ripped and my head burned when I realized Chrissy was telling me that she was pregnant by my boyfriend. To say that I didn't want to murder him would have been a lie. Knowing how much it would hurt NyQuest if I took him from his father kept me from dumping his body into the Aliners River in front of the police. In the distance, I could see the river bubbling as that thought popped into my head.

"Chillz, since NyQuest has been in this world, I have changed four diapers. Maybe five if you count the one the nurse taught me how to change in the hospital. As angry as I am with him for what he did to us, I could never be a parent without him. I wanted a baby, because I wanted to hook him, and I thought it would be cute to be known as his baby's mother. But I didn't know it came with all this. Now that I do, I can't do parenthood without him." When he had no rebuttal, I added, "Even before that, he's been showing me since our first date how great of a father he is, starting with getting those kids at G-Ma's house to school every day. So you can chill. I'm not taking his baby away from him ever."

"I want to believe that, but that look in your eyes that night gave me nightmares," he said.

I shrugged. "I don't know what to say."

"That whole scene was scary for me, because I didn't realize you knew Marvine," he added.

I scrunched my face. "How do you know my aunt? Where would you even meet her?"

He eyed me like he was surprised that I asked that question.

"Nyir had an accident when he was a baby that causes him to have to go to the hospital a lot. Marvine used to work at the hospital. It's out in Abolition Town."

His mention of that suburb jolted me. He stared at me, but I didn't make eye contact with him. Then, I got nervous and thought that made me look suspicious, so I looked at him. His eyes glazed as they twitched. That made me nervous, so I looked at his dimples instead. It was so quiet in that car that I could hear the guilt making my heart thud.

"Have you seen me out there or something? Why are you looking at me like that?" I asked.

Through gritted teeth, he answered, "You know I saw you."

I sucked my teeth and groaned. "When I was going up for that promotion at my job, they had me doing all kinds of stupid stuff on my lunch break that would cost me money just to see how much free work they could get out of me in the name of getting a job there that paid some big money. The lady who's my boss now is also in charge of the Miss Junior Sanford Pageant, so she had me running out to Abolition Town on my lunch break and doing all the banking for them with this creepy man with this nerdy name. Tisha said it the other night at Big Grams' house. She said she didn't like sitting at the dinner table with him when his wife wasn't there."

Relief filled that man's face and lifted his hooded eyes. "I thought you had a secret account out there or something. I mean, you should always have a hidden account, just not at that bank."

"That bank is the creepiest place I've ever been. It's like a horror film!" I whispered.

"You don't know how long I've been wanting to ask you what the fuck you were doing out there!" he whispered.

"Does Banger know that I've been out there?" I asked.

"Not that I know of. I didn't want you to think I was stalking you, but I was in that doctor's office that's between that specialty toy store you went into and that bank. Then, Marvine was following you..."

"She was?" I hoped he couldn't see me shaking while I

wondered who else saw me. "How did I miss all of this? Probably was concentrating too hard on getting back to work on time. They were hazing the hell out of me to get that little job. Was I doing something wrong, do you think? I thought it was just a deposit. The cops went through my bags and went through all of my bank cards and credit cards and asked if I had any other accounts anywhere else."

"No, sweetheart. You did nothing wrong." He exhaled. "Aight, so as far as Marvine goes, she used to work at that hospital and sometimes brought her daughter with her. I thought maybe her daughter was a patient there, but she seemed to just be coming to work with her mother to see if she'd see Nyir. They were talking at one point. She came to the house regularly once she got old enough to drive. That's how she knew about me frying chicken. I should have cleared that up with you right then and there, but Nyir was flipping out about her being pregnant. I have to look out for him when he gets like that. I didn't mean to treat you like you didn't matter. I was hoping to just wire you some money when you got to Paris to make you forget that we treated you like shit that night and apologize to you when you came back."

"Oh." It felt a little weird to know I was a problem he could throw money at to control.

He exhaled again and put his hand on the gear to merge back into traffic. "I think I've questioned you and pressured you enough today, but this talk relieved me. Please let me know what you need me to do for you, and I'll make sure that you have it. And think about what I said about the store too. These kids need something to do after school. I could get you a classroom at the community centers, and you could really do your thing and help some other little girls do it too."

"That might be nice," I said, "but won't that open me up to getting my shop broken into by the police so that they can tell the news that somebody from down here did it?" I looked at him and waited for him to tell me no.

"We can always rebuild," was his reply. "We always do."

I frowned at thought of Banger working three jobs just to have to go out and do it all over again because someone destroyed it. Then, I decided I didn't want to be done with our conversation. "What was my Aunt Marvine doing when she was following me?"

"Not going into any stores. She just stood outside the bank until she saw you coming out. Then, she acted weird for the rest of the day, but she's always been a little strange to me," he replied. "She never wanted to bring her daughter across the bridge all the years she was friends with Nyir, but all of a sudden wanted to come to the store and look around every single day. That's where Chrissy heard all that complaining Banger did about you. She made it sound like he was confiding in her, but it wasn't like that. Your mother didn't even remember who I was until they got to the cash register and saw Quest's picture. Actually, it wasn't even Quest's picture. It was a picture of your family that we took on Mother's Day that jogged her memory. Then Marvine started getting really pushy about going to see where you lived."

"Is this conversation gonna end with you telling me Banger didn't fuck her?" I asked him.

"I wish I could, but I really don't understand what was going on and can't get a straight answer from anybody." He looked at me and added, "I just need you to tell me what you need me to do to make whatever choice you're gonna make easier."

I got into the car after he opened the door for me and waited until he got in before I started talking again. "Do you think that I should try to work it out with him?"

"Honestly? No. Y'all are toxic as hell for no reason. And that look in your eyes when you were sitting at that table. That's a hurt that you'll never get over. I can tell," he said.

"You keep taking it back to the dinner. What about the broken promises on Valentine's Day Weekend?" I asked. "The bitches who came to me claiming that they were with him? What about getting left at a shootout in a club on my birthday? Being told that it was none of my business what happened in The Spot."

"I'm gonna tell you what that was about, but I'd appreciate it if you kept it on the low. I don't even want Banger knowing that I let you in on it," he said.

"Are you making up something to make me be quiet about it?" I asked.

"Wouldn't that have been done a long time ago?" he pointed out.

I shrugged.

"I ain't got no reason to lie to you, Shorty. Squeak and Shanae, if you notice, I don't treat the same way I treat everybody else. I try to do for their kids, but it ain't but so much I can do for them without their parents trying to find a way to milk it. I hate that shit, because they have no interest in paying it forward. They just wanna sit up and complain about what I don't *give* them," he said.

"How is that any different from what everybody else in the hood does to you?" I asked.

"It's way different. All they do is fight and fuck," he replied.

"Then why do you keep him around?" I asked.

"You ever heard that saying 'Keep your friends close and your enemies closer'? I'm watching that one real close. I think he's tryna kill my son," Chillz declared.

"What?" I asked.

"Ain't too much that gets by me, Monaysia. That's why I'm out here begging you to tell me what you want," he said.

"Because you think I'm gonna kill Banger?" I asked. "Chillz, you don't have to worry about that. I'm not a murderer."

That time, his grin made me shudder. "Remember when you weren't a fighter either?"

It was my turn to beg. "I'm not laughing, Chillz. I thought I was starting to love Banger. I want him to love me, but for more reasons than because I'm NyQuest's mother. I want him to like me as a person; not me, the model; not me, the chick who brought his child into the world. Me. Monaysia Denise Giles. Rize used to say that I wanted Banger to worship me, but he kind of already does. I want him to love me for real, and I want to love him back. Can you give me that?"

Chillz's head bent, and he sighed. "I saw the night of that dinner that you wouldn't take it even if he gave it to you."

The rest of the ride was silent. My seatbelt was choking me. I couldn't stop tugging at it or shifting around in my seat. It upset me that Chillz thought I'd risk my own freedom. I had a little bit of an attitude when I walked into the house. Banger and Rize were there. Rize sat at the table with Joy, highlighting something in a book. She glanced at me and pointed to the dining room chair she wanted me to sit in. I followed her command and waited for them to finish their conversation. During that time, NyQuest ran to me and climbed into my lap.

"Hi, baby!" I squealed at him.

He took my face in both hands and kissed my forehead. "Hi, Mommy. I need to go potty."

"You do?" I asked and popped up from my seat.

He took me to the bathroom and showed me that he didn't need any help other than getting the door opened. I couldn't help it. I had to call somebody to let them know that my baby was walking and going to the potty at just a year old. Midway through dialing my mother's number, I realized I was just like her, talking about my son because I could brag about him. But then I looked at him pulling up his Pull-Up and going to get disinfectant wipes from the cabinet under the sink just in case he dripped on the bowl, and somebody had to hear about that and see the pictures of him and his shapes. I called my dad instead of my mom, knowing that he'd brag to all of his friends. Quickly it would make it back to the friends they still shared, and she'd be hurt that she didn't have any pictures of him with his drawings.

NyQuest sat in the chair next to me and colored while Joy talked to me about what she'd found out for my case. Someone high on Jackson's legal team had pressed charges against Yolanda and Brooke, but had my name mixed up. According to the attorney, "Monaysia sounded like the name of an aggressor, not a victim." When Joy gave me that detail, the corners of her mouth turned downward. A storm brewed in her eyes. Chillz assured me that meant that she was going to bury the attorney for that comment.

"Onto the second charge, Kevin lied to you about deleting the charges. Jewana Marnes' attorney refuses to speak with me or anyone on my team until our day in court," Joy said.

"That means that they're scared, right, Joy?" Chillz asked with a slight grin on his face.

"William, do you have something better to do?" she asked him.

"What's better than watching the future president of the United States do her thing?" he asked with a smile, and she actually returned the smile with just as much warmth.

The sternness returned to her face quicker than the smile pushed it out.

"I've done some digging to see how she was able to find your name to press charges against you. The claim is that Rahshaan gave it to her, but that's not the South Ridge way. The police concocted that story to get under your skin. That leads me to believe that they already knew there was a sensitive point. I'm told what that point was. Rahshaan, get me a wooden spoon," she commanded.

"We ain't got none," he said.

She peered at him with her mouth taut. "Pardon me?"

"We don't have any, Joy Gilead," he corrected himself. "We don't cook."

"And why not?" she demanded to know.

"Because G-Ma and Chillz cook for us. Why? You jealous?" he quipped.

"Don't be an ass, Rahshaan Bailey."

I don't know how this happened so fast or why, but she snatched a wooden spoon from her briefcase and smacked his hand with it from across the table. The yelp he let out was more satisfying than the sizzle of the rim of that hot spaghetti pot against his skin. I tried to pull my lips in to keep the grin from spreading across my face while he rubbed the spot on his hand that she just popped. She slid the spoon back into her briefcase and went back to talking like nothing happened.

"I want you to understand that you are being monitored," Joy told me sternly. "Everything that you say and do is being watched and twisted into an evil web of scheming and plotting to take down every single member of your son's family. It's been brought to my attention that your ass of a boyfriend didn't tell you that I'm moving to take over this county. That's no longer my problem since you've been informed. If you do anything that stops me from becoming mayor so that I can get to county executive and bring this side of the bridge to its full potential, I will cut you. I'm told that you carry a butterfly knife. That's my weapon of choice, but you're from Sapphire Cadre. I assure you that you cannot pull yours faster than me. I have no need to confirm you understand. Lisa's already given me the final word on you."

She picked up her briefcase and left the house with Chillz. A breeze blew through the apartment, even after the door closed. I wanted to sleep on the pullout couch that night, but Rize was there. I slept in the recliner next to NyQuest's bed. My body automatically woke up at 2 to feed him, but he was asleep and

completely dry. Unable to sleep, I got up to go to get my knitting needles until I fell asleep, but I heard tapping and a man
singing. I walked into the living room where Rize's eyes were
shut, but he was singing that same Spanish lullaby that Melinda's cleaning woman sang. His fingers tapped out the rhythm
those patent leather shoes made when running above my head
at the bank. My heart thumped. The closer I got to him, the
more intense his singing became. I was about to touch him to
wake him up, but the doorbell rang. I leapt backward across the
room and screamed.

The bedroom door opened. Banger's face came toward me.
He then turned on the lights. Rize stirred and then stretched.

"What happened?" he asked, looking around.

"You was singing that spooky ass song again," Banger
replied.

"My bad, Chief. I don't even know I be doing it," he said.

The doorbell rang again.

"That's what woke me up," Banger remarked and went to the
door shirtless.

I wish I would have never watched him walk across that
living room to get the door. The muscles in his back had
mounted into a cobra's head. I wanted to lick it, despite
knowing how toxic that snake's venom could be. He snatched
the door open. Marcus stood there with crimson stained eyes
and looked like he could tumble if the wind blew too hard.

"Where's your coat?" Banger asked him.

Marcus didn't answer.

"How did you get here?" Banger asked him.

"I walked," he said.

"What you doing walking across the bridge? Why you ain't
stop at G-Ma's crib instead of coming all the way up here?"
Banger exclaimed while he pulled his younger brother into the
house.

Marcus said, "I was chasing Mommy, tryna get her to come

home."

Banger put his hands on both of Marcus' shoulders and shook him. "Stop putting your life in danger over her. Do you hear me? She ain't gonna come around until she wants to. You can't make her stay clean, and it ain't your fault if she don't."

"She's just sick," Marcus whimpered.

"She ain't *just* nothing, Marc. You can't save her. Come in here and get warm and eat. Just stay here, or go stay in our room at Chillz's crib. Don't do this shit no more." Banger pulled Marcus into the kitchen. Rize was already pulling the bed out of the loveseat for him and getting him a blanket.

By dinner the next day, Siraya's number had displayed on my Caller ID seven times. I finally picked it up while Banger and Rize were sitting on the couch playing video games.

"What do you want? I'm *extremely* busy. Mothering the smartest little boy in the world is *very* hard work." I exaggerated each syllable and then giggled.

"Bitch, I have two papers to write and an exam tomorrow. I know you still got Denise blocked, but you need to answer this phone when I call you back so that her and Siobhan can get off my 3-way bothering me about my cute ass godson and those adorable pictures. I better have a set by Friday to put up in my cubicle. That little boy's picture got me a date and my big boss talking to me. Her husband works for a real record label. I need that connection, so answer the phone when I call you back, hoe!"

Ten minutes later, Siraya had a 3-way call with Denise Giles and me. Denise Giles was crying about me giving my father pictures of her grandson before her while Siobhan preached to me about solidarity between mothers. Denise never apologized, so I didn't care. I just put NyQuest on the phone so that he could recite his alphabet and then hung up the phone. That put a curl in my lips.

"I need a video camera. I should have *been* recording you,

especially knowing I was going away for so long and how I get when I'm away from you," I remarked.

I bathed NyQuest and listened to him sing his alphabet, spell his name and both of his parents' full names with the tub letters that were stuck to the tile on the wall, and write his name on the wall with the soap crayons. I must have taken a trillion pictures of him. His fingers and toes were completely shriveled by the time I took him out of the tub and put on his pajamas. We colored a picture and read a book that I fell asleep in the middle of. He rested on my chest until I woke up and heard Rize singing that creepy ass song. Banger's eyes stared at me from the doorway. I jumped.

"What's wrong with you?" I snapped at him. Before he could answer, I asked, "What the hell is Rize's problem?"

"Chillz said something that got him shook about staying home." He came and took NyQuest from me. "And Rico kept bitching about that song he's singing. Their mother used to sing it to them when they were little, and it used to scare the shit out of them."

"So he's staying over here to scare the shit out of me, singing about a long sleep coming?" I pulled a blanket that was draped over the recliner down over me and got comfortable.

"Nay-Nay," Banger whispered.

"What?"

"Come get in our bed. It's cold."

I turned over and grumbled, "Call Chrissy to warm you up."

He sucked his teeth and gently laid NyQuest in his crib. Then, he came to me and ran his fingers down my neck.

"I took the shit too far. Come here and let me make it up to you."

I snatched away from him. He scooped me up and waited to see if I would resist. When I didn't, he took me into our bedroom and turned Monica on just loud enough to drown out Marcus' snoring and Rize's singing.

MONAYSIA'S STORY CONTINUES
OCTOBER 2021

Sign up for my newsletter to receive teasers, free chapters, exclusive novellas, to learn more about Sanford County, and to be the first to know about new releases.

https://www.kimanilaurenbooks.com

ABOUT THE AUTHOR

Kimani has had the pleasure of calling Harlem, NY, Columbia, SC, and Memphis, TN, her homes. Currently, she's back in Syracuse with her husband and 5 of their 6 children. This is her fifth book. Through her writing, she works to raise awareness about the issues of teen suicide, food deserts in America, human trafficking, how classism mirrors racism. Her hope is that she can help to bring an end to these issues through her writing.

If you loved this book, please tell somebody, and please leave a review. The best way to connect with Kimani Lauren is by signing up for her email list on her website: Kimanilaurenbooks.com

You can also email kimanilauren@kimanilaurenbooks.com

- facebook.com/kimanilaurenbooks
- twitter.com/kimanilaurenppw
- instagram.com/kimanilaurenbooks
- pinterest.com/kimanilaurenbooks
- youtube.com/kimanilaurenbooks
- amazon.com/author/kimanilauren
- goodreads.com/kimanilauren
- bookbub.com/authors/kimanilauren

ACKNOWLEDGMENTS

Book number five, I could not have written you without God Almighty leading me, guiding me, and directing me. My steps on this author journey are divinely ordered in your word. Thank you for being the all-knowing, all-present, all-powerful force that you are.

Mommy, thank you for how your support of me has grown since I brought my first paperback to you. You've always been the most amazing woman in my life. Thank you for making the trials and tribulations of motherhood look easy to maneuver.

My father-in-law, Rupert, you have been a wonderful, beautiful blessing to me from the day your son became a part of my life. Thank you for every single thing you have done for us.

My husband, Richard, thank you for being part of my well oiled machine and for not making me push this car uphill by myself. I love you. Also, thank you and the kids for whatever you did that delayed the completion of this book. It came out at the perfect age and time. Jemaine, Shateek, Riccardo, Raymoan, Rahmeelo, and Richara, I love you. Every single thing that I do is working toward giving you the life I always dreamed of giving my children.

My Perfectly Polished Words editing clientele, you all help me to stretch and grow in ways I never knew I needed. You all are going to be New York Times bestsellers, and will go down in history as the greatest in your genres. Thank you for choosing me to be a part of that journey.

My spiritual family, there was a day this year where I cried out for a grandmother to pray for me in the absence of my own. Four women from The City and a pastor from New Jersey came into my house and anointed my family with oil. My life will never be the same because of you. Thank you. I love you. I thank God for you.

My friends have been my friends nearly my entire life, and I thank you for continuing to show up for me. Kaii, in this season in my life, you have no idea how badly I've needed everything that you've given. Tasha, Tiffany, and Tyshecia, thank you for your continuous support. Subira, thank you for giving my character a name (and for not being as confrontational as the Subira in this book).

The people who helped breathe life into this book, I thank you. Kaye, I appreciate you never charging me to answer my undying list of questions. Nicole Watts, your mind is absolutely perfect. Natasha, you have x-ray vision. Quenci, you're a musical genius. Radiah Hubert, every single thing you do is priceless. Sip & Flip Book Club, Juicy Reads, She Reads Fire, Sistah Girls Book Club, Robert's Reading Room, Bourbon Street Book Club, and Diverse Shelves, your support means the world to us authors.

My literary sisters — Jincey, Takara, TK, Markeshia, and E — I don't take lightly how available you've made your ears to listen and your shoulders to cry on. D'Artanya, Carmen, Red, K. Sherrie, Mel, Shonda, and True to Urban Lit, the ways that you continue to show up for me are invaluable and will forever be cherished.

Skylyn of Team Skyward, one day I am going to be able to

pay you back at least 1/4 of the support you've shown me over the past decade.

As I write these, I am also enjoying a bottle of apple cranberry wine. If I forget you, your name is somewhere close to the bottom of the bottle and buried deep within my heart. I do love you.

ALSO BY KIMANI LAUREN

Red Danger Days

Consider Your Ways

Here I Lay Part 1: I've Gotta Have It

Here I Lay Part 3: Don't Take This Personal (Coming October 13, 2021)